ROBERT'S SOUL

A Quidell Brothers
ROMANCE

"*You deserve... a real girlfriend.*" *Her hand works into the waistband of my jeans.* "*Not someone who...*" *She sucks in her breath before my lips steal more of her air.* "*... leaves for months.*"

I pull back enough to see her eyes. She's serious. She doesn't think we can do this long distance.

Maybe she's right. Maybe she's not. But tonight, I'm proving to her how much she means to me....

ROBERT'S SOUL

Quidell Brothers Book 3

KRIS AUSTEN RADCLIFFE

Six Love Erotic Romance

THE WORLDS OF
KRIS AUSTEN RADCLIFFE

ROBERT'S SOUL

A Quidell Brothers
ROMANCE

By
Kris Austen Radcliffe

Six Love Erotic Romance
Minneapolis

www.krisaustenradcliffe.com

ROBERT'S SOUL

A Quidell Brothers
ROMANCE

CHAPTER 1

Robert

"**A** *stopwatch was used to measure the interval of perambulation through the pre-determined social interaction area...*"

I rub my glove's scratchy palm over my face. It's fifteen degrees outside and the bus's heater is busted, but at least I had the ride to read journal articles about the culturally anthropological implications of leisurely walks.

I rub my face again. Who the hell uses the verb *perambulate*?

The bus takes the last corner before my stop. I grip the side of the seat as I attempt to counter the inevitable sway. The moment the bus stops and my boots hit the concrete, I'm scampering my ass through the bus fumes to my drafty but warm apartment.

The University bus drops off seven blocks from home. I could wait the fifteen minutes for the city bus. Or I could trot the sidewalks with a laptop and twenty-five pounds of textbooks on my back, toasty warm from the effort and fully deserving of the beer awaiting me in my fridge.

The better choice, I do believe.

I stuff the article into my backpack before yanking the flaps of my prize yellow-and-black-striped, pointy-tipped winter hat over my ears. When one has a gift-bearing, almost-five-year-old nephew, one must wear one's badge of uncle-hood with pride. Which I do. Every day. And will continue to do so, until spring comes and the wind chill goes away.

Some days I wonder if I should have chosen a graduate school in a warmer climate. But I like it here, even if the weather is too much like home. This university offers a fresh start.

The bus groans and shudders as it pulls up to my stop. I jog down the steps to the cold concrete, and breathe in the crisp night air. I'm already halfway up the block when the bus rumbles away.

The stop is on the very edge of the university property, just beyond two old and huge dorms. The energy of academia wanes out here, off campus. We all sleep away from the grand and imposing structures of the University, but we don't *live* here. We live in our labs and offices, in our buildings and student unions. The beds are for sleep and sex.

More sleep than sex, at least for me.

New city, new school. A new reputation of seriousness and depth. Yet my dates continue to find the wonders of my undergrad years on the internet. I'm fully aware that I'm a "bad boy." And that women have expectations for how I am to express my badness.

Sometimes social media has its... drawbacks.

Cold air dances over my lips, to my cheeks, and then onto my eyeballs. The chill makes the buildings and the streets look cleaner, as if I'm looking through blue ice at a dust-free world. All the moisture in the air froze out and nothing floats on the wind anymore. The world stopped being human-built and is a faery-land cleansed of all the grit and grime.

Or my corneas crystalized and I'm too fucking cold to realize it.

I stuff my hands into the pockets of my jacket. The cold makes me thirsty and I focus on my awaiting beer.

The books in my bag press the slab of my laptop against my back and I wish I didn't have to carry the entire contents of my PhD program every time I go into campus. Plus today, I'm also carrying the twenty-three student assignments I need to grade over the weekend.

The teaching assistant gig pays tuition and fees, and nets me enough to pay rent and to eat. It's fun, too. Most undergrads take Intro to Cultural Anthropology to fulfill distribution requirements, making it a class they choose, so we don't get a lot of whining. At least my section didn't last semester. On the other hand, Mack, my roommate, told me stories: A drug arrest his first semester, a student who plagiarized and got off because his daddy's a big shot lawyer, the creepy male student who stalked the woman who TA'ed before me.

On the road next to the sidewalk, a car drifts by, obviously looking for an address. My breath clouds the air and I feel a little warmer now that I'm moving, so I push my bumblebee hat back, to get a better look at the world around me.

A musical beat bounces down the street. I hear faint and distant laughter.

Mack said something about a party tonight. I'd declined his invite, citing the contents of my backpack as my reason.

But mostly I'm trying not to meet women at parties anymore.

A new life needs new ways of living. And I no longer want alcohol to be a factor in how women assess what I have to offer.

My phone chimes. I try not to have it out in the open while I walk because there've been a few snatch and grabs around campus. Last week, a woman got held up at knife-point. So I glance around before pulling it out.

I pull off my glove and sweep my finger across my phone to unlock the screen. *Left the party. Headache*, pops up.

Mack must have just left the party. I immediately glance around again because my brain thinks it might see him leave. Except the apartment is a block west and on the other side of the party house.

My sister stayed, appears.

I stare at the message for a moment. Sister?

Then I remember: The photographer.

Isolde

MY TWIN BROTHER ONCE ASKED ME WHAT I SEE WHEN I LOOK AT

the world. We were kids playing in the woods, me in front and Mack following, climbing over fallen logs and dancing around holes and hollows. The trees smelled summer fresh and the sunlight flickered over leaves and vines and our upturned faces.

Before I answered, I turned my face to the sky, my eyes closed. Warmth smoothed over my skin. Clean air tasted as good as the water from a cool, bubbling fountain. I stood perfectly still, a child with her toes in the moss and her twin brother an arm's length away, weak before the truth: I don't see the truth.

The world is so much more than my eyes telling me "Don't trip on that," or "Watch out for the spider!" I don't *see* because what's around me is much more beautiful than my sorry eyes can measure.

Which is why I take pictures.

I'm not an artist. I'm a scientist. I take readings with my lenses and I run analyses with my processing software. I can't resist digging in and uncovering the truth. The pull to know—to experience—is too powerful.

So when my dear twin brother tells me to put away my brand-spanking-new, ultra-high-resolution, megapixel camera phone and "enjoy the party" I tell him to go away.

He stands close because bad pop music thumps through the house and if his lips were more than a foot away I wouldn't be able to hear him. Which, when I think about it, might be preferable.

"Isa, come on." Mack pushes his wire-rims up his nose and gives me one of his narrow, one-eyebrow-cocked eye rolls. It's meant to convey annoyance but mostly it shows condescension.

"You better not give that look to your students or you're going to get a ton of bad evaluations." I poke at his nose with my camera phone. Winter semester started last week and the party is supposed to be some sort "welcome back from break" celebration.

His look changes to one of perplexity as he leans closer. "What?"

Now I roll my eyes, knowing full well my face looks identical to his. Same muscle pulls. Same eyebrow arch. Same dirty blue eyes under the same dirty blonde hair. At least on him, the "dirty" looks more like verdigris in his eyes and copper in his hair. It makes him handsome under his glasses. Under mine, I just look like every other semi-chubby boring chick with a phone in her hand.

My dear brother rubs his forehead and his fingers shadow his face. The party's lights are low, with most of the house's illumination coming from the multitude of twinkling fairy lights woven through banisters, stapled up along the house's crown molding, and thrown over the random fifties art hanging on the walls.

The house must have been built in the thirties. The rooms circle the central stairwell and are all separated by grand double doors. Leaded glass panels top all the windows. I need to get a few shots of the moonlight through the bevels before I go.

"Why don't you talk to someone?" Mack waves his beer bottle. It's the same random microbrew I'm drinking and the stuff smells like piss.

Mack takes a sip out of his bottle and makes a *this is gross* face. "It's not an undergrad party, you know. They're all adults. Some have jobs."

I know a few people here. I come and go from this part of the world, and right now I'm in town for three days before I'm off to Namibia for my next shoot. It's a big deal—I'm assisting one of the best photojournalists working in the field and every time I think about the gig my stomach does flip-flops. Which is why Mack dragged me to this party. To take my mind off business.

But for me, my upcoming shoot is as much graduate school as Mack's current road toward a PhD. He's in cultural anthropology. I'm documenting "the cultural" for the anthropologists and the magazines.

It was nice of him, though, to store my stuff on such short notice during the month I'll be gone. One should have a permanent address, even if one is permanently not at home.

I had my fill of our mother's house when her new boyfriend moved in. Codependency is not my cup of tea. I'd rather be out in the world falling victim to my need to see instead of locked down in California.

I don't know what Mack told his roommate, though. Mack says he's a first-year student in his department. Called him "the new kid" and said he's charming. His name's Rob or Bob or maybe Cob. I don't remember, but I do remember the slight tick moving across Mack's cheek when he said "charming."

The twitch means the same thing now as it did in high school and our undergraduate years: Stay away, sister. We've got a player on our hands.

Not that players pay attention to me. I'm not their type, with the glasses and the ubiquitous camera equipment and the general round-ness to my hips and breasts. I glance down at my chest. My knit top's a little tight and my chosen-for-comfort-while-traveling black skirt and tights show more of my roundness than I generally like. Half a month in the wilds of Africa might just be what I need to finish thinning out. I dropped thirty pounds the last time I was overseas.

Not that I need thinning, really. Sometimes I wonder why my brain still thinks these thoughts.

Mack rubs his forehead again.

I touch his arm, drawing his attention. "One's starting, isn't it?"

Migraines began for my brother less than a week after we turned thirteen. They were pretty bad in high school, and it took him vomiting in the nurse's office to get him to admit something was wrong. I dragged him home and made Mom sober up enough to take him to the doctor.

He's been on meds ever since. Once we got into college, the headaches lessened, and he's been doing well lately, but I can tell when one starts.

If he goes home now, takes a med, and sleeps, he'll be fine tomorrow.

He nods yes.

"Do you want me to walk with you back to the apartment?" The party house is about five blocks from Mack's place. I stowed my stuff this afternoon, taking the key he gave me, before he dragged me here to see old friends and introduce me to his new ones.

Except the roommate. Rob-Bob-Cob was off somewhere. Mack said studying.

Mack waves me off before setting his bad beer on a low table against a wall. "No use you leaving as well. You haven't seen your friends in ages." He nods toward the living room. "I'll walk my own sorry ass home. The fresh air will do me good. The headache will clear up before I get back to the apartment. I promise."

He waves at the party again. "Just be quiet when you come in, okay? If you find Rob passed out on the couch, don't poke him. He has bad breath."

I snicker. So the player has his flaws.

But I can't abandon my brother. "I don't need to stay."

Mack pinches the bridge of his nose. "You want to get some more shots with that wonder of digital precision, don't you?" He points at my camera phone. "I know you do."

I do. I'm as fascinated by the new and developing language of social media photography as I am by the wilds of the planet and the cultures of humanity. It's another property of the world that needs documenting, measuring, and analyzing.

Mack nods over his shoulder. "Lisa was asking about you. She's in the living room. Go say hi."

I squeeze his hand. "Are you sure?" We all went to the same college in our undergraduate days and Lisa also came to this university with Mack. It'd be nice to talk to her.

Mack squeezes back. "Promise me you'll be careful walking back to the apartment, okay? See if someone will walk with you."

I frown. I can handle myself. You need skills if you're going to do fieldwork.

Mack frowns back at me. "Please."

"Yes, Dad."

He chuckles, but stops when it obviously hurts.

"Text me the moment you get home." I pat his arm. "I want to make sure you're okay."

My poor twin brother nods one last time. He pulls out his phone, swiping at the screen, and the sudden blue haze lights up his face. He waves the device in my general direction and makes his way toward the door, leaving me to fend for myself in the cultural jungle of a grad student party.

CHAPTER 2

Robert

I stare at Mack's text. We now have a semi-permanent house guest. Permanent in that she's technically moving in, but semi in that she rarely sets foot in the United States.

When he asked if she could crash in our apartment, I just shrugged and returned my nose to reading articles and grading papers. Mack's sister can sleep on the floor if she wants. Who am I to say no?

The screen fogs around my grip and an extra hint of blue creeps out from under my fingertips. And up my flesh. I stuff my hand into my pocket as I watch the texts from Mack roll in.

I need a pair of touchscreen gloves. Otherwise I'm going to lose a digit to frostbite before the winter's over. I pull my hand from my pocket again. *Does she have someone to walk her home?* I text. Five blocks in the cold by herself isn't likely to cause problems, but still.

She said she'd find someone.

The party is a block up and one over. I wasn't planning on walking by it, but I could. *Do you want me to ask her?*

Mack doesn't respond for a long moment. I stuff my ungloved hand into my pocket again and resume walking. But I dodge up the side street, knowing I'm going to end up at that party, no matter what he says.

Took my med. Off to sleep. She'll frown but don't let her walk home alone.

Okay, I text back, feeling more relieved than I probably should. It's not my place to butt into his family, or to swoop in, but I'd hate for something to happen.

Especially since we haven't yet been introduced.

Shit, I think. He showed me pictures a couple of nights ago. She's his twin sister, and I'll be looking for a sweeter, prettier version of Mack.

A nice, lovely Wellington whose first name I don't remember.

Send me a photo, I text. *What's her name again?*

I stuff my phone into my pocket and pull on my glove, hoping my roommate hasn't gone off to bed yet.

But he still hasn't answered by the time I round the fence into the front yard of the party house.

It's a semi-rundown place, like all the other student-rented houses around campus. The concrete front steps settled a long time ago and are now uneven. The porch sags and needs painting. But, like the apartment I share with Mack, the rent's probably cheap.

Music thumps through the hallway of the big house full of partying grad students. It shakes my eyeballs and my perception of people talking in tight huddles, causing a slight visual bump, making it difficult to distinguish faces in the too-dim light.

I press into the crowd and slowly make my way toward the back of the house.

Mack's photos of his sister were from their early undergrad years. In every single one, she was slightly out of the frame, or slightly blurry, or slightly behind something. None of the photos gave me a good sense of her features, her hair, how she stands, what her smile looks like.

I push into the back room of the house and sling my pack off my back. The hostess is a socially-oriented person, a woman aptly named Sunnie, who'd put a cruise ship entertainment director to shame. She wouldn't appreciate me smacking around her guests with twenty-five pounds of textbooks. Sunnie is a fellow grad student's wife and in the process of starting her own social media public relations company. No one was surprised when they learned she'd already landed three big clients.

A week into my first semester, one of her parties landed Mara in my bed. Then Olivia, a couple weeks later. Neither relationship lasted more than two weeks.

I met my brother Tom's hot new woman over winter break. Looked at all his new paintings, many of which were studies of her graceful curves and the lovely line of her jaw.

They smiled at each other. I watched them hold hands without realizing they were holding hands. And I wondered if a woman could see me that way.

Not that I'm jealous. I'm not. Both my brothers are better at commitment. I learned to accept my little relationship-deficit issue a long time ago, but I don't need to feed it right now. Which is why I stopped going to parties.

New town. New standing with the female half of the human race. At least I keep telling myself that.

I rub my face as I walk through the dim halls of the grad-student-filled house, wondering about building that new reputation.

I used to bring one or two, maybe three, brilliant evenings to as many women as I could. I'm their nova, their bright point of physical pleasure, the memory they use to make their long-term committed boyfriend feel inadequate.

I took my job seriously. Or so I like to tell myself.

I don't do that anymore. Maybe it's boring now. Maybe I'm worried about finishing my degree. Or maybe somewhere in the back of my mind I'm irritated that my brother, who wasn't dating, is now engaged to a woman he swears is the love of his life.

I circle through the house's dining area, scouting the crowd as I make my way toward the dining room. The house twinkles tonight. Layers and layers of tiny lights cover the ceiling and every surface in the interior. At least six or seven strands wind around the bar, making it look like an ice giant puked on the booze. I push in and lean on the counter.

The bar is an add-on to the house and probably put in by a former owner sometime in the seventies. The counter top is an ugly orange-tinted laminate full of pot marks and scratches. The tiny fridge underneath is probably the same age as my father. And the five bar stools are sticky black vinyl numbers that feel like they came from a dollar store.

Sunnie, our hostess, leans forward, her elbow on the bar, and her ample bosom flattens against her chest. She's a lovely woman, slightly older than me, with a sweet round face and a wit she normally keeps to herself. Says "commentary" doesn't help keep the clients.

"Nice to see ya, handsome." Sunnie winks as she wipes the counter with a rag, playing up her hostess-slash-bartender role. "Why you wearing the buzz cap and carrying your books?" She points at the bee stripes pulled over my hair.

"Just walking by on my way home from the library." I hold up the bag. "Studying."

She's not watching the bag. She's watching my bicep. I stifle a head shake. It's not like she can see anything under my jacket, so I don't know what she's actually thinking. But I can guess. I get a lot of looks like that.

"Ah..." Sunnie smiles and hands me a beer. "I'll keep the bag back here if you want to relax a little."

I grin but keep the tight hold on the straps. "Mack asked me to walk his sister home."

Sunnie nods toward the crowd. "She's probably in the living room." A bottle appears.

I take it, adhering to the student motto of never passing up free beer, and lean closer. "Do you, by chance, remember her name?"

Sunnie laughs and wipes down the bar again. "Sadly, not this time, handsome. Sorry."

I toss my hostess a salute before turning back to the crowd. I take a sip of the beer. *Chilled* is about all it is. Frowning, I stare for a long moment at the amber liquid in the bottle gripped by my fingers. Not all microbrews make the grade.

I take another sip anyway, and scan the crowd.

A knot of three women stand off to the side, in a corner. They laugh, and one I recognize—Mack's friend Lisa—touches the arm of one I don't.

The new woman looks up from her phone and the lenses of her glasses momentarily mirror the blue light of her screen.

But it highlights her face.

The party blanks out. Lisa and the other woman laugh but I don't pay attention. I don't care that one pushes a strand of hair behind her ear or that the other sips at her wine. I see only the set of the new woman's shoulders. The lush roundness of her hips and how they balance her two mounds of female perfection on her chest.

I notice her ease with the tech in her hand. But mostly I wonder how that sweep of her finger would feel on my skin. I want to know if her voice is as smooth as her body. If I'll hear the same layers of brilliance I see.

I want to know what color her eyes are. If her lips are dark and rosy, or light and pink. I want to see her smile.

My head tips to the side, my brain wanting to see around the glare bouncing off the glasses hiding her eyes.

And I finally recognize my mystery lady.

CHAPTER 3

Isolde

Mack's old friend Lisa leans closer. They dated for a year before grad school. Now they're buds. "Have you met Rob yet?" she says.

Robert Quidell. It took Lisa and her friend Anne to nail down his name, along with a few other traits my brother's roommate seems to possess.

"Not yet," I say, and take a sip of my beer. It's weak and bitter, and tastes more like what I used to drink out of a plastic cup in high school.

Anne sighs and nods her head like she's in the know. "He's God's gift, by the way."

Lisa laughs and touches my arm. "So you're warned. For when you do meet him. Best to know what to expect."

Anne laughs.

I watch them both, marveling at the similarity of expression on the faces of these two very different women. Lisa is tall, thin, and more blonde than me. Anne is short but also thin, and dark. But their lips both curl into the same sardonic, knowing grin.

I snap a photo and glance down at my phone. This new camera is doing a pretty good job in the low light. Though I wish I had fill flash.

"God's gift?" I ask, making conversation.

Anne nods. "He's easy on the eyes."

Lisa laughs again. "And other parts."

I look up at her face, shocked. Lisa's not the sleeping around type.

She laughs again. "Or so I've heard."

I think they've both had too much to drink. "I'm not looking for a relationship." I'll be leaving town in a couple of weeks.

"No one said anything about a relationship." Anne sips at her beer.

I roll my eyes. I try not to, but it happens anyway. "Dear Penthouse Letters," I say. "I never thought it would happen to me. But when I walked into my brother's apartment—"

A warm baritone flows over me from behind. A wonderful voice, one more musical and resonant than the song blaring from the speakers in the corner. "Hello, ladies," the mystery man says.

I turn around and look up at a textbook handsome face topped off by the most ridiculous hat I've ever seen. It's yellow and black, with a pointed top and two earflaps that look suspiciously like bee wings, and it makes his pale eyes all but glow.

The new guy grins and points at his head. "Nephew gave it to me." A look of pure joy flashes over his face as if thinking about his nephew makes him happier than anything else in the world.

But the look of joy vanishes quickly. And I think that I just glimpsed something most other people aren't allowed to see.

Or don't see, because they don't look beyond the perfection of his strong, square features and his shadow of stubble. I glance at Lisa and Anne. Neither of them seemed to have noticed his expression. They're both staring at the new guy with eyes full of dismissive lust. As if they see only the wonderfully masculine jaw exactly proportioned to balance the broadness of his shoulders. He's not particularly big, or extra tall, though he's tall enough I need to tilt up my head when I look at him.

When I glance back, he's looking at Lisa and Anne. And I think he looks faintly disappointed.

My body skips a beat. Not just my heart, but my entire body. How could they have missed the happiness he flashed when he mentioned his nephew?

I want to touch his face to make sure the muscle movements I saw dart across his cheeks were real. A part of me wants to push my fingers under the bumblebee hat and run my fingers through the dark hair poking out under its edge. It's the part that saunters onto a scene and often does exactly what it wants to, no matter what my responsible brain says. But listening to the *Bad idea!* thoughts often gets me shitty pictures.

Warm and slick creeps between my thighs. I want to nuzzle my face against his neck and breathe in his skin, smell its scent, feel its softness. My tongue wakes up too and somewhere in my head I hear *Lick his abs.*

God damn, I'm a freak.

Deep in my brain a little voice is saying *see* this one. There's more to that look. More than Anne and Lisa give him credit for. I want to understand this man's world. His body. How he moves. The things my cameras can't capture. Get a full sensory understanding of what's right in front of me.

He's watching me. Not Anne, who is arguably the prettiest of the three of us, or Lisa, the thinnest. He's looking at me.

"Rob," he says, and holds out his hand.

I blink. My mouth must be open. I don't shake back even though I know I should be friendly. But *goddamn* this man is magnetic and I don't dare touch him.

"No you don't, Robert. Shoo." Lisa waves her hand at him.

He smiles and his pale eyes twinkle. I almost melt. What the hell is wrong with me?

"Are you Mack's sister?" He holds out his hand again and his gaze stays glued to me.

His name's Robert. Rob. He's the mysterious roommate.

"Yes," I say. I take his offered hand this time, unable to resist the need to feel his skin. To know if his touch is as focused as his gaze.

His fingers glide first over the tips of mine. A tingle fires into the tight array of small muscles and tendons holding together my joints. When his grip tightens and his fingers press into the flesh of my wrist, I feel his electricity merge into my bones and flow through my veins.

And realize that his hand is ice cold. Startled, I let go, and wave my fingers in the air. "Did you just come in from outside?"

Rob laughs and stuffs his hand into his pocket. "Sorry. Texting with your brother. Don't have good gloves."

I swear his eyes twinkle again.

He leans close. "What's your name?"

Lisa and Anne look at each other and I see a plan forming. A slightly mean plan, as if they think, for some reason, that he needs a lesson.

Part of me thinks the undeniably hot guy smiling at me right now probably doesn't deserve to be played. But another part of me gets a thrill. If he has to figure out my name, his attention will stay on me.

"We are not giving you *any* information, Robert Quidell." Anne pokes his shoulder. "No name. No likes and dislikes. Nothing. Now go find someone else to charm."

He doesn't look at my friends. He watches me, assessing. Mapping, I think, every angle my body twists into as a response to his presence. Looking for patterns in my small movements, my twitches. He's reading me the way he'd read a book.

I feel the same twinge I do when I peel back the shadows and photograph a truth. When I find a moment, a small point in the universe, and I document what is truly there. When I know what's in front of me isn't simply a picture.

Robert Quidell is as real and alive and full of the pushes and pulls of the universe as any subject who has ever crossed through the focal plane of my lens.

He knows it, too. "I provide only an opportunity to be charmed," he says, his face open yet sardonic, his posture friendly yet cocky.

The man in front of me is no idiot.

I laugh and shake my head, wishing I had enough light to see the true color of his eyes. His irises glimmer and I wonder if I'm looking at reflected starlight.

I grin. He's too delicious an opportunity to pass up, even if he is my brother's bad boy roommate. "Hmmm... I'm sensing a... reputation?"

Rob laughs. But his face falls a bit too, and the laugh seems to be more to cover what I suspect is, for him, a sore spot. I said "reputation" and his shoulders slumped like a fugitive who'd just been caught by the FBI. Rob Quidell stands in front of me, a man carrying the weight of his sins.

Or it seems so to me.

My thighs press together and I wiggle where I stand. My neck and cheeks heat and I thank all that's good in the universe for the low lighting. My nipples tighten and my breasts feel as if he's already dancing those exquisite fingers over my flesh.

Am I feeling empathy? I don't know. But I do, deep inside, think this man needs a second chance.

CHAPTER 4

Robert

Lisa and Anne must have warned Mack's sister about me because the moment she figured out who I am, her posture changed.

If the music wasn't so loud, I suspect I'd be hearing a little voice in the back of my head whispering sentences like *Feel that drop in your stomach? Your rep turns every new encounter into the same old, same old.* And *This is what you get for being an ass.*

But I'm not an ass. I'm honest about what I have to give and I always give what I promise.

Yet that little whisper jabbing its fingers into the back sides of my eyeballs yells *The women just delineated, laid out, highlighted, and bullet-pointed for Mack's sister the schema you built yourself, dumbass.*

The look I see on my roommate's sister's face is exactly the same look I see on every woman's face. It's the same *Oh, I know your type.*

I suppose I shouldn't be surprised.

I grin though, and laugh, when she mentions my "reputation." What else am I to do? This script's been written. Welcome to the new episode of *Educating Rob Quidell*, everyone's favorite sitcom.

It takes energy to break through a woman's walls and, honestly, I'm tired. And she's Mack's sister, so it really doesn't matter. Let the ladies have their moment of poking at little old me, because it gives Lisa and Anne a sense of power.

It's funny how it's always the ones I don't sleep with who play the mean games.

I don't frown. I control the tics and the twitches. And I watch Mack's sister do her best not to be affected by the promised lust my reputation carries with it. But she squirms.

Because she knows my type.

So we all fall into the game we're expected to play, because the game is what we all expect. Me included.

"Living life nameless must be tough." I grin again and nod, doing my best to say *I understand the game*, as I set down my tasteless beer on the table to the side of Mack's sister's hip. Her skirt's short and I can't help but stare at the hem of the dark fabric brushing her thigh. She's beautifully proportioned.

I twist a little, angling my chest toward her body, and make a show of looking at her ass.

But her grin looks more open than I expect.

Lisa and Anne vanish from my perception. I stand straight and relaxed, focusing on the woman in front of me. The drop in my stomach eases as I look at the lovely planes of her face. I see the same bone structure as Mack, but softer and feminine. Exquisite. Her glasses don't hide the intelligence in her eyes, or her obvious ability to perceive the world around her.

I doubt anything is lost on this woman. My gut does a little dance, but not to push off the costume Lisa and Anne placed on my shoulders, or to stop feeling sorry for myself. It dances because I'm in the presence of brilliance.

Nothing is sexier than a mind as agile as the body.

I don't think I will have a problem walking my roommate's twin sister home tonight.

"You have one of the new ultra-pixel phones?" I point at the small bag strapped around her shoulder. She'd dropped her gadget into it when I walked up. "I have one." I pull mine from my pocket. "No clue how to use the camera."

She blinks and shivers a little, as if I surprised her. When she turns her back on Lisa and Anne, aligning with me, I almost smirk at the other women. But I don't need to be the bad boy they think I am.

I drop my lips close to Mack's sister's ear. "Did you see the stained glass window on the porch? The moon is shining through it. I'd like to take a picture."

The smile she gives me is wonderful and beautiful and beyond any I could imagine. The game, for the moment, vanishes.

When she reaches for my phone, I don't touch her again. I don't know why. I usually stroke a woman's elbow or her shoulder. Small movements to make her comfortable with me. But with Mack's sister, for some reason, it feels disingenuous.

Maybe because I've touched so many women so many times I don't believe I'd feel her skin, her body, under my fingers. I'd feel all the other elbows and shoulders the way I feel every steering wheel in my hands whenever I drive a new car.

It's never the moment I'm in. It's always all the moments where I've been.

But I want to touch. I want to be somewhere I can hear her clearly. Someplace with fresh air so I know it's her scent, her perfume I smell, and not Lisa's.

The porch should give us a moment to recalibrate.

And maybe I can get her to tell me her name.

She grins and holds up my phone, looking at the screen. "I'm still learning the limits of mine." She tilts it side to side like it's one of those sloshing water toys that makes new images when you wiggle it.

I step back and hoist my backpack onto my shoulders. She picks up the coat that's sitting next to her on the table where we dropped our tasteless beers, and I shepherd her into the crowd. Lisa throws me a dirty look, one meant to say *I'm telling Mack*, but my roommate will know I've made friends with his sister soon enough. The desire to make kissy lips at Lisa almost overcomes my control. Instead, I wave and walk into the crowd with the beautiful woman whose name I don't remember, on our way to a moment of privacy.

And I can no longer keep my fingers away.

CHAPTER 5

Isolde

Rob spreads his fingers over my lower back, his palm resting where my spine curves out toward my ass, as he guides me through the crowded hallway toward the house's front door.

His hand's no longer cold. Warmth flows through the fabric of my shirt, to my flesh, and up my backbone. His fingers press but don't dig, and his hand flows with the movements of my body.

He's learning. I see it on his face when I look up, too. He's watching and adjusting and figuring out how to understand the best way to interact with me.

Like I'm a puzzle.

I hold his phone in my hand. I feel, strangely, as if this man handed over part of his soul. That allowing me to touch the device I grip between my fingers and my palm—and allowing me to carry it— symbolizes something. I just don't know what.

Or maybe I'm reading more into it than there is. Maybe I'm reading a whole lot of what I want into a whole lot of nothing. My body is attracted, for sure. How could it not be? He's spectacularly gorgeous. Firm and well-angled, with a nice shadow of stubble on his chin. Where I should be behind the camera, he should be in front of it. But I've been around beautiful men before. Fashion shoots tend to be flooded with beautiful men.

Shoots have production plans. Scripts, basically, of the story that needs to be told via the produced visuals. Perhaps my brain is making up a script for the pretty bad boy with the bee hat and a hand on my back.

Rob leans close so that I can hear him over the music. His breath dances over the top curve of my ear, across the sensitive inner folds, shifting the few strands of my hair that have fallen from my ponytail.

I close my eyes for a moment, letting the sensation wash over me, and allow him to escort me through the crowd toward a place without distractions.

The responsible part of my brain wants to stop this game right now. But we have five blocks until we reach the apartment and, damn it, I want to enjoy his touches while I can.

"What should I call you? Since I'm barred from learning your real name." he asks, his lips still only inches from my ear.

He could nibble, if he wanted. Right here in full view of all the partygoers. Nibble on my ear and work his hand under my shirt and I don't think I'd stop him no matter how annoyed my Responsible Brain got.

"What do you want to call me?" I say. We're playing a game, so a game we will play.

Rob chuckles as he pushes some drunk guy out of the way. Grad students, for the most part, behave better than undergrads, but parties are still parties.

The drunk guy blinks and gives Rob the finger.

We both chuckle as we fall out onto the front porch. The music drops to just the *thump thump* of the beat. I slip on my jacket, transferring his phone from one hand to the other, as the cold air hits. The world takes on the real colors of night—the soft shadows of pinks and greens that the twinkling electric fairy lights hid. The moon shines in the sky, surrounded by a spray of clouds, and the streetlights throw pools along the sidewalk leading away from the party.

It's as crisp and blue as the chill in the air.

"The window is over there." Rob points off to the side, where the porch takes a turn and wraps around the side of the house, to another door, on the side. I think it used to be a servant entrance.

He tips his head as if trying to see around the corner, and smiles as he takes my hand. He pulls me toward the promised stained glass window.

The tug moves me forward, but his grip flows up my arm. All I see, all I feel, is the strength of his arms. How it's *there*; how it's part of him. It's not a feature he scrubs clean or plays up because he wants to attract women. He doesn't present it to the world as a part of his uniform.

It's in his bones.

It's what I need to photograph.

We turn the corner and blocks of colored moonglow dance over his face. He smiles, pointing at his phone, which I still hold. "What do I do?"

He's playing. He understands how to use the camera. I can tell the moment he unlocks the screen for me. When I turn toward the window, he moves behind me, watching over my shoulder. I half expect him to stroke my arms the way a tennis pro would while whispering things like "Your grip needs to be firmer."

I must be smirking because he chuckles in my ear. "I think I shall call you Diana, goddess of the moon."

The tone in his voice carries the perfect amount of wry humor. A big hearty laugh rolls from my belly and I bend over, giggling. "You are a freak, you know that, Rob Quidell? A total freak of nature."

He laughs too, and his pale eyes glimmer in the colored light, still brilliantly intelligent and still hiding their true color from me. "I promised your brother that I'd walk you to the apartment, so hopefully I'm not *too* freaky."

I snap a picture of the window and hold up his phone so he can see. "If you set it like this..." I swipe my finger over the screen. "...and use this filter..." I swipe again. "...you'll get a nice image."

Rob nods. "Ah."

Yeah, I'm pretty sure he knew exactly how to take a good photo with his camera phone. "Mack asked you to walk me home?" I snap another one for him, framing the window just right to get a nice image of the moon.

"I volunteered. I was walking by anyway." He reaches over his head and pats his backpack.

An image of him making the exact same move, but shirtless, flickers through my mind's eye. I see the wonderful elongation and tightening of a man's abdomen that happens when he curls a bicep and holds an arm next to his ear.

Something must have flickered across my face because Rob smirks.

My shoulders tighten. "You didn't need to stop. I can handle myself." The words snap from my mouth a little tighter and a little higher pitched than I meant them to. The last remnants of the terrible beer must be messing with my head.

Either that, or I'm embarrassed about ogling him.

His mouth rounds and he steps back. He looks a little shocked. "Sorry if I offended."

"No offense." My responses to him confound me. I'm not used to feeling this way. So I smile. "So you're my knight in shining bumblebee armor?"

I flick through the filters on his phone, looking for something that will get me a good image. Not of the moonlight flowing through the window, but of Rob standing here with the window's reds and blues dancing over his skin, a beautiful boy draped under a blanket of beautiful colors, topped off by a ridiculous hat.

He's much more interesting than the moon and I might as well concentrate on photographing the wonder standing next to me than on how he makes me feel.

He doesn't answer. No stupid crack about knights or armor or slaying dragons falls out of his luscious mouth. He just grins and I swear his eyes soften.

Maybe it's a trick of the light. Maybe, like before, I don't see what I think I do. But I swear, for a second, I see a very different desire in his eyes than what he expects me to see.

I snap a picture.

He blinks, stunned, and the look disappears underneath his façade. I check the image, hoping.

I didn't catch it. His eyes are in the process of hardening. The tilt of his head is changing to add distance. I missed it by a microsecond.

"Damn," I whisper.

"What?" He leans closer. "My nostrils too big?"

Chuckling, I hand over his phone. "You going to walk me home, pretty boy?"

"Nice to know the photographer thinks I'm pretty enough to photograph." Rob nods in a way that says *uh-huh* and crosses his arms. "Are you going to tell me your name?"

My brother and this man have been living in the same apartment for a semester, so I *know* Mack has told him my name. It's his problem he doesn't remember, not mine.

"Do you have a middle name?" I ask. For some reason, I'm expecting something ridiculous and elaborate, like Maximillian or Rachenthrall. Probably because of the ridiculous and elaborate hat.

Rob narrows his eyes. "Why?"

I shrug. "Just wondering."

"What's yours?" He takes my hand again as if it's the most natural gesture ever and tugs me toward the side exit off the porch.

I only grin.

We round the front of the house, Rob still holding my hand. Out on the sidewalk, we walk toward the apartment. Rob unconsciously falls into a stride matching mine, one that seems a little too short for him, but not uncomfortable.

Maybe this isn't such a bad game. Touching and being touched isn't bad. He's my brother's roommate and, I think, a man worth knowing.

So I breathe. I let myself feel the tingling again, wondering about that air mattress Mack inflated and tossed on the floor of their "den" before we left for the party. That squishy, crinkly, baggie-full-of-air that I will be sleeping on for the next three nights.

Then I remember the tingle in my hand and arm when Rob took my hand. It resurfaces and fires across my shoulders and to my breasts.

And I wonder if Rob's bed is more comfortable.

He smirks and stuffs his phone into his pocket. Leaning back, he makes a show of checking out my ass again, then looks up at the sky. "This bumblebee says you are as lovely as a spring day." He leans close, his head turning as if he's about to kiss my neck, but he breathes in deeply instead. "Fresh scented and sweetly hued."

Rob's smirk widens into a full-on, smartass grin. "I think your middle name is Daffodil, like the flower." He smoothes his hand over his bee hat. "Daffy, for short."

I smack his arm. Not hard, but I can't help myself. I'm laughing too hard. "Mack should have warned me that you're a brat." Though Lisa did warn me about his charm.

"I thought I was a freak of nature." Rob and I walk along, him on the outside, between me and the street, his pack on his back.

Out here in the yellow glow of the streetlights, when we both pull on our gloves, I notice the black leather cord tied with what looks like an old, tight knot circling his left wrist. It's worn and I wonder how long he's kept it close to his skin.

His flawless, warm skin. Gorgeous, healthy, clean and fresh-smelling, lovely skin that is as perfect on his neck and jaw and forehead as it is on his arms. And it's all topped off by what I suspect is a mop of wrap-my-fingers-in black hair.

I skip ahead so I'm not looking at him anymore. I think my brain—responsible and not-so-responsible parts—needs a break from his scrumptiousness. It's causing me to need to fan myself.

A step or two ahead of Mr. Robert Quidell, I'm out in the open again, looking at the world. My fingers want to pull out my new camera toy and snap a few images. Stuff I'll look at later to see if I can manipulate it into moody, flowing wonders. Pieces that, by virtue of showing the sameness of this street with all other streets, might give some insight into what's *not* the same here. What's different in the world of the image-taker.

Like the man who's next to me again, less than an elbow away. Rob strides along, grinning and pointing out buildings so he has an excuse to touch my back. It feels like both a conscious and an unconscious effort on his part, as if he's learned how to play *my* game, and now he's an expert. He stopped thinking about it ages ago and now he's fallen into an easy automatic looseness.

He's Mack's height and he doesn't tower over me, which I like. He's probably six feet, maybe a fraction under, but his shoulders are broader than I'd expect for a guy his size. Not that he's over-muscled—I hate that—just that his bones look big.

The sense of strength returns. I see it in the power of his stride and the mesmerizing cords of his neck.

"So no Daffy?" Rob smiles a real smile, not the player smirk from earlier. He walks parallel with me, his eyes forward, except for the occasional glance down the front of my shirt.

My body reacts the way I suspect he engineered his attentions to make it respond: A blush rises across my neck and cheeks, and across my chest. I feel hot, even in the cold air. My belly tingles. And I suspect my hips sway more than my usual walk.

Perhaps I should admit to myself how desired I feel. How his ease and his smile make me think he doesn't have the shallow definitions of beauty I've encountered with many of the men who work in my field. The guys who allow their image aesthetics to shape their three dimensional world.

The irony of having this gorgeous man make me feel this way makes me smirk. Perhaps I drank more beer than I realized. Looking at him makes me feel a little drunk.

I push my glasses up my nose, to better see his face. "Perhaps I should call you Goofy."

I still can't tell the color of his eyes.

Rob laughs again. "Call me Pluto, Lord of the underworld. My Diana, goddess of the moon." He flicks his hand at the sky.

His eyes flash. Their silver tones burst with the moonlight and for a moment I wonder who the real moon god is. It's certainly not me.

He's enjoying himself and, I think, he wants me to enjoy myself too. I'm a puzzle. He's a puzzle. We're having fun. Even if I do call him on his bad memory when we return to the apartment, I think I'll play along for a little longer.

"The moon is my strobe, Lord Hades."

Another, heartier laugh rolls from Rob. "Where have you been all my life?"

I shake my head. But when his hand glides over my back again, his fingers moving slowly up from the low curve of my spine toward the spot just below my shoulder blades—and just below the clasp of my bra

—I find myself leaning toward him. My hips twist slightly as I walk. And the next thing I know, Rob Quidell has his arm around my waist as we walk.

His fingers glide over my hip and settle into a gentle hold. Is he acting possessive? Is he telling me with the pressure of his fingertips what he wants? I don't know.

But he smiles and I feel safe even though I just met him. Literally just met this man with a reputation of making women feel good without the guilt of attachment and I feel my not-so-Responsible Brain roll through all sorts of excuses: *Mack will protect me if Rob turns out to be an asshole.* And *He's freakin' gorgeous. When have you been with a freakin' gorgeous guy? You might work with them but they ignore you.*

"Home." Rob points at the apartment and his hand moves up my side to just under my breast. A quick, barely perceptible squeeze presses through my jacket before his hand lifts away.

I want it back. I'm not often on the receiving end of touches. Gentle, strong, firm, light, it doesn't matter. I'm behind the camera— behind a wall—and I'm not to be touched. And now I have a desirable man touching me.

I like it. I like it a lot.

And my not-so-Responsible Brain kicks out the ultimate rationalization: *You're leaving in three days. What difference does it make?*

His hand trails across my back before stroking my opposite elbow. He's watching my arm, not my face, as if seeing his fingers perform this dance makes him as happy as the sensations the skin on skin contact creates.

I don't breathe and I hold perfectly still. His gloved fingers make a soft, smooth sound as they glide down my arm toward my palm and I think of rain in moonlight. He blinks slowly. The glow of his eyes vanishes, but not the gentleness of his touch. The electricity. The cool fire of our nerve endings brushing against each other.

He's a magician. Beautiful beyond words or images and I don't think I dare photograph him again unless I know I'm capable of creating images that capture him in three dimensions. Because he's popping out of the background for me. Taking all my attention with his fingers. And everything else suddenly, completely flattens out.

When his hand settles into mine again, I'm lost. Hypnotized. I feel my fretting drop away. Right here on the concrete steps to the apartment I would have been sleeping in anyway, I decide this game is more important than good citizenship and appropriate behavior.

"You make me feel naughty, Lord Hades," I whisper. It's juvenile. But something tells me Rob Quidell understands "juvenile" better than any other adult I've ever met. That he knows what to do come morning, when we're staring at each other over our cereal and coffee. That he'll smile and wink and tell me he's happy he could be of service.

And that what we are about to do might feel naughty, but isn't. Feeling naughty only makes it more fun.

Hunger works from Rob's cheeks up to the muscles around his eyes and down to his jaw and neck. He tightens, but not in an angry way. In an "I'm about to pounce" way. And I think I gasp.

Out here, on the steps up to the building, the glow from the streetlight twenty feet away reflects off the concrete under our feet, and I'm sure that this time he sees the heat creeping from under my coat's collar and up my neck. And the blush deepening the color of my lips. Maybe also the lust building in my eyes, even behind my glasses.

I'm positive he sees it in how I wriggle. Or how my breasts involuntarily thrust out toward his chest. Or how my hip wants so very much to rub against his crotch.

He leans forward, his gaze tight on mine, as if measuring and re-measuring my consent with each heartbeat thundering inside my head. Each moment. Each of his warm, mint-scented breaths.

"I am at your service, my goddess," he whispers as his lips graze my cheek.

CHAPTER 6

Robert

I think she's been waiting for a "You must be tired from running through my mind all night" line or perhaps a straight-up "let's fuck" since we walked out of the party.

The little voice in the back of my head that presses its fists into its waist and frowns before yelling *Charming women is bad!* has been waving its arms since we walked off the porch, poking at me, saying it's my own damned fault I get treated the way I do. If I hadn't bedded every woman I met since I was a teenager, I wouldn't have the rep.

And maybe Mack's sister wouldn't be eyeing me as if my services are the begin-all end-all of my role in this world. The way she's been the entire time we've walked home.

When I took her hand, the game slid from my fingers to the delicate skin of her wrist the way the sheets will slide on my bed when I lay her down naked and flushed.

And I won.

Her invitation is right in front of me in the looseness of her cheeks and her half-closed eyelids. She moves closer and brushes against my front. Even through our coats, I know her nipples harden to little buds. I know she's wet, wanting me.

I could slide her tights off the perfect curve of her hips and down her legs. Maybe use them to tie her ankles together. Or maybe tie her legs wide open, spread for me, slick and waiting.

I could press my fingers into her breasts. Breathe in the warm bronze sheen to the full waves of her hair. See the secret depths of her eyes.

Because I won.

Part of me didn't want to win. Part of me wanted the schema dictating how a woman sees me to disintegrate and let the two of us play by a different set of expectations. Hell, I think I wanted *her* to win. Just this once, I wanted a woman to play by her rules. I wanted to open my eyes to a new way of seeing the world.

But it seems we both took the easy route.

I breathe in the curls of her breath and the cold makes her scent all the warmer.

She gives me a brilliant come-hither look. "I think we should go inside."

Am I disappointed? Am I angry? But why do I want to kiss her so much even though this was too easy? Even though she's my roommate's sister and should be, by all measures, off limits?

But I think "off limits" might be what's fueling my win. I'm the inaccessible bad boy. The male she's never allowed to touch. I represent all the men she's not supposed to play with.

So exactly whose rules are we playing by?

"You realize Mack will not be happy with either of us, don't you?" I say. Perhaps pointing out the obvious will break us out of this path we've both stepped onto.

"He's a big boy. I'm a big girl." She grins. "I'm here for three days. Then I'm gone."

Or reaffirm my suspicions.

Back on the porch, I thought maybe we were connecting at a level deeper than the expectations Lisa fed into her head. But now I'm back to being a woman's bright point of physical fun.

Yet I shouldn't want to kiss her as much as I do. I don't kiss my nova-ing stars, my lovely moon goddesses. It seems too personal, too blinding, too close to their brightness. But Mack's sister tips back her head, her lush, moist lips parting slightly. Her tongue appears for a fleeting microsecond, then vanishes again into her mouth. And I lose all sense of the game.

Her scent intoxicates me. Her touch more so. I don't want to think about the inevitable embarrassed laughter and sucked-up handshake coming tomorrow morning, when we eat breakfast across from each other, Mack scowling at us for our immaturity.

I whisper the word I've been thinking since I saw her standing with Mack's friends: *goddess*.

She's my goddess tonight.

My lips graze hers. I touch with pressure only gentle enough to let her know how much I want to lift the hem of her skirt and cup her ass, but not enough to demand. It's her choice. I may have won, but the rules are hers.

She glances around as if embarrassed by public displays of attraction. Or tempted by them.

"There's an alcove off the entryway," I nod toward the dark, glassed-in front of the building, "if you don't want to go upstairs."

Her eyes and mouth round. If she wants a bad boy, I'll play the bad boy and fuck her against the scratchy brick wall of the back of the alcove, my jeans around my ankles and her skirt yanked over her face. Mack will never need to know.

My cock responds, itching for attention. It knows the drill. The game. We fuck; it feels good. The itch is scratched. Then I go about my life the way I always do.

The fatigue I felt when she first indicated she knows of my "reputation" filters in. Fucking will happen. Gripping her ass is going to be glorious no matter if I take the path of least resistance and play to her expectations or if I try harder. If I take her under the stairs, or take her to my room and my bed. If I do what's expected, or if I become someone beyond a woman's expectations.

I know the rewards of expectation. I don't know the prizes of extra effort and diligence. Right now, my cock doesn't think it's worth the effort to figure it out.

"What if we get caught?" She stares at the door but she presses her ass against my crotch.

I feel myself slide into old habits as if I recorded all this and I'm watching a playback. Automatic desire tells my hand where to sit on her back, my lips the correct pressure to apply to the top edge of her ear. It tells my cock to stand at attention because I'm likely to get a quality blowjob tonight.

My habits feel comfortable. Warm and secure. This isn't a relationship—it can't be a relationship—so what difference does it make if I fall down to expectations? What difference does it make if I let my reputation give a woman a couple hours of joy?

So why is my back tightening up? She wants this.

"We won't get caught." The alcove is well-hidden.

"Are you going to take off the hat?" She takes my hand and pulls me toward the apartment vestibule.

We run up the steps and to the front of the creaking glass door. She pulls the extra key out of her little bag but fumbles it with her gloves. "Oh!"

My hand swings around her waist and I catch the key before it hits the ground. My chest is pressed firmly against her shoulder blades. My other hand splays over her belly. And carefully, gently, I press my erection against her ass.

She shivers. The cold exaggerates the vibration running from her hips to her breasts and up into her jaw, but it's the promise I press into her back that's making her moan.

"Here." I brush my lips against her ear. "Let me."

Slowly, I slide the key into the lock, mirroring the pressure I give the metal with the same force of my palm across her hip bone. She responds by wiggling her ass against my erection. I pull her against my front and yank open the door. Quickly, I roll us both in.

The vestibule of the apartment building is a dim, gray space full of mailboxes and creaky stairs. Sometime in the past, someone thought it a good idea to add a short wall blocking the sight lines to an empty space under the stairs. It's full of ladders and paint supplies now, and closed off by a mesh door, so no one can get in.

Unless you know the lock combo, which I do. I helped the super one day with a plumbing problem. He didn't think to change the numbers afterward.

I move her toward the stairs and around the short wall to the wire of the alcove door. Her fingers weave into the mesh and when she moans, the door rattles.

I don't turn her around. Don't demand a kiss. If we're playing the game this way, I'll play by the conventional rules. So I thread my hand under her jacket and slowly wiggle her shirt up underneath.

"I want to take pictures of you." Her voice is breathy. She leans into me, her back arching, and looks up at my face.

I want to spin her around. I want to taste those lovely lips. But that's not the game. "Now?"

Somewhere in the back of my head, my reputation is grinning like the cocky son of a bitch it is. What's a little more amateur porn going to hurt? My face isn't visible in any video that's online now. I know how to make sure it won't be this time, either.

It'll do her more harm than me.

She flips around and presses her back into the wire mesh. Her hands run over my chest and she rubs her lower belly against my cock. But her eyes narrow. "When I say I want pictures."

Oh, she's good. I grin. "With or without the hat?"

She answers by pulling off her gloves, unzipping my jacket and curling her fingers around my belt buckle.

CHAPTER 7

Isolde

Rob pulls my hands off his belt. His fingers stroke tiny circles on my hand before his skin lifts completely off mine and for a brief moment, all my perception zeroes in on my wrist. He touches just the right spot with just the exact amount of wispy pressure to set every single nerve ending in my body on fire.

My lips part and a minuscule, hitched breath passes over my tongue. Rob presses me against the cage and all I want to do is drop to my knees and find his cock under all the layers of jackets and clothes between us.

"Wait." Both his hands move away and he fiddles with the lock on the cage. The mechanism pops open and the door rocks under my weight.

Rob wraps his arm under my bottom and half-hoists, half-drags me to the side so he can open the door. It whines as it swings wide, so loud I think it's going to catch attention, but Rob doesn't seem to notice. He wiggles us inside, between two ladders leaning against the wall and a stack of what looks like industrial paint buckets.

A tarp spread over a stack of cans twists when his backpack drags over it. Rob frowns and closes the door, dropping his pack in front of it. We're trapped in here, behind a fence guarded by his books.

Only the dim light from the entrance area filters in. The paint smells astringent, with a little grease mixed in. A wheeled toolbox rattles when Rob pushes it against the wall opposite the ladders and he turns me around again, leaning me over its top.

His hands roam over my stuck-out ass, pinching and kneading, before he grabs my coat and pulls it off my shoulders. I hear it drop onto his backpack, followed by more rustling. He must be taking off his.

"Leave on the hat," I breathe. It makes this ridiculous moment all the more ridiculous. I'm about to fuck my brother's roommate. A man who doesn't know my name. A guy I'm going to be living with, if only randomly and temporarily.

A man with layers I want to see. But whose body is way, way too distracting.

So I'm letting this happen. I am, I think, getting it out of the way. Because if I don't, fucking him is all I'm going to think about as I lie on my air mattress staring at the ceiling. How he's one room over lying naked on his belly, his arm over the side of the bed, snoring softly instead of awake and hard and going down on me.

His roaming hands feel incredible. His touch is better than any other man's. And even if there's no relationship here, at least I've had a sample of what a gorgeous man has to offer. At least, for once in my life, I feel desired.

Rob chuckles but doesn't speak. He moves away for a second and I hear his backpack zipper open. Cellophane crinkles, then a strip of condoms appears on a step of the ladder next to my face.

Not one condom. Three.

My entire body quakes like I'm about to orgasm. Oh my god, what is he promising me? I turn around. His jacket lies on top of mine. He wears a dark-colored t-shirt that's tight around his chest but loose around his middle. He's backlit by the low light filtering in from the overhead globe in the entryway but his biceps pop. As do his forearms.

The arms of this man alone spark every single one of my deep, primal needs. A part of me wants to fight it, to dig for those special looks, but I want this, too.

I want both.

"Tomorrow at breakfast, we talk like adults, okay?" I say.

Rob chuckles again. "I aim only to please my goddess," he purrs.

He hoists me up onto the tool case, flicking my skirt at the same time so I'm not sitting on it. The fabric fans out over the cool metal and my perch rocks, but Rob presses his knees into it, holding it still. He's between my legs looking down like his cock is going to burst from his jeans on its own. As if my presence has set free his personal monster.

He works both hands under my skirt and up between the waistband and my tights. His fingers search for the elastic and when he finds the edge, his fingertips curl against my skin. But he doesn't yank them down. Not yet.

"Undo my belt," he says.

I immediately fumble with the leather, yanking as I try to work in the gloom of the alcove. His buckle rattles. Rob grins, fighting my pulls, and rubs small circles with the fingers he slid between my waistband and my skin.

The belt loosens and slides out of the buckle. The denim of his jeans feels softer than I expected, as does the cloth-covered waistband of the underwear peeking out the top. I close my eyes and work my fingers between the fabric and his skin, drinking in the lusciousness of this man's hard, firm muscles.

"Button and zipper," Rob sounds as if he's stalking me, playing with his prize. I'm the best he's ever caught and damn it, he's going to savor his toy.

I'm so wet I can barely think. I'll come the moment he flicks my clit with the pad of his thumb.

All I want is his cock. Fucking my pussy, fucking my mouth. Hell, pumping between my tits or my ass cheeks. I don't care. I just want to feel him lose control and come and come again.

I release the button on his jeans. His eyes half close. His mouth opens just a bit. And I slowly unzip his fly.

His fingers yank down my waistband at the same time, at the same speed. His thumbs flare out, pressing on my mound, and as the zipper of his jeans parts, his thumbs do their own opening. They curl down and inward, and stroke the edges of my inner lips.

"Oh, fuck," I groan. My head drops back but my hands rub his cock through the fabric of his boxer-briefs.

Rob leans into me and presses his thumbs together just below my clit, and he pinches closed my labia.

I moan and he chuckles into my ear. "You are freakin' sexy," he whispers. "I'm going to fuck you every night you're here. Every goddamned night."

He thinks I'm sexy? I pull back a little, and look at his wonderfully masculine face. Is he lying because we're hooking up? Does he mean what he's saying?

I can't tell in the low light. All I know is that his long, thick cock is rock hard and separated from my grip by too much fabric.

"You say that to all the girls, don't you?" I nip at his neck right along the collar of his shirt.

"Only the freakin' sexy ones." His lips press into the skin just below my earlobe. "And you are the by far the sexiest of the freaks."

His thumbs pull apart and I feel my pussy spread for him, even though my tights still strangle my hips.

But there's something off about how he's speaking. His face shifts a little again and he looks like he wants to kiss me. Or maybe he's disappointed that he can't. Or that he's saying weird, player things to me.

Because he's supposed to.

And I realize I still can't see the color of his eyes.

"Are you ready to do this?" Again, something is off about the pitch of his baritone. The way he speaks reminds me of how Mack talks to students.

Impersonal. Explicit. There's not to be any corner or point or fold of this encounter left open to interpretation. We may behave like juveniles, but he knows how to play the game.

Right now, looking up at his face, I wonder how ready *he* is to do this.

And I don't feel horny anymore.

Why are we here, like this? Why did I let—*lead*—this man into a dark corner so I can satisfy some primal need for hot sex? Because he's perfectly formed and excellently muscled? Because he's obviously a good person, even if he allows behaviors like what we are about to do? Because he has a reputation and I won't have to take any responsibility for my own lust?

"Are you?" I ask.

His thumbs pull away from my pussy. His fingers release my tights. He steps back. And the man I saw at the party resurfaces, if only for a brief flicker.

But it's gone. "Yes," he says. But he watches me with the semi-stern face of a soldier waiting for explicit confirmation of orders.

He won't proceed unless I make it clear I understand exactly what's happening. And I think the bit of Rob I saw earlier has been submerged into this other, sexual part. When his reputation took over, he became a different person, or an actor playing a role, or drummer keeping the beat.

I wonder what this means to him. And I wonder if I give in and feed my lust, what it will do to his soul, because I'm wondering about the slippery grains of his reputation. I'm wondering if I'll be the pebble that starts the final spill and if he'll ever be able to dig himself out from under it. From under what my selfishness might do to him.

The look that flashed across his face at the party can't get buried. I can't be the woman who starts the avalanche he can't escape from. No matter how weak I am, I won't do that to this man.

"How many times have you done this?" I ask.

CHAPTER 8

Robert

If only she knew how often women have asked me "how many times." What number am I? What notch am I on your belt? Have you fucked enough women to know how to do me right?

Or enough to leave me in peace tomorrow morning?

Mack's sister pulls her thighs together and drops off the cart. She runs her hand down the front of her shirt and stands up straight. Hitching up her skirt, she yanks her tights back where they should be. When she tips her head to the side, I see the frown on her lips.

I stand in front of her with my jeans open, but my auto anti-lust response kicks in and dampens my horniness. My cock presses painfully against the teeth of my fly as I zip up, irritated even through the cotton of my boxer-briefs, but with a little effort I can will away the discomfort. I have control. I can make my body behave.

The alcove takes on definition again and I see the ladders and the paint buckets. I smell the industrial chemicals instead of her incredible sexiness. I may want to rip those tights right off her hips and lick her to the best damned orgasm she's ever experienced just to prove to her she's made a mistake turning me down, but that's not going to happen.

If she changes her mind in this moment, then she changes her mind. And I need to change mine, too.

No sex for Robert tonight, though there ain't no harm in telling her exactly what she's going to miss. "You ever come twice while fucked?" I run my hand up the outside of her thigh. "Because I'll get you there. And a third, licked."

I'll find the right spot inside. The point which takes a thrust and gives back the shudders and the moans. The place where the friction makes a woman lose control and beg for more. I'll pound it just right.

"I'm sorry," she whispers. "I'm sorry I listened to Lisa and Anne and not what you were telling me."

Telling her? The only thing I told her was that I'll give her the orgasm she needs to make her life worth remembering.

"When did your nephew give you that hat?" She points at my head.

The edges of the earflaps rest just outside my perception but I know they're there. My preposterous hat. The symbol of family and connection I wouldn't trade for anything. And I was going to fuck a woman whose name I don't know while wearing it.

I close my eyes and take another step back.

"Last Christmas, when I was still an undergrad." I lived off campus then as well, the way I do here. At the time, my middle brother, Tom, was living with Dan, my oldest, and Dan's boy, my nephew Bart. The kid who gave me the hat because "Cold ears are bad, Uncle Robby."

Tom's out of Dan's basement now, and employed. And engaged. My brothers, the two responsible adults of our family.

The mood's gone and it didn't take the metal teeth of my zipper to do it, either.

I rebuckle my belt. My balls ache and the tiny, immature part of my brain screams *It's not fair! She's mean!*

Mack's sister touches my elbow. "I'm sorry. I just don't think either of us really wants this."

She's watching me the way she did on the porch, under the moonlight, when she snapped that photo of my nostrils. Watching me more like she's a therapist than a photographer.

It's weird and I look away. "We should go upstairs."

Time to sleep in the same apartment with the woman who just

cockblocked me because she's more in tune with my psyche than I am. Because she's right. I don't really want this. But a game is a game and you can't change the rules right in the middle.

But she did. Ripped them like short-and-curlies right off my balls.

Why?

She picks up her coat and drapes it over her arm. Watching me still, she swipes it with the palm of her hand. The fabric makes the same sound as the tarp did, when we groped each other in the alcove.

She brushes around me, doing her best not to touch, but I still feel the pressure of her body move across my abdomen. I still smell faint hints of that bad beer from the party, but also the dry, sterile smell of airplanes and airports. She's probably just as tired and loopy from traveling all day as I am from my epic ten-hour study-fit on campus.

So maybe she saw me as a way to release tension. I snort and reach to pick up my twenty-five pounds of backpack. That's me, the talking vibrator who cracks jokes.

She presses open the cage door, moving it slowly to minimize the squeaking, and her fingers curl into the mesh. Her lovely, tapered fingers that, I think, I would have enjoyed feeling in my hair and touching my face. I would have enjoyed her stuttered, soft moans. And, possibly, quite enjoyed the taste of her lips, even with the beer residue.

If I kissed my goddesses. Which I don't.

But it's not happening anyway, so I better push it out of my mind.

She walks out into the circle of dim light under the hanging fixture in the vestibule and looks over her shoulder, waiting. She's a bit taller than most women—the top of her head comes up to the bridge of my nose. Her lovely blonde ponytail glimmers with metallic undertones as if she's woven gold and bronze and copper threads into her hair. Her curves flow beautifully, proportioned to her frame and firm under my fingers, but I suspect she's a little heavier than she thinks she should be, mostly because every woman thinks she is heavier than she should be.

Her body makes her fuckable, but it's her mind that makes her attractive.

And the word *goddess* continues to dominate my thoughts.

At this point, I don't think I want to know her name. Might ruin the magic.

I close the cage and spin the lock. She waits, watching. I carry my jacket in one fist and my pack in the other, partly to occupy my hands. But we still climb the stairs next to each other, and they creak in unison, under our synchronized steps. Her black tights hug her long legs, but she pulls her arms close to her body. It's cold, even in here.

The lights in the hallway to the apartment glow brighter than in the vestibule and I step back enough to watch her walk. Her hips swing nicely, her back straight and her step assured.

Traits I noticed before, but didn't think about.

She pulls her key from her purse but doesn't unlock the door. "Thank you for walking me home safely, Mr. Robert Quidell."

I chuckle knowing full well I'd either run my hand over my head or stuff my hands in my pockets if I wasn't carrying my PhD program in my bag. "You are welcome, Daffy."

She chuckles too, and opens the door. "My name's Isa." She pauses and glances around the door, into our dark apartment. "It's short for Isolde. My parents were going to name Mack Tristan but I'm glad they had a fight about it and my dad won. Tristan would have been creepy."

Chuckling again, I follow her in and drop my bag on the floor. The apartment is set up like most apartments: you enter into the living room, the kitchen is off to the left and the hallway to the bedrooms and the bathroom is off to the right. I flip on the living room light as she glances down the dark corridor toward the bedrooms, her shoulders angled, obviously listening for signs of her brother.

Nodding once, she glances back at me. "I think he's asleep."

I toss my jacket on the couch before taking off my bumblebee hat. It feels warm in my hands, and the sudden exposure of my head feels cold. But Isa smiles.

"Your eyes are green," she says.

My right eyebrow does the chagrined arch-dance of confusion and she laughs.

"I couldn't see before." She waves her hands at my face.

"They're not quite green." I lean toward her. My brothers and I all inherited a mix of our mom's baby blues and our dad's crystal greens.

From a distance, I always thought we looked like we had storm clouds in our eyes.

"Ah." Isa steps closer, her nose and chin out, as if she's concentrating on the details of my irises. "Ocean."

"Statues in Paris." I point at her eyes. Where I have blue flecks, she has copper and fog and the depth of ages.

Isa blinks and I think a moment of connection passes between us. It feels as weird as her piercing gaze or her uncanny ability to read my soul.

Am I frightened by it? There are so many different ways I could be frightened. My stomach does a little dance of pushes and pulls and either I'm embarrassed by the whole evening, or petulant. Or perhaps I truly am scared. But whatever makes my body act like I'm a mad eight-year-old takes control.

And I open my stupid mouth. "No sneaking into my room tonight when you figure out what you missed. I need my beauty sleep." It comes out dripping with all that eight-year-old sarcasm.

I let my internal immature dickweed tell her how mean she is.

The moment of connection snaps like a twig. Snaps and snaps again because I just smashed my foot into it, heel first, before jumping up and down for good measure.

Isa closes her eyes. When she opens them again, her face takes on the hardness I associate with someone who sees their role in my life as a narrow and precise set of interactions. She's a teacher teaching a specific subject, or she's the police officer giving me a ticket. She might be that cute girl at the coffee shop who smiles at me the same way she smiles at all the professors and the undergrads. Or Isa might be one of the many women who, after a conquest, doesn't want anything more to do with me.

I had to open my mouth, didn't I?

"Good night, Robert." Isa nods once, succinctly, and walks away toward our apartment's tiny third bedroom, the place where Mack and I used to retreat to grade or study. She's about to drop her head onto her pillow. Alone.

Because there really isn't an alternative for either of us.

CHAPTER 9

Robert

Sun streams in through the window opposite the galley that passes as our kitchen. Mack left the curtains wide open last night. I blink, squinting, and hold my hand up to shade my eyes.

The glass in the window rattles. The wind picked up this morning and has been shrieking between the sashes and the frames of every one of our apartment's leaky portals to the exterior world. I woke up to a blast of cold whistling in from the window in my bedroom.

Which means the clouds will roll in soon. And snow.

And once again, I wonder why I didn't pick a school in a more pleasant climate.

I dump the coffee into the maker as I scratch at my belly and my sweatshirt rubs across my skin. It may be Saturday, but it's still a work day. I have papers to grade and six midterm exam questions to prep. As does Mack.

So a full pot of black hazelnut-tainted caffeine will do us good.

Isa, for her part, will be on her own today.

Coffee aroma wafts through the kitchen, caught on the cold-ass draft blasting through the window. Goosebumps rise on my forearms. Maybe I should turn up the heat.

A door opens down the hall. I hear shuffling, and a knock. Then the other door. Mack and Isa mumble at each other.

My back stiffens. What is she telling him? Not that I care. Or should care. We'd be acting cordial and nonchalant even if I had fucked her.

Which I didn't.

I slam the lid on the coffeemaker.

I hear shuffling toward me, down the hall, and another door slam, farther away. One of them walks toward the kitchen, the other into the bathroom.

The pipes grumble. The shower starts. And I'm alone with one of the twins.

"What'd you do to my sister last night?" I hear a chair pull back from the table and Mack's ass hit the seat.

I turn around. He looks like shit. Pale, eyes sunken, he hasn't shaved in three days and his hair's sticking out from his scalp like a halo of dirty fungus. "You need to go back to bed," I say.

Mack chuckles and rubs his face. His fingers pull on his cheeks and the skin around his eyes yanks down. "Papers to grade."

My roommate looks like he's about to puke. "Seriously, man. Go back to bed. You can't grade like that." I point at his chest.

He slumps down in the chair before leaning his head on the table. "It's the fucking weather." A hand snakes out from under his forehead and waves in the general vicinity of the window. "Low pressure system. Normally it's not a problem but this semester's been a bitch."

Mack's TA-ing two courses this term, plus juggling a full load of classes and starting to prep for his comps. Even without the weather and his sister showing up, he's under enough stress to trigger migraines for even the most normal among us.

"I'll grade some of your section." It pops out of my mouth before I realize what I'm saying. I have a ton of studying and a paper to write. I don't have time to grade his section.

But he really does look like shit.

I pour myself a mug of low-grade hazelnut-laced caffeine and drop into the chair next to him. "Listen," I say, "half the assignment is multiple choice. I'll breeze through it first. Leave the hard shit for you."

Mack chuckles but doesn't lift his head off his arms. "Don't expect me to help you cheat on your stats test."

It's not the statistics I hate about the course, it's the program we're using to run the data. The department uses an interface-less, shareware piece of shit because of, I suspect, the licensing fees. So I suffer. If I wanted to learn to program, I would have gone into computer science. Better chance of a job once I graduate if I had. But no, I had to go with my "passion" like all the other dumbshits in my generation.

"Oh, yes you are, my friend." I sit back and sip my cheap-but-serviceable coffee. It's bitter. I better clean the maker. "I grade your papers and tolerate your houseguest, and you program my stats assignments. That's the deal."

Mack chuckles again and sits up, but he keeps his eyes closed. "I'd appreciate it if you took care of some of the grading."

What else am I supposed to do? He's hurting. "Go back to bed."

After a moment, Mack slowly stands up. "The headaches usually go away by now. I'll be better by this evening."

Maybe. "Go back to bed." I wave him away.

Mack pinches the bridge of his nose. "Student assignments are in the front pocket of my bag." He points over his shoulder at the couch, where his backpack sits.

I wave him away again. "Dude. Go. Back. To. Bed."

My roommate shuffles across the carpet of the dining area toward the hallway, but stops in the center of the living room between the couch and the coffee table piled with books and empty beer bottles. "Did Lisa say something to Isa at the party?" He rubs his head again. "She's mopey this morning."

I sip my coffee and try not to look suspicious. "How the hell would I know?" But my retort sounds as bitchy as Lisa's *I'm telling Mack* evil glare last night.

The pain cinching tight around Mack's forehead must be bad because he doesn't notice. "Be nice." He waves at me again. "She's leaving Tuesday. I don't want her to think she needs to move back into Mom's house, okay? That's not a good situation."

But he shuffles off before I can ask.

I set down my mug. I don't know a lot about what's happening in California. Only that their parents have been divorced since they were ten and their mom and dad continue to fight. Mom had a parade of boyfriends through their house while they were growing up. Dad jetsets. I get the impression Mack thinks their father is a selfish son of a bitch.

Mack always makes a face when he talks about their parents. And he seems quite protective of his twin sister.

I almost fucked her last night. Almost did my player bullshit and lived a little too much in the moment.

If my oldest brother, Dan, knew what I'd done, he'd smack me upside the head. He's the family man. The one who took up the slack when our mom died. The one who says "the hedonistic crap you pull is going to get you either dead or alone." Then he calls me an immature, weak-willed, self-centered shit.

I'm fully aware of the distancing outcomes of my behavior. What Dan doesn't seem to understand is that I like it that way.

Unlike him, I get all the sweet tail I want. And I get it without all the extra fun leftovers like emotional fallout and children.

I sip my coffee again, listening to the shower turn off.

But maybe I'd still like a new reputation. One that doesn't end with upturned noses and rolled eyes from the ladies.

Then again, maybe those rolled eyes save me from a whole mountain of bullshit I don't need. Or want. Or can handle right now. With the grading. And the classes.

I set down my mug. If I admit it to myself, the coffee tastes more like woodchips than hazelnut. But caffeine is caffeine and sometimes you need to take the burned pulpiness with the positives hitting the bloodstream. Because sometimes your body needs what it needs, no matter how bad it tastes.

Down the hall, the bathroom door creaks open. I hear the fan running, drawing out of our apartment the air sodden by ten minutes of a running hot shower. The whirring, electrically stimulated blades vomit the moisture out through the tubes and the vents into the low pressure system outside. The same weather that's giving my roommate a migraine. The same uncaring wider world that doesn't give a shit if I fuck a new woman every week.

So why the hell should I care? Why the hell should I make an effort to change my ways?

I don't care how beautiful she is, with all her copper flecks and her sweet curves. How bright and intelligent her eyes are. How, I suspect, she might be able to hold up her end of a conversation for more than five minutes.

How, most likely, she'd tell me something fascinating and wonderful and worthy of thinking about. Because she's Mack's sister and if she's not as smart as him, I'll eat my own socks.

It doesn't matter.

Because I have shit to do.

I tap the side of my mug as I reach for one of the many red pens we have sitting in the middle of our rickety table. It's time to get to work.

CHAPTER 10

Isolde

It's hard not to fantasize about him. I have a silly school-girl dominance daydream swirling around in my head. One about a pretty boy who needs a lesson on how to treat a woman. How if he wants the best, he needs to step out of his ego and look at what's in front of him.

It's oh-so-difficult not to go back into my room, lie down on my air mattress, and rub one out while thinking about teaching Mr. Robert Quidell the lesson he very much deserves.

Warm water runs over my shoulders and steam expands through my throat and sinuses. I should be washing my hair. But in my mind's eye I see his slightly skewed smirk as he explains to me his view of the world: *I'm a god, baby. A hard-bodied, gorgeous god and I control the vertical just as much as I control all the... horizontals.*

I smirk right back at him. *Keep telling yourself that, big boy. One is the loneliest number, you know.*

He grins and chuckles and runs those strong fingers through his luscious dark hair before he leans closer. *Are you going to be the one to break through my hard exterior?*

I open my eyes. I'm wasting water. In two days I'm going to be in a part of the world where the clean, clear water running over my nipples would keep a family of four alive for a goddamned week. And yet here I am letting it swirl away because I'm fantasizing about my brother's immature but lust-worthy roommate.

Even if he does have a sweet, soft interior under his crunchy outer shell. One he doesn't want anyone to see. He made that abundantly clear last night with his little snide comment. The choice is his, not mine.

His game, his rules.

If there's one thing I've learned from growing up in the same house as my mother and her constant stream of boyfriends in need of fixing, it's that, if their idiotic behaviors keep their dicks happy, they don't give a shit about how dysfunctional they are. Or how much pollution they spread into the world around them.

So the charming, intelligent, obviously deeply-scarred-by-something-or-other Mr. Quidell can suck his thumb and hold tight to his teddy bear of ouchiness for all I care. With guys like him—the entitled boys with everything going for them—the pain usually comes from something pathetic. Like they're still mad about their second grade crush rejecting them. Or they couldn't have a new car at sixteen. Because in their worlds, that pain is by far the worst thing they have ever experienced.

I soap up my hair as I curse the horrors of first world problems.

Though he really didn't seem like an entitled dickbag. A brat, yes. A dickbag, no. Frowning, I rinse off and step out of the shower. After toweling off, I slather on my nice moisturizer, knowing full well that today and tomorrow morning's showers will be the last I get for a while. And the last time I'll get to keep the skin of my shins buttery soft.

I could shave. Doesn't seem worth the effort, though. And being hairy might make that semi-dirtbag Aaron, the other assistant accompanying on this trip, not leer at me.

He's married. Never tried to touch when we worked together in Paris eight months ago. But the fucker stares.

I'm half tempted to write "Isa's boyfriend" on Rob's chest and take a picture. Set it as my phone's wallpaper so every time I get a leer I can hold it up. Make the son of a bitch who wants to make *me* feel small, feel totally, utterly inadequate.

But that, too, is another school girl fantasy. A shallow, insecure fantasy.

I pull on my t-shirt and sweats. No make-up, no blow-dried hair, no bra. Glasses perched on my nose. I may be semi-living with boys, but one's my brother and the other needs to get over himself.

When I swing open the bathroom door, the scent of hazelnut coffee slaps me full on the face. I breathe in deep. This, too, is another of life's little pleasures I'm about to say good-bye to for two and a half weeks.

Part of me likes the slimming down of my life to just my duffle and my equipment. To the mandatory malaria shots and the massive, bush-worthy hiking boots. Aaron can look at my ass all he wants when we are out on the back of our Range Rover, but he's nothing. I'm in the world and I'm seeing what needs to be seen.

It's cold in the hallway. I rub my arms. My nipples tighten, doing their usual response to the cold, and goosebumps rise on my flesh.

I need to find a sweater.

Mack's door is closed when I go by. I almost knock, but I know what it means. The storm moving in is probably giving him shit. This, too, is a familiar pattern. He needs about another eight or so hours of quiet dark to recover.

Rob sits hunched over the table when I walk into the living room, and all I see is the wide expanse of his broad back. He's wearing a ratty sweatshirt but I swear I see the cut and definition of his shoulders through the fabric. Which I can't. Because it's a sweatshirt. And no man's that perfect.

I push away thoughts of pulling up his sweatshirt and kissing between his strong, muscular shoulder blades.

He looks up when he hears me shuffle in. Blinking, he squints for a second, and I swear those wondrous, ocean-filled eyes do the same twinkle they did at the party.

Or maybe I just need coffee.

"Good mornin'," Rob mumbles. His hand wiggles toward the

kitchen. "Mugs are in the cabinet to the left of the sink. Coffee's sort of fresh." He drops his face back to whatever it is he's doing.

"Did Mack go back to bed?" I walk into the kitchen and pour myself some liquid gold. I take it black, more because the extras are just that—extras. And I'm not going to turn down caffeine because I have delicate tastebuds.

Rob nods. "Ah-huh." He doesn't look up from the assignment he's grading.

"It's the storm." I point at the whistling window. At least I'm about to go someplace warm. Hot, actually. Still better than blistering wind so cold your skin feels like it's about to freeze solid.

Rob nods again. "That's what he said."

I almost hold out my hand for a high-five, an involuntary reaction to hearing the words *That's what he said*. I snort instead.

Chuckling, Rob drops his red pen. "Sorry. Not enough coffee in me to make good jokes."

When he looks up, his face is open and happy again, the way it was for that moment last night, right after we entered the apartment. When I finally saw the color of his eyes.

But it vanishes in very much the same way it vanished last night.

I sip my coffee. The lukewarm liquid glides over my tongue and I await the inevitable snarky princess bitching that always drops off the lips of a spurned boy.

Rob sits back in his chair, his face stern yet complex, and crosses his arms over his chest. One eyebrow arches. The other draws in. And one corner of his mouth rises higher than the other. "You look angry," he says.

Do I? "Why would I be angry?" I set my mug on the counter. His gaze follows my hand as it drops away from my mouth but his eye movements stop when his focus reaches my chest. His eyes don't follow the arch of my arm. He notices my braless breasts and I swear he looks like he just saw Jesus. Not that immature Aaron leering at boobies, but a full-on look of happy wonder as if he'd just gotten a glimpse of a priceless work of art.

But he looks back at his papers before I know for sure I understand correctly what I was seeing. "I don't know," he says. "Maybe because you were expecting the bee hat?" He shrugs and pats his head. "It *is* cold in here."

He glances at my chest again.

"Look." I take a deep breath and grab Mack's sweatshirt off the back of the other chair. Quickly, I pull it on and drop my ass across from him. "I'm going to be living here on and off, okay? I don't have a lot of stuff and I won't be in the way when I'm here. I promise. So can we act like adults? Not get on each other's nerves?"

It's bad enough I can't stop thinking about him without also thinking about him bending me over a chair, or setting me on the counter in the kitchen and pounding me so hard the coffeemaker falls off the edge.

Across from me, wheels turn and I think Rob's trying very hard to *not* say something about my breasts. He only glances at me. "Sure." A quick pout moves across his mouth.

A very sexy, very small pout where his wonderful, gorgeous lower lip poked out just a tiny bit for a just-as-tiny moment.

God*damn* the man is photogenic. And an ass. My thighs tingle looking at him.

"You want to go back to my room right now, Rob?" I sit back in my chair, too. "Get it out of the way? Scratch that itch so you don't have an unfilled notch on your belt?"

I think I suggest it more for me than him. Because I think part of me regrets saying no last night. The part that fantasizes. But on the other hand, Responsible Brain did the right thing.

He rolls his eyes and without answering, goes back to grading his papers.

I lean closer. I don't know why I'm mad, but I am. "You think you're the first hot guy to get his hand under my skirt?" I'm exaggerating about the hotness of the guys who try with me, but Rob doesn't need to know that. "I work with models, many of whom are way, way hotter than you. Men who are *paid* to be hot."

Surprise flickers over Rob's face as if he doesn't think there are guys hotter than him out there in the wider world. Or maybe it's surprise because I think he's hot.

I'd rather think his ego wasn't so ginormous he thinks of himself as Prince Hottie, so I'll go with my second choice and hope I'm right.

A sniff twitches my nose. I don't mean it to happen, but it does. "I know the kind of fun you offer. I fully understand the rules of the game. But I also know what I saw in your eyes last night. I *know* you know when you're acting like a player. And for a moment, I thought maybe you were smart enough to get beyond it."

Rob pinches the bridge of his nose. "If you know the rules, then why the hell would you care if I got beyond my childhood traumas?"

So he knows the root causes of his behavior. Yet he won't do the work to change it. "Maybe I thought getting to know you might be worth the effort."

He blinks and his mouth opens, but he doesn't respond.

I push back my chair. "My connector flight to JFK goes out Tuesday morning. Mack's taking me to the airport before teaching his section. I need to make sure my equipment's secure."

Still silent, Rob waves me away.

In the living room, I look over my shoulder. He hunches over the papers, his attention fully on his students' needs.

Mack said his new roommate impressed him. That Rob had a mind quicker and sharper than anyone he'd ever met. My brother had seen Rob in action at a department function at the beginning of last semester. Rob, the new kid, spent three hours arguing with the department head about ethnocentrism and the emerging cyber-based subcultures formed around social media.

So the gorgeous guy sitting at the table making a point of ignoring me has a fire in his belly. And a hidden trauma.

I turn away. Someday, he might feel safe enough to get beyond his issues and find a way of living that's whole. One that meets all his needs, not just the ones easily sated.

A twinge makes me blink and I wonder, deep inside, if I'm sad that when it happens, I won't be part of his world.

Or, perhaps, I wonder if I'm worthy.

CHAPTER 11

Robert

The snow starts in the late afternoon. I frown out the leaky window at the big flakes bouncing off the glass, wondering if we're going to get snowed in. The flipping flakes tinkle against the window, each one its own little chime. The storm's brought the faery land to life at the same time it might be trapping me in a drafty apartment with the migraine twins.

One twin with a headache that's all his, and the other making a new pain in the neck for me.

I hear shuffling in the hallway and turn around in my chair half expecting to see my roommate, but Isa glides into the living room, still fresh faced and braless, her hair in a messy ponytail, a tablet in one hand and her empty coffee mug in the other.

She extends a finger, lifting it off the handle of the mug, and slides it across her tablet. The reflected light playing over her lovely face shifts, as does the mirage dancing over her glasses.

She moves into the room, looking more at what's on her screen than where she's going.

And Isa almost trips over the coffee table.

"Shit." She stands up straight a little too fast. Her old coffee sloshes out of the mug and onto a stack of student assignments on the table.

I jump off my chair, a napkin in my hand, before the "—it" part of her swearing is out of her mouth. I dab at the top assignment, swearing softly myself, somewhat grateful that this stack has been graded and they're my students, not Mack's. My section has a pretty good sense of humor, so they won't care.

"I'm sorry." Isa sets down the mug. She blinks her huge eyes and bites her lip. "I didn't ruin them, did I?" The tablet, she tucks under her arm. "I wasn't looking."

I wad up the napkin. She looks genuinely embarrassed. And she's hiding the tablet under her arm.

I point. "You looking at porn on that thing?"

Isa's brows crunch up and she frowns just like my mom used to when I was a kid and I said something bratty to my brother Tom. Stuff like, "Nice tulip you're painting. 'Cause real artists draw pretty flowers."

I was a brat who hadn't yet developed a good instinct for insults.

Isa pulls the tablet out from under her arm. "I'm applying for a position with a studio in L.A. It's steady work. Less travel." She waves the little screen in the air between us, but too fast for me to get a sense of what's on it.

But I don't see color, just gray. She must be looking at black and whites.

I don't respond. I walk away instead, to throw out the coffee-soaked napkin.

"Are you like this with Mack?" she asks. "So obnoxious?"

I stop, one hand on the cabinet where we keep the stinky garbage can. The fingers of my other tightened around the edge of the countertop.

Why do women think they have the right to psychoanalyze me? I'm just their good time evening. Why do they care? "I don't need you poking your fingers at me," I say. "Because my life's not your business."

"Your life?" Isa points at the stack of coffee-stained assignments. "I thought it was about your students' now-difficult-to-read papers."

I feel my eyes narrow. Part of me wants to yell "You started it!" but then I *would* be acting like a child. So I stay quiet.

Isa sighs, pulling in a deep lung-full of air. She holds it for a long moment, then releases it slowly. But her shoulders stay tight. And her nose scrunches up. She picks up her now-empty coffee mug. "Excuse me. I'd like to make lunch. I heard Mack moving around and my sick brother is probably hungry."

She brushes by me. Her hip bumps into my thigh and I step to the side, a little off balance, but I catch myself on the back of the chair I'd just jumped out of to save my students' assignments.

I smell her shampoo when she rubs against my side. Wisps of a sweet essential oil curl around my head—something warmly honeyed with just enough floral blended into it to make me want to inhale all the way to the bottom of my diaphragm.

Isa blinks as she glances over her shoulder, but she doesn't say more. The tablet balances closer to the edge of the counter than makes me comfortable and I stare at it, waiting for it to go tumbling the way her coffee did earlier.

But it doesn't. And I have an excellent view of the black and white she was studying when she bumped the table.

It's a young couple. They look younger than us, probably high school, and the boy is wrapped around the girl, his head on her shoulder and his arms around her waist. She leans her head toward his, her nose in his hair, and she looks as if she's breathing in his love.

There's no mistaking the story the photo tells. For the girl, the boy outlines the world. His edges are the edges of her space. And for the boy, the girl fills a space that if empty, would rip him to shreds. He'd be eaten by emptiness.

Isa doesn't comment or offer a glance in my direction or even ask where we keep the bread. She walks around our narrow kitchen, opening and closing cabinets, pulling out dishes, finding utensils. And makes a peanut butter sandwich on whole wheat toast for her suffering brother.

She walks by again, the sandwich's plate held in one hand and a glass of water in the other, and her tablet now under her arm. Isa, who knew in her bones exactly when to take that photo, how to stand to capture the image. The woman who instructed her camera and her models in how to make a moment worth capturing. A good sister who now takes into another room her ability to read humanity's deep secrets.

Away from me. Toward a man she feels is worth caring about.

I watch her go to offer a kind gesture of food to her in-pain brother.

And I feel suddenly, completely, alone.

CHAPTER 12

Robert

Mack took Isa to the airport seventeen days, six hours and twenty minutes ago. Not that I'm counting. I just remember the moment peace returned to our apartment.

Quiet that's been filled with glorious, gorgeous photos of African life sent to her brother whenever she's somewhere with service. Her eye for people continues to astound me, but also her eye for landscapes and animals. Every snap is a story in and of itself, many of which are taken with her phone camera.

Mack says she's experimenting with a "low-fidelity aesthetic." I just think she's talented. And that I really do need to learn how to use the camera on my phone.

The last picture, an orange and gold sunset over the African plain, I stared at for a full ten minutes. It's now my phone's background.

I'll take it off before she gets back. Don't need the hell of her seeing one of her photos on my phone.

Mack tidied her room, sticking the clothes she left behind into a cheap dresser he bought and stacking her boxes of software and drives and SD cards against the wall. He deflated the air bed, rolled it up, and set it on top of the boxes next to the sheets, which he washed and folded.

I think my roommate misses his sister.

I study and I don't think about her talent or her smile or her spectacular breasts.

But now it's my turn to run off. I'm flying home for the weekend, to celebrate my nephew's fifth birthday. Tom's first gallery show is Tuesday, but I can't stay. My first test of the term is Monday. So I fly home, party with the brothers, and fly back, all while reading journal articles on my phone.

Ugly, difficult to parse articles without the glorious yellows and wondrous reds of a sunset over the savanna.

I'm leaving, but Isa is coming home. I almost ask Mack if he could ask her to share more of her photos while I'm gone, but I doubt she'd appreciate my interest. So I keep my mouth shut.

Mack pats my shoulder as we walk into the ubiquitous airport bustle. "Getting sick of dropping off and picking up." He hitches the straps on his backpack and frowns at a loud family walking by. "I'm going to make her buy her own car and leave it in long term parking when she goes on these trips."

He didn't seem all that happy about taking me to the airport, either. "Why the hell don't you have on your coat?" Mack pushed up his glasses before flicking his hand at me.

"Because Minnesota is warmer than here, that's why." And my brothers have everything I need. No use packing shit I might leave behind.

Mack snorts. "Sure, buddy. Whatever you say."

Isa's coming in about an hour after my plane takes off, so Mack's spending the rest of the afternoon in an airport coffee shop grading papers, reading journal articles, and sipping syrupy coffee.

"You're a good brother," I say. At least someone is. I'll be home by the evening and in the presence of my two better-than-me brothers, meeting their new women-of-quality. And, most likely, rolling around on the floor playing superhero with the world's greatest nephew.

Mack laughs when I smile. "You're the one who dropped almost three hundred dollars on a camera for your kindergarten-aged nephew." He points at my duffle. "Why didn't you ask Isa to help you pick out something? She's opinionated, you know."

Yes, Isa has a full set of opinions. "She wasn't here."

Mack stops walking. "Give me your phone."

I stop as well. "Why?" He doesn't need to fuck around with my phone.

My roommate wiggles his fingers.

"Don't download porn." I pull the phone from my pocket and unlock the screen before slowly setting it on his palm.

"Figure out how to use the camera yet?" Mack swipes and tilts and taps in something or other.

"What are you doing?" I grab for my phone put he pulls it away.

"Not so fast, lover boy." He holds it up above his head. "How many women's numbers do you have in here?" He swipes again.

"Plenty." More than I need, that's for sure. More than will ever talk to me again. More than I want.

"You could share, you know." Mack hands back my phone.

I swipe through it but I can't tell what he did. "What did you do?"

"I added Isa's number. Take a picture of your nephew using his birthday present and send it to her. It'll make her month."

Her number's not obvious in my contacts. "Where'd you put it?" If it's in the notes, I'll need to transfer it.

Mack chuckles. "It's there with all the other ladies, Casanova." He walks ahead, shepherding me toward the self-serve check-in. "You don't have a girlfriend because you're a pig. They can smell it on you a mile away." He makes grunting noises.

I give him the finger, but quickly hide my hand when an old lady pulling a huge wheeled bag throws me a stern disapproving grandma look. Her bag *thump thumps* away and Mack laughs and laughs.

"You're twelve courses of dumbass," he says.

I tuck my phone in my pocket and jog to catch up. "You'll pick me up Monday afternoon?" I ask, determined to change the subject.

Mack grins like a cocky son of a bitch and flicks his finger across the tip of his nose. "Sending Isa. So you two love birds can have some quality time together."

I stop walking again. "Your sister does not like me, Mack."

His look transforms into a slightly annoyed frown. "I thought that whole social media issue you had when you got here might have made you reconsider how you interact with women. Not that it's my business." He shakes his head. "Which it's not. Until you started treating my sister like she's unwelcomed."

I feel my back bristle. "You're bringing this up now? I have a plane to catch." But I don't point over my shoulder or turn away. Some part of me wants a fight. To, I think, yell and punch because she keeps getting under my skin.

And I refuse to think about her. "She wants indifference. So I'm indifferent."

Mack snorts. "You are far, far from indifferent." He gives me the finger as he turns away. "How the hell are you going to do participant observations if you can't see the obvious right in front of you?"

I see the world just fine. Mack's body language is clear and precise —he's more indignant than angry. And, like so many other times I've seen him interact with people, he's backing off of a potential conflict by walking away from me.

Which is his choice. But my gut tells me he's going to stew about it while I'm home.

"Mack!"

He hitches his pack up his back and points toward the check-in before walking back to me. "Looks like the line's long. Better queue up."

He stands straight and slaps my shoulder. "One day a woman may actually *like* you. Could happen, you know."

"Fuck off, Mack." Plenty of women like me.

He laughs, but his face instantly turns stone cold serious. "You mess with my sister and I'm kicking your ass to the curb."

"You put her number on my phone, not me." Now I'm more confused than anything else. I think my mouth opens. He might be joking, but I don't think he's *joking*. This is the first time I've seen my roommate look... menacing.

"I told you why I put her number on your phone. Send her a photo of your nephew. It will make her millennium." His eyes go spacey for a second and part of me wonders if he's having another migraine. But he seems to be remembering something.

"She used to do a lot of volunteer work teaching kids how to take photos." Mack waves his hand at me. "She'll like it." But his face turns stony again. "I meant what I said about you fucking with her."

I want to snarl. To get my back up and get into a fight, but that won't help anyone. "I don't fuck *with* women, dude." Anything short of clarity of intention is rude at the best and seriously shitty at the worst. And I don't do that.

Mack sniffs. He slaps my shoulder again as he nods toward his awaiting café seat. "And that, my friend, is the true source of your problems."

He shakes his head one last time and walks away.

Shit, I think. *What the hell did that mean?* Now what?

Maybe I should move out, anyway.

No, I won't think about it. I won't think about Isa, either. I'm going home to visit my family and women are not my concern right now.

I make it through the wonders of automated ticket check-in without difficulty, then thread my way through security. At the gate, I pull out my phone and practice taking photos of the planes, telling myself they're for Bart, my nephew. But mostly I suspect I just want to take photos.

Because I'm not going to look for her number. I'm not going to admit she's under my skin. Or that I don't understand Mack's comment about not fucking with women being my problem.

I snap photos and wait for my boarding group to be called.

On the plane, I listen to music instead of studying. The kid sitting behind me kicks my seat with a rhythm worthy of an A-list rock drummer and the obese woman across the aisle keeps ordering tiny bottles of vodka. The plane roars as planes do, and the air smells not-quite-clean, as plane air always does.

When we land, I turn on my phone to text my oldest brother, Dan, who should be at the airport by now to pick me up. My phone boots, making the jingle noise of my carrier, and a text pops up.

It's a selfie of Mack and Isa in the coffee shop at the airport, but it's not from his phone. It's from a number labeled as 'Iseult.' *If your nephew has questions about his new camera, text me.*

Why did Mack label her number 'Iseult'? It must be some variation of her name.

Confusion hops from one of my shoulders to the other, digging in its claws and biting at my ears. *I thought you didn't like me*, I text back.

It's off into the ether before I realize just how juvenile it sounds. But it's on her phone now and there's nothing I can do about it.

I like your nephew. He gave you the bee hat.

Which I left in the apartment. Didn't want to lose it.

A new photo pops up. It's Mack wearing my hat and smiling a big, happy smile. *Show Bart.*

I will, I text back. I want to ask why she's doing this. Why she's not indifferent.

But I don't think that's Isa. I don't think she'd be able to take the photos she does if she were indifferent. If she didn't see what needs to be seen.

I touch the screen as if, somehow, touching the photo she sent was touching the woman.

And I don't know what to do.

CHAPTER 13

Robert

It didn't matter how many times I checked my phone, Isa didn't send more texts. I dropped my ass into the passenger seat of my brother's truck and she didn't send more. I helped read bedtime stories to my nephew, and still no new texts. I set up the whole "video chat the gallery opening" situation with Tom's smart-but-impulsive fiancé, Sammie, but still no texts.

Until I send a picture of Bart taking pictures with his birthday gift: *It's okay if Bart wants to share his photos with me.* Then all of a sudden my little nephew is talking more with the professional photographer than I am.

Dan tapped Isa's email into his tablet and Bart "submitted his first piece to a professional." The smile on my nephew's face made the whole family smile, too. But I think I got a little jealous.

Then the noise of my brothers' relationships drowned out the rest of the world, including all the bits of jealousy. I wondered how my laid-back brother Tom fell so completely for the high-energy Sammie. And how the hell my adult-in-the-room brother Dan can be such an idiot with his new girlfriend, Camille.

I rub the top of my head as I walk through the Minneapolis International Airport on my way back to school. I dodge old men and tourists and school groups off to God knows where. The airport smells the same every time I'm here—fakely fresh but cleaner than the huge ports on the East Coast. And full of happy people returning home from their journeys.

I rub my head again and stop in front of the coffee shop down from my gate. The airport bustles around me, loud with indistinct chatter and the grind of wheeled luggage on the tiled floors and the background roar of planes. It mirrors my life.

I shake my head and look up at the menu, wondering if I want some sugar with my caffeine.

Until a stupid and stray thought bumps through my head: *You get fat and Isa won't want to take pictures of you.* A pang of indignation comes with it, and for a flash, I wonder if I'm more like my five-year-old nephew than my mature-enough-to-maintain-relationships brothers.

I chuckle at what my little-boy brain spit up. Or maybe it came out a snort because the girl behind the coffee shop counter is giving me a look. I smile and order, doing my best to charm, and by the time our interaction is done, she's smiling back at me.

But part of me wonders why I would have such a shallow thought in the first place.

On the plane, I read articles. I study for my test. And I stare at the selfie of Isa and her brother that's still on my phone.

Why can't I make my way through the haze of my reputation and build something better? Why can't I use the same rigor I need to finish my degree and apply it to the rest of my life?

Why do I act like a child around Isa?

Good thing my test tomorrow's easy or I'd be in trouble.

When the plane lands, I take my phone out of airplane mode and wait for the *I'm here* or *I'm in traffic* text, hoping it's from Mack. But it's not. It's from Isa.

I brought your coat, it says.

So Mack stuck to his word and I'm about to spend forty-five minutes in a car with a woman who thinks I'm an asshole. Who will be giving me the lust-filled stink-eye the entire drive. Because she still wants me but decided I'm not worth her time. Even if my nephew is.

Because I'm a brat and Bart isn't.

I so enjoy getting the stink-eye. I love how it raises my blood pressure while at the same time making me want to punch the nearest wall. Or the car's dash.

Women are a pain in the ass.

I really don't want to spend forty-five minutes of frowning from a woman who smells like I could cuddle up to her on a nice spring afternoon, swinging in a hammock and listening to the birds dart and chirp.

Screen says luggage pick-up six, the next text says.

I only have my duffle, I text back. *Don't need to go to luggage.*

After a moment, a new text pops up: *Glad you landed safe. I'm at door three.*

I stare at my phone as everyone in the aisle seats elbow each other so they can get their bags out of the overhead bins first. There's small talk and there's impatience and I know I'll need to walk the concourse to door three any second now.

And my gut feels like shit. I'm pretty sure she's still mad and I feel like shit.

I need to figure out what the fuck is wrong with me. No woman should make me feel like this.

I stop for an overly sweet coffee at the stand next to the escalators, saying to myself it's because I have more studying to do and not because I'm avoiding. Because that would be bratty.

The annoying airport voice rolls through the concourse telling everyone to attend to their luggage. People meeting loved ones scream with arm-flailing joy while others scurry on by, more exhausted than happy.

I hear at least four different languages; see at least six expressions of non-continental US cultures. I smell sterile airport air and taste sterile, bland pseudo-coffee. I watch a tired woman shepherd her children toward a man the kids don't seem interested in greeting. And I walk toward the door, continuing to do my damnedest to not think about my roommate's sister.

Three days in my apartment eighteen days ago and the woman

managed to burrow her way down to my bones like a damned parasite and now I can't get rid of her. I need to figure out how to live with her because as long as I'm Mack's roommate, she's going to be a chronic condition.

So yeah, I had better "treat her right" or I'll be out on my ass.

I ride down the long escalator from the gates with a knot of business types and other exhausted travelers. I hear plenty of New York-accented complaints, as well as several local people happy to be home. But mostly I see Isa waiting by the door.

Her hair is up in a ponytail but it halos her lovely face like a wonderful bit of the sun she's carried back with her from her trip to Africa. Her skin glows too, bronzed and bright. She looks exhausted, but it's not weight-of-the-world exhaustion. She looks as if she just finished climbing a mountain. Or whitewater rafting. Or uncovering a long-buried secret.

She smiles when she sees me. An actual, real, bright smile and I think I must be blinking. I expected the lust-filled stink-eye. The coldest, nastiest lust-filled stink-eye Mack's sister could muster.

Instead, I get a smile.

"Rob," she says. "Coat." She hands over my winter jacket. "It's cold."

Isa shakes her head and points over her shoulder at the tunnel to visitor parking. "Ready?"

I smile back, and make small talk as I slip on my jacket. "Mack showed me the images you sent from your trip before I left." I nod toward the bag strapped over her shoulder. "Very nice."

She grins and shakes her head. "I got a couple good ones this time."

I'm sure she did. In fact, I suspect she got a couple hundred good ones.

She's staring at my arms as I pull on my jacket. One of her eyebrows arches and I'm suddenly reminded of my surprise at the lack of unhappy looks. Part of me figures it'll show, probably sooner than later, and I almost flex, just to be embarrassing. Somehow I find the strength not to be too much of a dumbass.

Behind us, a siren screeches the start of a luggage carousel. A blue light flashes. I smile and nod toward the tunnel. "Shall we?"

We walk side by side through the flickering fluorescent lights of the tunnel, me carrying my duffle and my coffee, not really talking. She comments on Bart's photos. I smile and nod. I ask her about Africa. She smiles and nods.

It's going to be a long ride back.

I dutifully situate my duffle in the trunk before plopping my ass in the passenger seat and drop my coffee into the cup holder. As she pulls out of the ramp, she doesn't say a lot.

"Want me to turn on the radio?" Anything to break up the awkward silence and the knocking of her brother's car's engine.

She pulls us onto the freeway. "How have you been, Rob?"

I scowl. I don't mean to. So the stink-eye's going to start with her acting like she's my therapist. "Why?"

Isa shrugs. "Because I think it would be best for everyone if you and I got along."

"Mack agrees."

"Do you?" Isa, the photographing therapist.

I want to say something snarky like *I'm not a child who needs guidance.* Or tell her she's condescending.

But that's childish.

When I don't answer right away, her mouth scrunches up like my sister and my mom used to scrunch up their faces after I did something dumb, like saying mean things and making the neighbor kid cry, or getting exactly the median scores on three homeworks in a row, or describing in detail for my brother Tom what was wrong with his middle school attempts at art.

Isa looks as if she clearly sees the effort I put into wiggling myself below the lowest expectations anyone cares to put out for me.

And she changes the subject. "Your nephew has a great deal of talent. Is your brother fostering it?"

I nod and take a sip of my airport coffee.

Isa grins. "You look like that stuff hurts your teeth."

I blink. "I didn't know I was making a weird face."

She takes the ramp onto the freeway. My coffee sloshes against the side of the cup and I juggle to keep it from spilling.

Isa settles us into traffic before she glances over. "Sometimes I wonder if you're aware of your body language." She shakes her head the way someone who just had a eureka moment. "You have tells."

"What?" I don't have tells. I return the too-sweet coffee to the cup holder.

Isa laughs and swirls her finger in the air between us. "You're like a kindergartner who can't decide if he wants to play nice or steal all the toys."

"Excuse me? I'm not stealing your toys." I thought maybe we could get along, but she has to go and be insulting. "I do *not* like you anymore." It pops out of my mouth before I realize I sound like the kid she just accused me of being. And that I'm pouting. I thin my lips and clamp my mouth shut.

How the hell can Mack's sister be so... mean? Because that's what she is. Plain old mean. I didn't do anything to deserve her being *mean*.

Isa stops laughing. She stares for a long moment, both her eyes and her mouth round. "I'm going to be in your apartment for two weeks before I'm off to L.A. for a month."

She's changing the subject again. I glance at her, wondering if I should be frowning or giving her the finger.

Isa tips her head, watching me again the way she did that night at the party. "I'm sorry I pay attention. I'm a photographer. It's what we do." Her finger swirls in the air again. "That hat Bart gave you brings out something in your eyes. Something I don't think you let other people know is there." She shakes like a bug crawled up her back and flops against the seat. "I want to photograph it."

"Hell *no*." This time, I don't glower. I won't give her the satisfaction of showing a "tell."

Isa shrugs. And frowns. But she doesn't ask again.

Traffic picks up again and she takes the exit toward campus and the apartment. Where we will both be living. Mack, me, and his mean sister.

She's watching me in her weird therapist way again. Like she's looking for the correct angle to snap my photo so she can steal my soul.

That's Isa, Mack's witchy woman sister.

I can't deny that the desire to fuck her still lingers. Arguments always get the blood pumping and pumping blood makes me horny. The desires of my body color how I perceive the movements of her fingers and the flutters of her lips. They draw my attention to the rise and fall of her breasts as she breathes and to the tension in the muscles around her eyes. They make me want to bury my face in her hair and sniff along the nape of her neck. And to rub my entire body against hers.

But she's not a woman whose company I enjoy. In fact, I think, right now, I truly, honestly, all the way to my bones feel something very unlike *like* for Isa Wellington. Something that's going to monopolize several areas of my brain while I figure out what it is, even though I need to study for my upcoming test. And figure out these "tells" she accused me of having. Because I can't walk through life with tells. Tells don't help you get what you want.

She parks the car in the lot behind the apartment building and unbuckles her seatbelt. The car dings for a moment until she pulls out the key. Then she hops out and stretches next to the car, her arms up and her breasts thrust out.

No, I do not like this woman. I particularly don't like how she sees into parts of my psyche she shouldn't be able to see. I don't need a woman shining her strobe into my head. Don't need the complications.

But something tells me keeping Isa out of my soul is going to take considerable effort.

CHAPTER 14

Isolde

For the next two days, Rob and I dance around each other. We're cordial. He makes coffee; I drink the coffee. I make popcorn; he sits on the other side of Mack and nods approvingly at my photos. We eat breakfast; he goes to class and takes his tests. I spend my time networking and hoping I get an interview for the L.A. position when I'm in town. And wondering why he still fuels my fantasies.

Because he does. My trip to Namibia was days filled with landscapes and nights filled with dreams of Rob licking me to blinding orgasm after orgasm under the bright African moon.

Every goddamned night. I don't think I've ever masturbated so much while on another continent.

I truly am a freak. And I think I need a hook-up. Some random guy who's in it just for the fuck.

Or I could sneak into Rob's room. Be the one who's only in it for the fuck. Which, if I'm honest, is the main bit of my cognitive dissonance that keeps my fantasies at the front of my mind. How is it that I harangue Mr. Robert Quidell about being a shallow dickbag when my body wants to hold him down and ride his cock until I come and come again? He and I are too much alike. So I keep thinking about him.

I just wish he'd make up his mind. One second, he's open and friendly and... I don't know. Supportive? Wanting to connect? Then the next, he's behind his wall of childish asshole-ery. If I'm going to set up a relationship—committed, not-committed, hook-ups, whatever—I need to know. I won't be like my mother. I'm not out to fix every dumbass who needs fixing. I like my men to be *men* and not indecisive asshats, like my father.

Probably the safest thing to do is to ignore Mr. Quidell and his perfectly proportioned abs. Right now, he's off somewhere in the warming outdoors, presumably exercising. Mack left at the same time, his bag on his back and his own hat pulled down over his ears. Said something about an appointment with a student.

So I settle back into my laptop and my networking. I have the shoot in L.A. set for the end of the week, and inroads with the studio. If this shoot goes well, they may call me back and I may end up with a consistent position. It'd mean returning to California, but with a full-time job, I could get my own apartment. Maybe upgrade my equipment, too.

I have several other options to consider as well, including a possible three-month shoot in South America at the end of the year. Lots of portfolio work to do today even if I'd rather be outside taking end-of-winter photos of Rob standing shirtless in front of the melting snow.

I stifle a sigh and force my brain back to the work at hand: finding jobs.

I could "settle down" here. Take a position with the local studio and work out of this city. I'd be living in the same apartment as my brother. And his tasty roommate. And making a lot less—and garnering less prestige—than I would with the studio in California.

I throw my head against the back of the couch, groaning. My grandma's hand-knitted, Irish fisherman afghan—the one Mack took when he moved out because I don't stay in one place long enough to have heirlooms around—the one grandma made for grandpa, curls around my arms and my torso. Grandpa, the love of my grandma's life. God, even as kids, their relationship was obvious to Mack and me.

Maybe Grams and Gramps were why Mom's post-divorce parade of idiots always made me recoil like someone had thrown a bug into my hair.

I rub the yarn. It's thick and warm, the color of the cream I never add to my coffee, and made of intricate stitchwork and more love than any human should be able to muster.

The kind of connective love I saw flash over Rob's face that night at the party. That moment when he first spoke of his nephew.

The kid really does have a massive amount of raw talent which I'm more than happy to support. If Rob lets me. I remember Mack saying something about Rob's brother's gallery opening tonight. And that Tom Quidell is quite the artist. Little Bart will be "live blogging" for uncle Robby tonight.

Rob also set up something to share the event with his father in Sedona.

I think part of me is jealous. And another part is annoyed that I wasn't invited to participate, like Mack.

Rob really can be an asshole.

He doesn't see me when he bursts panting through the apartment door, his wonderful bee hat pushed back on his gorgeous head and his running clothes shimmering over his square, perfect ass. The door almost slams against the wall but he catches it, his hand curled tight around its edge as he bends over, his other hand on his knee.

A blast of still-cold springtime air follows him in, along with the scent of sweaty man, but iced-over. My brain makes images of a fur-wearing, ax-wielding Norse god under all that black spandex and high-tech running armor.

He stands up, still breathing hard, and closes the door. The hat flies toward me, smacking me in the face, but he's not looking at the couch. He's pulling off his jacket.

And his skin-tight, dark gray, long-sleeved undershirt. It peels off his torso, then up, over his head. The fabric rolls down his arms and his biceps pop.

I think I must have wiggled. Or moaned. Or dropped his hat. Because Rob Quidell is looking at me wide-eyed and shocked.

"What are you doing out here?" he says between two breaths.

"What the hell are you doing not cooling down?" I toss his hat back at him as I try not to look at his chest.

His sculpted, muscled, exceptionally lickable chest.

Rob pouts as he fumbles the hat. "It's cold. I came in. I was going to do my pushups in here to cool down but now I have an audience."

"Don't let me stop you."

Rob walks in a circle, his running shirt in his hand and I swear steam rising off his shoulders. He watches me with his ocean-in-moonlight eyes, his dark hair messy and spiky from his workout, and a sheen of sweat shimmering on his skin.

I pick up my phone. Concentrating on making an image will give me back some perspective on Rob Quidell. No thoughts of touching. No thinking about how good he smells, even sweaty, or how salty his skin likely tastes. How wonderful his breathing sounds. Or how comforting, even if it shouldn't be.

I snap a photo. "Hmm..." I say. It looks flat. I need fill light. And a better background than the apartment's ugly door. Because I need to capture the wonder he brings to all five senses.

I close my eyes and breathe my own air. I don't like this. I don't like *him*. He's a distracting ass who probably isn't really an ass, just playing one in real life because it's easier than *not* being an ass.

Rob stops walking. He stares at me, his hands on his hips and his chest calming to normal breathing.

Didn't take him long to cool down. Which means he's got stamina. A lot of stamina.

"Why did you take a picture of me?" He pouts and points at my phone. "It's invasive."

Invasive? "Yeah, that's me. I'm the kudzu in your life, Rob. Get used to it." Maybe I won't move out just so I can continue to be irritating.

Rob smirks. The muscles around his eyes change. And I swear he puffs out his chest. "You want me naked? You know, since I need to get used to you invading my life. Best to make the most of the photos you're going to take anyway." He wiggles down the waistband of his running tights.

Fuck, I think. I see the defined invitation V of his lower abs drawing my attention down his well-trimmed happy trail. Down toward the top of the now-visible shadow of trimmed pubic hair.

The tingle starts in my breasts and moves very quickly through my chest. It fires into my throat and down between my legs. And I want to yank down those running tights. I want to free what I know has been confined and held secure this past hour while he ran around the neighborhood, his legs pumping and his body working.

The memory of his hard cock rubbing against my thighs plays over my skin and I focus on not wiggling. Because every part of me wants to be wet and to wiggle along every inch of his brilliant body. Wet, wiggling, licking, and sucking.

But I can't think of him that way. I can't give in. He's a goddamned immature brat and fucking him will cause many more problems than it will solve.

Even if I have to go into my room and take care of it myself.

"Why do you do that?" I'm off the couch and walking toward him before I realize what I'm doing. "Why the bluster?" My hands gesture without me willing them to fly around in the air. But there's something about Rob Quidell that gets me worked up.

"Bluster?" Still half naked, he crosses his arms over his chest. "I'm not the one poking my nose in other people's business."

My lip wiggles. On its own. Wiggles like I want to cry or hit him or run away. Why do I care what this man thinks?

Rob snorts like a little boy who just won his game of bullying.

"I'd rather you were indifferent to me." My words roll out of my mouth soft and low, almost a whisper. I'm not thinking about them. I'm not even sure why I'm saying what I'm saying. But it all comes out anyway.

Because I think he's *not* indifferent. Every sideways glance signals the exact opposite of indifference. Every moment he watches me for longer than an indifferent man would. Every hurt-puppy, snarky remark.

But I don't think he's mad about not getting sex after the party. His posture is the wrong kind of belligerent—sad instead of mad. Frowning instead of chest out, puffed up intimidation. Rob Quidell isn't oppressive. He's, I think, lonely.

And I think his body language screaming how much he wants connection is exactly the lack of indifference that's been fueling my attention and my fantasies and my poking at him. Because he's always poking at me. In the car back from the airport, he acted as if every word I said was a bone-cutting insult. But every time he glances in my direction or unconsciously orients his body toward me, he's showing interest.

I don't know if I'm reading him correctly. I don't know if trying to get through will lead to seeing the caring I see when he talks about his family. Or, maybe, it will lead to another one of his barbs. Does he want connection or does my presence fill him with disdain? Or maybe the disdain is for himself.

"If you were truly indifferent, I'd fuck you," I say. "Scratch that itch and get it behind us. We could at least be roommates then, even if we were never friends. But being around you is like being in a traffic accident. It bangs me up and leaves bruises and I know I need to go to the emergency room because you might be doing some deep, hidden damage and I won't know until I'm bleeding internally and end up in intensive care."

Rob blinks, his face blank, and he steps back a little bit.

He pulls his shirt over his head.

I continue. "It's not in what you say. Hell, you barely talk to me. It's in how you move. How you look at me. In how you ignore me."

"You spurned me, not the other way around." He's pouting again.

"I did not *spurn* you. If anything, I did the opposite of spurning you." I wish he understood. "The worst part of all this is I don't think you realize what you're doing. I don't think you have any sense at all of the information your body shows the rest of the world. I think you've got your 'ignore emotional resonance' set so high you refuse to see it in yourself."

Rob's brow crinkles up. "Photographer or therapist? Which are you?"

I close my eyes. "I don't think you understand what either photographers or therapists do. And here you are in school to learn how humans interact with each other."

When my feet turn me toward my laptop, I pick up my life and I carry it toward my room. I think it's time to move back to California, with or without the job. I can't live with Robert Quidell.

"I don't think you understand what anthropologists do!" Rob calls down the hall as I close my door.

At this point, I don't know if I care.

CHAPTER 15

Robert

I follow her down the hall as I pull my sweaty running shirt back over my sweaty running tights. I know I shouldn't follow her. It's stupid. I should go take a damned shower because my clothes feel sticky and clammy. She stomps away and I follow her like a confused puppy because she's confusing.

Very, very confusing.

"You'd fuck me if I was *indifferent*? What the fuck are you talking about?" I yell. God, now I'm *yelling*. The entire building has to be hearing this.

Isa stops in the shadows filling our hallway. The light bouncing out from her room sets off the copper glints in her hair. All that bullshit about me not detecting emotions doesn't mean a thing because her body posture clearly screams *angry*.

"I'd fuck you if you were indifferent. I'd *sleep with you* if you stopped acting like a wounded kitten." She stomps off into her room and slams her door.

"Now I'm a wounded kitten?" I pace back and forth in front of her door, doing my damnedest not to pound on the frame with my fists. "You don't want to fuck me. You want to fuck with my head!"

Why am I putting all this effort into arguing with her? She's just going to call me another name. I pace again.

Isa opens her door. It slowly swings into her room, the hinges squeaking like wounded little creatures—*kittens*—and she stands in the threshold, her lovely hair messy and her pretty eyes wide behind her glasses. Her lips quiver as if she's about to cry.

Isa is about to *cry* like I'm the mean one here.

"I hope your brothers are better role models for your nephew than you are, Robert." She slams the door again.

"Better role models? I'm the one who stuck with his education." Why can't I stop pacing?

The door swings open again. "You *know* that's not what I'm talking about!" She pokes a finger at my chest. If I'd been close enough, she probably would have left a bruise.

"Then why don't you tell me, Isolde? Because I'm such a wounded kitten I can't see beyond my own widdle biddy paws." I fight the urge to rub my wrist behind my ear and keep my hands on my hips. I won't give her the satisfaction of seeing me act like an animal.

She stands in her door, her head tipped to the side, watching me. Her eyelids descend slowly, and her mouth opens just a little bit. And she finally speaks. "Do you push away all your male friends the way you push away women?"

"I don't push anyone away." It rolls out of my mouth automatically the same way it has so many times before. All the many times growing up that my many therapists asked the same question. Or when my brothers walk away because they don't have the patience anymore to deal with me complaining about my girlfriends.

Not like it's Isa's business, anyway.

"When you walked up to me at the party and I asked you about your hat, you made this wonderful face when you said 'my nephew gave it to me.' A beautiful, brilliant face. That's the face I want to photograph. Not Mr. Snarky McSpurny." She moves to close the door again.

But I put out my hand to stop it. I don't touch her. I just stop the door. "Isa," I whisper.

I don't know what I'm doing. I don't understand at all why I'm reacting this way, but I do think I know why she's gotten under my skin. "Please." It's all I can say. I don't know if I mean "don't close the door," or "don't stop talking," or maybe "don't walk away."

"That's why, when we were in the alcove and I was acting weak and full of lust I said stop, Rob. Not because I changed my mind. I just wanted to see that face again."

I think my mouth opens and closes. I think maybe I mumble something, but I'm not sure. Because Isa still looks like she wants to cry and I realize, I think for the first time, that I'm the reason.

"I'm sorry I've been mean to you. I didn't understand well enough how to articulate it until now." She steps into her room again. "When your reputation took over I thought I'd never see that beautiful, brilliant face again if we stayed on the course we were on."

I don't know what to say. I just know I'm the reason she's going to cry.

She turns her body away from me but she doesn't really. Her shoulders still sweep like she's attempting to pull herself into the hallway. "Will you stop poking at me, Rob? Can we be civil? Mack doesn't need us fighting."

Why the hell have I been fighting with her? She's about to *cry* and I feel nauseous and I think it's because I'm a dick. "Then we don't fight anymore."

I never thought about her reason for stopping. I didn't consider that maybe she sees me as a person and not just some random player she didn't want anything to do with. I didn't think that maybe she had higher expectations.

"Don't you have a family thing tonight?" She still looks like she's going to cry. "Mack said something about your brother's gallery opening."

She's changing the subject. Again. She did the same thing in the car. Frustration crawls out of the discomfort in my gut and that childish part of my brain wants to scream *Pay attention to me!* But that won't help. And I think it's part of the problem. I listen a little too much to my whiny inner child.

"I'm video chatting with Dan and Bart." I feel a smile wash across my face even though I didn't mean to. I shouldn't be smiling right now. Isa's on the verge of crying.

Isa eyes round and I hear her suck in her breath. But then she sighs and looks down at her feet. "I don't want to move back in with my mom." She looks up but I can't see her eyes in the shadows. "I'll move out as soon as I can afford it."

With that, with her final words that sound as if she's given up on me, she closes her door.

CHAPTER 16

Robert

On the other side of the video connection lighting up my laptop screen, my brother Tom gives me the finger. "If you weren't my brother, I'd smack you upside the head."

I wiggle in my room's desk chair and I fiddle with my screen so Tom can see me well. "Dan tells me the same thing every single day." My brothers feign a great deal of lack-of-patience with me. Neither wants to hear about my roommate problems.

Thing is, they're the only people I can talk to about this. Mack's partial, and I'm sure he's not interested in knowing I made his sister cry. Though part of me thinks he's guessed. But I doubt he wants to hear about it. If she were my sister, I wouldn't want to hear about it.

So I asked Tom what he'd do. He pursed his lips and looked over his shoulder at his lovely fiancé as she scurried around behind him adjusting his paintings.

"Take her on a date. You obviously want to."

I can't blame either Tom or Dan for not wanting to hear about my "wounded kitten" issues. This is Tom's big night. And Dan still hasn't fixed his Camille problem. "You need to slap Dan, not me," I say.

Tom frowns. "Look, I need to finish here." Tom straightens his tie. Sammie darts around behind him, an indigo burst of energy in a very sexy dress. My brother is one lucky man. "We open in fifteen minutes."

Sammie's friend, a dark-haired guy named Andrew, waves over Tom's shoulder. "Hi, Rob!" he calls. We haven't officially met, but he seems like a good guy. And he's been a major player in my brother's blooming career as a much-sought-after artist.

"Hi, Andy," I say.

"Dan's here!" Sammie vanishes from the connection.

"I'll have Dan reconnect, okay?" Tom aims his phone at my older brother. Then a swing back so I can see his face, and he cuts the call.

I sit back. They're both offline.

I hear shuffling in the hall and as I turn around, Mack knocks on my door. "You coming out? We want to see the show."

I've been talking up Tom's opening for two months but I didn't think Mack actually *cared*. But he has a bowl of popcorn under his arm and a couple of beers in his hand.

I almost ask about Isa. If she's coming out of her room. If I did make her cry. I should have knocked again. Made sure. But I'm a dumbass.

I nod to Mack and gather up my laptop. Time to move to the kitchen table and be social.

Isa sits on the couch with her own laptop in front of her on the coffee table. She glances up but doesn't say anything. Or ask to be included. I walk by. Because I'm a dumbass.

By the time I set up again, my brother Dan's online. He sniffs and holds out the phone. "This working?" he says.

"Hey, Dan." Mack drops the beers on the table and pulls up a chair. He leans toward me and whispers so my brother doesn't hear. "He looks uncomfortable."

I shake my head and adjust the screen. My brother's been uncomfortable in a suit since the hearings he went through to get full custody of his son. I think he associates a tie with lawyer-based hell.

Dan peers at his screen. "That Mack?"

Both Mack and I chuckle.

"I'm sorry you got saddled with my little shit of a brother." Dan turns the phone around and does a panorama of the room. "Show looks good. Andy says they expect a big crowd."

Colors and forms and glorious patterns swirl across my screen as Dan adjusts his phone and I can't help but be proud of Tom. Part of me hopes that somewhere inside, I have a sliver of the talent he possesses.

"Hold on." I take a pull on my beer more for the hydration than the flavor or the alcohol, and call up our father's number.

Dan knows what I'm doing. Tom, not so much. There's not a lot of good history there. After Mom and Jeanie died, it got complicated.

I hear a little kid voice. "Uncle Robby!" From below, the top of a young head bounces into the frame. "Uncle Robby!" My nephew jumps up and down in front of his daddy's phone and his hair appears again.

Mack laughs and looks over his shoulder. "Isa! Look at this." He waves her over. "You want to meet Bart? He's here."

My back stiffens, but my dad is coming online and I can't deal with Isa and him at the same time. Too much stress from too many faces.

In the bottom corner of my screen, the silver hair and long face of the other Quidell artist appears, our dad, Jeremiah. The man my brothers are still getting used to having in their lives again.

My poor father. The fallout of depression is difficult for an entire family to deal with. But he's been making attempts these past few years. I do what I can.

My dad fiddles with his screen and leans forward. "Did I hear Bart?"

"Grandpa!" I hear squealing.

From behind me, the sweet laughter of a happy woman. "Bart's the cutest little boy I have ever seen in my entire life." Isa smacks me on the back. "Why can't you be like that? You'd be easier to live with."

Mack snorts.

Bart takes Dan's phone and for the next twenty minutes we're neck deep in Bart-isms. My nephew's nonstop commentary gives me an excuse to ignore Isa even though she pulls up a chair right next to me. So close our arms touch and I smell the organic floral notes of her shampoo. And see clearly the joy in her eyes as she quizzes Bart about the paintings and what he likes most about drawing and taking pictures.

Mack and I pretty much sit back and drink our beers.

Few words exchange between Dad and Dan, but at least there's some. When Sammie walks Bart to his "Young Artist Corner" Dan takes us through the nudes section of the show. Dad asks a few things, mostly art and composition questions. Dan doesn't know what to say so he shrugs a lot. He's obviously distracted, probably by *his* woman problems.

Dad falls silent. As does Dan. Things get awkward.

"Will you have a show soon, Mr. Quidell?" Isa leans into me and toward the screen. I think my family has charmed her to the point she's forgotten she doesn't like me. And that I made her cry.

I don't know why but I don't lean away. The outside of her leg presses against mine and it feels different than any other contact I've ever had with a woman, except maybe my sister and my mom. It feels affectionate and genuine and friendly.

And I really do think she's forgotten how much she dislikes me.

My dad laughs but it's sad and my attention flits back to the screen. Dan's looking away. His wide-eyed gaze turns up and across the room as if an angel descended into the gallery directly from Heaven above.

I lean toward Isa. I don't mean to, but I know what the look on Dan's face means. I saw it again and again while I visited over the weekend.

"Ten bucks his girlfriend just walked in," I whisper.

Isa frowns like I'm the biggest lout in the world, but keeps her eyes on the screen. "You need a lesson in manners."

"Camille's here," Dan says.

Isa bites her lip. When she sits back, I swear she looks as if she's going to cry again.

On my screen, Camille appears and waves hello. Dan is still looking at her like a goddamned puppy. "Gotta go," he says, and cuts the call.

My dad blinks a couple of times and visibly moves back from his screen. He says good-bye and cuts too. He knows about the trouble Dan and Camille are having right now. I don't think he likes seeing his boys having lady issues.

"You all look like your dad," Isa says. She's still watching my now dark screen.

We do, Dan more so than Tom and me. We get our big and broad frames from him. But the pretty is all from our mom.

Dad still misses her and Jeanie. We all miss them. It's been over a decade but my dad's heart hasn't healed yet.

Mack pats Isa on the shoulder as he stands up. "Make him buy you ice cream with that ten bucks. He deserves to get fat." Stretching first, my roommate picks up the empty beers and popcorn bowl off the table. "I'm going to bed."

I doubt Isa would go for ice cream with me. I snort and close my laptop.

Isa frowns but she doesn't move. "I like caramel chocolate."

She doesn't look angry. Just sad, like Mack. But I think maybe this might be my chance. "The coffee shop next to the florist on the corner sells ice cream." Maybe we can be friends.

Isa watches her brother saunter down the hall. He looks more sad than I've seen him in a while, like her.

"Do you think he's got another headache coming on?" I ask. We both teach tomorrow. A migraine will just cause him a new and different set of headaches.

"No." Isa turns toward me when we hear Mack's door close. "Let's get that ice cream."

CHAPTER 17

Isolde

Rob stuffs his hands into his pockets. It's warmed up enough his hat looks uncomfortably hot, but it stays where it is, a bumblebee stinger-butt perched on the top of his head. His breath curls in front of us as we walk, the same as mine. The streetlights make it glow from above and it fogs the air, a brief cloud of our warmth lingering for only a moment.

Then it's gone.

He's been quiet. Watching me, mostly, with keen eyes and his body angled toward me. I'm beginning to wonder if maybe, possibly, he understood what I said before his brother's gallery opening.

I don't want to fight with him. I don't want to have to move out before I can afford to either, or run off to my mom's place because I can't get along with my brother's roommate. But at this point, I'm wondering if I can tolerate my mom's drunk-ass douchey boyfriends asking me if I want to "make it a threesome" better than Rob's belligerence.

"I deserved you yelling at me earlier." He does a little sidestep dance to accent his comment.

It's odd and out of place. It's as if he's happy I called him on his behavior.

He does another little two-step dance and twirls around. "You're right and I'm sorry."

I tap my foot. I can't help it; watching him makes me want to dance, too. "That's it? You're sorry?" He could just be saying it. "The last thing I want is to come out of the shower to find you standing there all pouty and huffy because I'm mean and you think I used your soap or something."

Rob laughs, but his face is serious. "You were crying."

He noticed. "You were dense."

The cold tickles my nose and I turn away, not feeling like dancing anymore. Maybe ice cream wasn't a good idea.

"Still am. Doesn't mean I can't learn." He bops in front of me, his hands still in his pockets. "I resolve to be a good roommate. You don't need to move out."

He's smiling but his eyes are serious. And he's tapping his foot like he wants to fidget.

I think he honestly wants to try.

"Thank you," I say.

Rob takes a small bow. "Were you really going to cry?"

A micro-expression of terror flashes across his face the way I'd expect to see it on someone before that moment when they realize the thing on the path in front of them is a stick and not a snake. Or that pre-understanding moment when they hear a loud pop and somewhere in their amygdala they think it's gunfire and not a car or a firecracker.

That fear moment that for most people vanishes once their rational brain takes over, but for a few unlucky souls, develops into something nasty and ongoing.

Rob twitches. Not a lot. Just a little. And I wonder.

"You did a good thing tonight." He needs to know. It might help. "I think your dad smiled more in the forty minutes you facilitated the chat than I ever saw mine in the entire time he lived in the same house as us."

Now Rob frowns. "Really? That's sad."

I laugh. I can't help it any more than I could help the dancing.

"Dad's got impulse control issues." I shrug. "Which I sometimes think I inherited."

Rob pulls a hand out of his pocket and adjusts his hat. "Quick thinking gets you the good photos."

"Yeah, but we be the sad twins, aye?" I do a sidestep the way he did earlier, my footwork opposite his. "You and I."

"I do say we be." He nods approvingly at my feet. "You that good with your camera, miz photographer person?" He does a different, more complicated step, one shuffling him backward first, then to the side. His foot thrusts out.

I tap my chin, wondering just how much I can get this man to dance. Because I like this new and improved, non-ass, open version of Rob. "Of course." I imitate his steps and flick out my foot to tap my heel on the cold concrete.

"Oh no you don't." Rob does a full arm swing and a hip circle before taking my hands and spinning me around in the cold night air. He's smiling and I feel light like the sun's shining. Warm like it's summer and not the tips of spring's ears.

"You're laughing." Rob stops twirling us around.

The surprise on his face makes me feel silly. Or sad that I let our issues get to where they did. Because I think my first impression was right: He's a good person.

"I'm sorry I was a dick." He's blinking sort of like he expects me to slap him right across the face.

"Can we be friends now?" Stroking describes much better the action my fingers want to take. Stroke his chin, touch his cheek, caress his hair. Pull him down on top of me and kiss him until he moans into my mouth. Until he can't take it anymore and pumps into me with his incredible granite-hard cock.

But if we're to be friends, I can't have these fantasies about him anymore. Because they're not going to happen.

"Friends." Rob stands erect, his chin up and his bee hat perched on the back of his head, and pulls off his thin and ratty glove. He extends his hand to shake.

He looks ridiculous, but I like it. And I smile. "You need new gloves." I pull mine off too, and glide my fingers over his palm.

Even in the cold, his skin feels like a dream. He's warm. Gentle. Soft but firm and masculine. I stare at his fingers as he curls his hand around mine and I don't want him to let go. But we're friends, not lovers. So I allow my hand to slide away from his.

He slams his hands into his pockets again. "Coffee shop's down the street."

Rob's gorgeous eyes gleam in the light reflecting off the sidewalk and his black hair pokes out from under his hat. He's a handsome god of a bee-filled underworld and part of me can't help but wonder if he's serious about changing. If he really does want to be friends.

We walk for a few minutes, Rob next to me. He's quiet, watching the street, until I start asking questions about his brothers.

Rob lights up. "I swear Tom's painted twenty portraits since he met Sammie." He kicks a small stone out of the way and leans closer. "She moved in with him a week after they met. Can you believe that? One week and now they're engaged."

A smirk moves across his face and once again I don't think he realizes what his body language says. The square shoulders and the raised chin show confidence. The slight skip to his walk signals he's proud of his behavior. The glances toward me show that he wants to share.

And that he likes the idea of knowing immediately when someone's the right one.

"Sometimes that's what happens," I say. "Other times, it takes years. Every couple's journey is different." His brother Tom seems to have a good head on his shoulders. None of the distancing Rob does, or the workaholic behaviors Rob says his other brother shows.

When we walk under another streetlight, he glances around, his eyes bright and watching. "Hey," he says, his voice louder than usual, and authoritative, and he wraps his arm around my waist. "I changed my mind. Let's go to the other coffee shop. The one closer to campus."

He won't let go, either. His hand pulls me close and the next thing I know, we're jaywalking across the street, walking quickly toward the major road next to the dorms.

"Don't take out your phone and don't let go of my hand." He grips my fingers so tight it hurts.

"What's wrong?" What did he see? Then I notice the figure in the shadows about a hundred feet in front of us, or what would have been in front of us, if we'd stayed on that side of the street.

A skinny person dressed head to toe in dark colors with his or her head completely hidden in a hood. No distinguishing features. No indication that there's even a face in there at all.

"Shit," I mutter. "I didn't see him."

"Doesn't mean he's up to anything, but I'd rather trust my gut." Rob's fingers tense and for a second, I think he might want to weave them through mine. "I'm not going to let anything happen to you. Mack will kick me out. Then what will I do?"

His grin is more disarming than any I've seen from him.

"Thank you," I whisper.

He grins again. "See? I'm not a complete dickbag." We walk along faster than my usual pace until we're out of sight of the shadowy figure. "Do you still want ice cream?"

I think, more than anything, I want to spend time with this new Rob. The one not hiding anything anymore. The man with the bright eyes and the happy smile. "I think I want to take pictures."

Rob stops walking but doesn't let go of my hand. "Now?" He looks around. "I'm not taking off my shirt out here," he says, but he's grinning and I know if I asked, he probably would.

I grin, too. I *have* to take pictures. I can't let this openness get away. "Where should we go? I don't want to go back to get my equipment so it'll have to be the phone." I nod toward the shadowy figure.

"The fountain in front of the Alumni Center has floodlights. Will that work?" God, his eyes sparkle in the moonlight, the same way they did the night we met.

"Yes," I say, and pull Rob Quidell toward the center of campus.

CHAPTER 18

Robert

Isa screws up her face and closes one eye as she looks me over. Her phone rises through the air, riding on the sensual curve of her lively fingers, and I hear the electronic shutter sound. She screws up her face again and shakes her head "no."

I'm beginning to think I'm not as photogenic as all my dates tell me I am.

The Alumni Center fountain covers a massive open concrete field that spits water out onto a flat surface, but in the winter they shut it off. This year, a melting exhibition of student ice sculptures dots the open concrete. The floodlights make all the ice glow and Isa has me on the edge of the fountain space, my toes inches from a wet, slick area of very cold water.

I frown at my feet. "I don't want to stand in slush." Frozen toes don't sound like fun.

Isa laughs and twists my shoulders toward one of the floodlights. "You pout a lot."

"Says the crybaby." I grin and shift to the side, the way she wants.

The floods make everything unearthly and too bright. Her hair glows almost white. Our breath curls like cotton candy. And the gold and copper flecks in her eyes fluoresce.

And I can't help but hear *goddess* echoing in my mind again. Diana rode a moonbeam to the Earth and now she's posing me in front of ice sculptures.

"This crybaby wants a good picture, so hold still. And don't stiffen up like that. You look like a damned robot." She wiggles my arms like a massage therapist loosening up a football player.

It feels good. It's not sexual but it's intimate in a way I'm not used to. Her fingers—her touch—focuses on me and I don't give a damn if it's because she wants a certain look for her picture. I just want her to wrap her long, graceful fingers around my arm again.

When I glance up, she's not looking at my arm. She's looking at my face. And she's smiling. "Yeah, I'm pretty sure you're clueless about your body language."

She dances a few steps back and snaps another photo before I can respond. This time, her smile only grows.

"I take it my nostrils aren't too big this time?" I stick a knuckle into each side of my nose and stick out my tongue.

Isa chuckles. The phone's fake shutter sound rings through the chilly air. Somewhere behind us, an undergrad laughs at her date's silly joke. I look over my shoulder in time to see the young woman lean against the kid.

My dates always narrowed their eyes, assessing mutual lust, and straddled my lap. Sometimes they take a selfie with me pressed against their back, to make all their shallow friends jealous. No one ever leans against my shoulder.

When I look back, Isa snaps another photo. Shaking my head, I pull the bee hat over my eyes and grin like a fool, hoping to give her some fun photos, too. I don't want to think about shallow right now. Now that for once in my life, I think I'm friends with a woman.

A wonderful, talented woman who the immature part of my brain thought was mean. But I see the truth now. Only immature assholes make women cry.

Isa grins and steps right up to me, her back against my shoulder. She holds out her phone to allow me to see the screen but I lose any interest in the photos. I breathe in her sweet and warm scent. I feel the weight of her hips against mine as she moves closer. All I want is to pull her against my body and kiss her deeply.

But I was a dick. I should thank the stars I've been allowed to be her friend.

She swipes through the photos. "I like this one."

It's the moment before I pulled the hat over my eyes. The undergrads behind me are out of focus, one blurry smudge of two people happy together. I'm glancing away, looking down, my hand rising to yank the hat down, my shoulders slumping, like the moment's too much. My face looks like regret rooted into my soul long ago and seeing the undergrads has made it blossom into something massive and entangling but strangely lovely.

"Wow," I say. How did she capture all that with a camera phone?

"We need to work on your stiffness, mistah cyborg maaann." Isa elbows my stomach.

"Most of the time, when women take photos of me, it's to make me look bad on social media." I shrug.

She tucks her phone into her pocket. We walk side by side toward the apartment, silent for a long moment.

At the corner, we wait for the light to change. Cars buzz by. Exhaust fills the air. But Isa still fills my senses.

"I have no interest in posting photos like that, Rob." Her head angles up and away, her eyes focused on a sign across the street. "You deserve better." I barely hear what she says.

Part of me doesn't believe it, anyway. The part that yells and screams and says women like to be cruel because I do deserve it.

The streetlight glints in Isa's beautiful eyes when she turns to me, and I know she's not lying. I know she speaks the truth. And the schema I built for myself—that fuck-buddy bad boy reputation that's kept me confined to the women who want bad boy fuck-buddies—crumbles. I feel it crack and I see it fall away from how I see the world and I have Isa to thank for it.

But it's new. And it's terrifying. I don't know if I can breathe through this. Or if I can let go of what's become the only way I know how to live, no matter how much I want to be free of it.

"Thank you," I whisper.

Isa's hand curls around mine. And we walk across the street, hand in hand, as friends.

CHAPTER 19

Robert

Three days later, Isa left for an eight-day gig in California. She mumbled something about the studio being a major operation and that working with the lead photographer was going to do wonders for her career. When she gets home, she'll be here for two weeks, then off again, away to somewhere else.

I gave her a hug and squeezed her fingers and tried not to look like a kitten. She smiled and squeezed back and disappeared into her room, to pack.

The evening of the first day without her, the creaks and the rattles of the building drowned out everything else. Mack and I ate our pizza and graded our students' assignments. Isa messaged me photos of her room at her mother's house outside L.A. Wide doors open onto a panoramic view of the hills separated from the house by a vast wrought iron fence. Off-white curtains billow in a breeze. A long shadow falls over a large bed made up with a flat white coverlet and a gigantic, generic painting that to me, looks like a drop of blood.

Her room looks more like a mausoleum than any place a human with so much brilliant creativity should live.

When I asked why her photos weren't displayed on every surface, I got only the texted version of a shrug.

If it were my house, I'd freakin' project her photos onto every single goddamned wall. I already ordered a big print of one of her Africa photos and bought a frame. It's going to be hanging over the couch when she gets home.

The second evening, she wanted to video chat so she could show me the sunset. We talked for six hours about her mom and her life growing up and how everyone in her family but Mack rushes headlong into situations. The worst of it caused her parents' divorce.

That night, I didn't go to bed until two a.m. and ended up sleep-walking through teaching the next day.

The third evening, she had a dinner she needed to attend. Mack and I spent our meal in stitches because of her two-hour-long, under-the-table messaged commentary on the grandiose douchebaggery of the shoot's client.

On the fourth night, I called. We talked for three hours about my classes and her production boredom and the differences in the flavors of California and Florida oranges.

On the fifth, I joked I was mad she took her shampoo but that her pillow, the one sitting on top of her rolled-up air mattress next to the cheap dresser full of her clothes, still smells like her. I know this because I needed printer paper from the closet in what used to be our den. Which is the only reason I went into her room. I don't want to be creepy.

She laughed and laughed and laughed.

The next evening, we texted all through dinner and the four hours it took me to grade my student's latest assignments. She sent me a new photo of the Los Angeles sunset each time I made it through ten essays. The last one is the new wallpaper on my laptop.

Mack's eyed me the whole week. We teach and we grade, and we both keep our noses to the grad school grindstone, but I think he wonders about my intentions toward his sister.

The truth is, I miss her, too.

Last night, she told us she had news she'd share when she got back. Mack scratched at his beard and said she probably got another big shoot someplace where she might get cholera or kidnapped or a bullet in her head.

I spent the night staring at the ceiling with his words echoing in my head, trying very hard not to let my mind wander from one horrible scenario to another.

This morning, Mack got mad when I grabbed the keys from his hand. He frowned, but I think a new migraine had started knocking on the inside of his skull. So I sent him to bed with a promise that I'd fetch Isa from the airport.

I sped all the way. I'm lucky I didn't get a ticket. But today's the first day driving with the window down that wouldn't ice over my corneas.

The weather's beautiful—warm and sunny. The birds sing their loud springtime songs and the trees try to rustle in the breeze as if they all wish their leaves had unfurled weeks ago. Puddles cover every street and sidewalk. Isa comes home today.

I stare at my phone as I stand next to the benches between the two luggage carousels of her carrier, numbers six and seven. The airport's the same as always—loud and cleaned-by-bleach smelling. The coffee is unsurprisingly bitter. Exhausted people mill about. The fluorescent lights blink.

And Isa's coming home.

A text pops up: *Landed.*

I smile and text back *Waiting by luggage pick-up.*

A little thumbs-up symbol and a smiley face appear followed by *I got some shots I'm really proud of.*

Pride rushes through my veins even though I have no right to feel the way I do. But supporting her talent feels right. *I can't wait to see them*, I tap out.

Just you here?

In the back of my head, I hear that little voice again. The one that used to call her mean. This time it's scared. *Sorry to disappoint*, I type. *Mack had a proto-headache so I sent him to bed.* What if she doesn't want me here?

I'm not disappointed.

My breath releases and I close my eyes. What's wrong with me? I'm acting like a high schooler. We're friends and I don't think we can be anything else. Not after the way I treated her for the first month she lived in the apartment.

I fucked up and I need to live with it.

Every time I visit my family, Dan points out my flaws. Between him, Tom, and my many therapists, I have a pretty good understanding of my behavior with women. It used to work for me. It worked for the women, too. I may have disappointed, but in my undergrad days, I never made anyone cry.

Another text pops up: *Off the plane. There in a minute.*

For the last ten days, we've been friends. Good friends. And maybe, I think, Isa might be becoming my best friend. So she can't cry again because of me.

Heads bob along in the sea of people. I watch the crowd, looking for Isa's beautiful goldspun hair. Her confident gait.

A knot parts. Fifteen feet down the concourse, Isa walks between a big guy wearing a cowboy hat and a slow moving little old lady, her main gear bag on her back and her second case in her hand. She bends forward a little under the weight and I think the bags throw her balance off. She shifts to the side and the guy in the cowboy hat almost bumps into her.

The look he throws borders on vicious. He's less than five feet from my best friend and every muscle in my body tightens. "Isa!" I shout.

She looks up but I'm not looking at her. I'm glaring at the asshole in the hat as I stride toward her, making sure he sees me. She glances at him then back at me, and her expression changes. Something I don't recognize moves across her cheeks and settles in her eyes. And when I'm close enough, she reaches for my hand.

Every other sound in the airport blanks out. Every sight and every scent. Isa looks up through her glasses with her big eyes and I don't think. I take her bag and pull her close and wrap my arms around her waist. The sweet notes of her scent fill my nose when I bury my face in her hair and the wonder of her skin covers my lips when I kiss her forehead.

Her hands grip my back. "I missed you, too," she whispers.

My hold tightens and again I don't think about what I'm doing.

About where we are or who's around us. About her luggage or how tired she is. She's against me and she missed me too. I kiss her on the lips like the silly stupid high school kid I'm trying not to be. Right here, in the middle of the fucking airport, I kiss a woman who's my friend because she means more to me than I realized.

"Rob!" Isa pulls back. Her mouth rounds and she glances around. But she smiles and slaps my shoulder.

"Sorry," I say. She's beautiful beyond reason with her hair in the chaotic ponytail and her clothes wrinkled and disheveled. All I want is to kiss her again, but she's right. Not here.

Her eyes narrow. "Robert Quidell, you are a *terrible* kisser." She slaps my shoulder again.

"I am not." The immature part of me wants out again. It's miffed. But I'm just being stupid. Because I'm pretty sure another kiss, one somewhere more private, would go over better.

But it's hard for me not to kiss her again, just to prove my point. I may not kiss my dates, but I know my skills. Skills I want to use to bring Isa to the exact opposite of crying.

I didn't realize how deeply I missed her until I felt her touch again. Until I breathed in her honeyed and slightly rosewater scent. How much I wanted our relationship to be more than friend and roommate.

She grins and takes my hand, but doesn't say much more. I hold her bag and we get her luggage and Isa watches me with concerned eyes. She clutches my hand, but she's far enough away our arms bow out like a rope between us. When I move to close the distance, she moves away, first to get her luggage, then to lead me toward the car.

And now I'm wondering if she wants another kiss as much as I do.

Isa pulls her seat belt across her lap and I press the key into the ignition but I don't start the car. I rub the top of my head instead. "Do you want to get dinner tonight? Not at home. At a restaurant. You and me?" I rub my head again. It'd be nice to spend an evening away from the apartment. Someplace where Mack can't stare accusingly at the back of my head. "I thought maybe we could spend some time together." I pluck at my t-shirt. "I'll put on a decent shirt. Promise."

"Rob..." Isa folds her hands over her lap. Her face does the same drawn, pale look it did when we argued in the hallway. When I made her cry.

"What's wrong?" My mind goes to all those catastrophic places with cholera and bullets even though she's sitting here right now so close that if I leaned over the shift I could kiss her cheek.

Why is my mind flipping over to thoughts of her sick or hurt? Why do I feel helpless? She may be exhausted but she's home and I can spend the next two weeks making up for the terrible behavior of our first month.

Isa opens her mouth, but it closes again and she looks down at her hands.

"Did I do something?" She's everything. I didn't realize until she walked up the concourse and that a-hole in the hat looked like he might hurt her, but it's true. Absolutely true. I think it's been true since the party.

I won't hurt her again. I won't.

Isa presses her lips together. "I'm moving out, Rob. I'm going back to California."

CHAPTER 20

Isolde

We spent the past eight days talking and texting and becoming better friends. We talked about sunsets and shampoo and I didn't tell him I'd been offered a position with the studio in L.A. That taking it would boost my career to the next level and might, if I'm lucky, lead to major magazine deals. Maybe gallery shows like his brother, Tom.

I don't know why I didn't tell him. Why I didn't ask his opinion.

Rob sits on the other side of the apartment's dining room table, an uneaten slice of pizza on a paper plate in front of him and two empty bottles of beer next to his twitching fingers. He's barely looked at me since we got home, and has said even less.

I think, maybe, I didn't say anything because I knew I'd break his heart.

Mack, on the other hand, took it well. My brother shrugged and ate his pepperoni pizza, though he did suck down an extra beer, just like Rob.

But Mack's sideways glances at Rob all through dinner bothered me. The slightly narrowed eyes. The tightening of his neck and his shoulders. My brother looked like he wanted to punch his roommate.

The man I'm pretty sure feels more than friendship for me.

Gorgeous Rob, a guy who, two weeks ago, acted more like a child than a man. Who pouted and poked and would have thrown sand if we were preschoolers on a playground because he likes me and he didn't understand any other way to respond. Beautiful, handsome, family-oriented Rob who, I think, uses his looks and his bluster to distance people.

But I wanted to see the real Rob. I wanted to take his picture. And I wanted to lean against his shoulder, safe and happy and, I think, sharing in his moments of strength. In his sense of family.

I wanted to be part of his life even though I kept telling myself it wasn't possible. How could I be part of his life? I'm just another conquest. Even when men change, they don't change. *Friends* was the best I could hope for.

So in the airport, when he kissed me, I thought he was teasing. How could Rob Quidell see me as someone other than the woman who forced him to see her as a friend?

Yet he sits in his chair two feet from me, his eyes averted. Every time our feet touch, or we rub knees, electricity fires through my limbs. But Rob won't look at me and pulls back as if I just cut him with a knife.

All I want to do is crawl onto his lap and kiss away his hurt. I want to see his beautiful eyes gleam and I want to spend hours feeling his hands roam over my body.

But I'm moving back to California.

Rob will be three time zones away.

Mack drops his napkin on the table. He looks at Rob, then me, then Rob again, frowning the entire time. "Opportunities like Isa's don't come around often." His words come out as narrow as his eyes. He means it for Rob, not me.

"If this works out, I could be well on my way to my own studio in a couple of years. Shooting for myself. I'll have more control of when and where I travel." Maybe settle down, at least a little. But I don't say it.

Rob looks up and I swear I see *Really?* play through his eyes. I can almost see the calculations bounce around in his head. Semesters he has left. Time to write a dissertation. Job hunting.

The possibility of moving to California.

It's all there, on his face and in his body posture. And I don't know what to do.

Years in reality are very different than years in fantasy, and I can't do that to him. To me. I can't expect Rob to change and sacrifice. I can't be worrying about a boyfriend on another coast.

"Work." Mack slaps his knee. "Must do." He jabs a finger at Rob's nose. "Don't be a dick and fall behind in grading."

He's up and dumping his paper plate into the garbage. After a moment or so, he walks away toward his room.

Rob watches him go. "I have all weekend to grade." He sounds tired. His words rolled out of his mouth slow and sad, and I wonder just how much beer's going to be consumed over the next two days.

Over the next two weeks, to be honest. Two weeks before I permanently move out and temporarily move into my mom's house again.

I refuse to stay with her longer than I need to. My new gig will get me steady work and income and I'm going to get my own place. How my mother has managed to keep her house both sterile and terrifyingly clean at the same time it's full of alcohol-filled chaos and yelling and weird boyfriends, I don't know.

Rob doesn't move from his place at the table. He stares at the hallway, frowning.

"I'm getting my own place. In L.A." I rotate on my chair so I'm facing him. "Come visit, okay?" Though having Rob sleeping on my couch is going to be a hell all its own. Friend or not, relationship or not, I have my own set of fantasies and many of them star my favorite ocean-eyed bad boy.

I think every time I close my eyes and imagine his tongue working across my nipples, or down my belly, or buried in my pussy, it makes him a little less real and a little more distant. He becomes inaccessible in real life, and it makes moving out easier.

Fantasy Rob and real, my-friend Rob, are two different men.

"I'll fly out every weekend, if you want me, Isa." Rob takes a pull on his beer.

If I want him. I blink wondering if what I feel is as obvious on my body as his emotions are on his.

"My dad used to travel a lot," I say. "Business." Slowly, I stand and pick up my plate to clean up some of the mess. "Our parents say they had an open relationship." I shrug and point down the hall, toward my brother's bedroom. "Mack and I know they didn't. They both cheated. Dad was—is still, really—a player. So's Mom. New lovers every few weeks for both of them. So we're sensitive."

Rob stands and helps finish clearing the table. "My parents never strayed. I don't think my father ever looked at other women." He smiles and chuckles. "I still remember the moms at my soccer games eyeing him. I don't think he noticed." His plate lands in the garbage. "My mom got harassed all the time." He waves his hand at his face as if he's a magician. "My excellent bone structure comes from my mom's side of the family."

I chuckle, too. "You *are* a pretty one."

Rob smiles big and throws a pose worthy of a perfume ad. "Maybe after I'm done with school, I'll model. God knows I'll need a job."

"You'll need to take a shower, first." I give him a little push before pinching my nose and crossing my eyes even though Rob smells warm and deep, like his voice. Masculine and fresh, and a little like clean ocean spray. It's his natural scent. No body sprays or perfumes. With Rob, what you see and smell and hear—and touch—is what you get.

I was so surprised by his kiss at the airport, I didn't think about how he tasted. Now I wonder.

Rob drops onto the couch, his beer in his hand. He sets it on the coffee table and pats the cushion next to his side.

I flop close, but not too close, my own beer in my hand. Friend close. Because we need to establish our boundaries. Or at least I'll keep telling myself that. I think, though, that I'm being weird about things. "I should have been more open about my moving out." I'm as confused as Rob looks.

His nose wiggles and he looks away. "Before I flew home for Bart's birthday, Mack told me that if I fucked with you he'd kick my ass to the curb." Another sniff works across his face. "I don't think he trusts me to act like a gentleman."

CHAPTER 21

Isolde

Rob picks up his beer but doesn't drink. "He's probably right."

His shoulders slump and he blinks slowly, his lids dropping over his beautiful eyes before snapping open. A shiver runs through his entire body. Rob sits up straight, a masking grin on his face, and puts on his best player face.

Seeing him fake not caring makes my stomach drop.

Rob leans back against the couch. "Tom has one of those magic relationships. The kind that happens fast and perfect and the next thing you know you're living with the love of your life." Rob's nose and eyebrow twitch.

He does the little shoulder roll men do when they don't believe someone's telling the truth.

"I take it you don't think so?" I wiggle on the couch, trying to get comfortable. My brother's shitty sofa has lumps.

Rob shrugs and takes a long pull on his beer. How the man stays as fit as he does while drinking so much is beyond me. Must be his handsome Quidell genes.

"I think Tom's artist mind wants his life with Sammie to be as exquisite a picture as the ones he paints."

"Oh?" I think he needs to get this out. To change the subject but not change it at the same time. Rob needs to talk about the social world he's part of, not just the social worlds he studies.

He scratches his cheek. "I think they have a lot more work to do than they realize. And I think they should wait longer before getting married."

"You don't believe in fairy tale romances?"

The day I took pictures of him by the fountain, he seemed to think his brother has a good thing going. But that may have been more about *liking* a woman than loving one.

I've seen fairy tale romances work as often as I've seen them fall apart. My mother is a serial fairy tale romancer, but I don't tell Rob that. My family's issues aren't his.

"It happened with our mom and dad. They eloped ten days after they met. Dan was born nine months later. Their marriage lasted through four kids and a lot of ups and downs." He stares at the coffee table instead of looking at me.

His lips thin, too. And his neck tenses. There's more to this than he's telling me.

"Dan's the family man, ya know?" Rob continues to stare at the table top. "The protector. He's clueless. Always has been and always will be." He chuckles and taps his beer against his thigh. "His new girl-friend is the first woman in his life since that psychotic twit Lori divorced him."

I take a sip of my beer. "They doing okay?" I haven't asked.

Rob shrugs again, but this time, he glances up. The look in his eyes takes me by surprise. Rob Quidell, the man okay with being on his own, looks as if every ounce of the world's loneliness has burrowed under his skin. As if somewhere in there, he misses his family more than he lets anyone see. More than he lets himself see. And that he wants, more than anything, for his brothers to be happy.

And his father, too. And his sweet little nephew, Bart.

"They are." He tips back his bottle but it's empty. He makes a face and it clinks when he sets it on the table. "But the moment she gets pregnant, he's going to become Mr. Super Protector Family Man again and become a bore."

Rob snorts and sits back against the throw on the back of the couch. His gaze stays on the one spot on the table, like he's drilling through the glass top with his heat vision.

"That's what happened after our mom and sister died. Dan stepped up. Became the dad Tom and I needed."

"I'm sorry."

He looks so distraught I want to pull him to my chest. Hug him until he smiles again. I squeeze his forearm.

When I don't let go, he covers my hand with his own. His palm slides over the back of my wrist, warm and strong and alive, but there's a tension I don't expect. His hand feels as distraught as his eyes look.

"My sister was three years younger than Dan and three years older than Tom. Her birthday falls almost exactly between my two brothers." Rob smiles. "She used to read me bedtime stories."

I swear he hiccups. Not a big one, not one that would be visible to another guy, but it's there. Right there, in front of me. And I didn't think my heart could ache any more than it does right now.

I move closer, to offer comfort. Rob leans toward me. He doesn't take his hand off mine. He doesn't ask for anything more.

"I heard the crash. I was in the front yard, bouncing my soccer ball against the garage door. I ran down the street. Dan got there after me. We were the first two people there, my brother and I." He blinked. "Dan and I saw it first."

"Rob—" I pull on him trying to draw him closer. I don't know if it's for me or for him, but it happens.

But Rob stiffens. He doesn't push me away. He just sucks in his breath.

"I did the therapy. I'm fine."

But I don't think so. Not really. How can he possibly be okay?

"Tom doesn't know. Dan and I never told him we were there first. It never came up. It..." His face scrunches up. "He was at a friend's house. Didn't seem to be necessary to tell him."

I lived through my mother's parade of shitty boyfriends. The ones who were better fathers than my real dad and who broke my heart when they left. The one who tried to grope me in middle school. The ones who didn't care either way.

But nothing like this.

"Rob—"

He sniffs and turns toward me, and the distraught look is gone. Vanished away into whatever space Rob puts it when he doesn't want to think about it.

I know all about those spaces. The pocket universes where we put the distress.

I'm relieved he has one. And that it looks strong enough to hold this for him. Some people would get mad at me for supporting what they see as a corrosive coping mechanism, but they can go to their little hug festival corner and whine to each other. We do what we need to do to get through the day.

"So," he says. He's changing the subject. Just like that, because he doesn't want to talk about the bad stuff anymore. Which is fine. "You want to do some night shoots?" He plucks at his shirt. "We better do them now before you're gone forever."

CHAPTER 22

Isolde

Rob stands next to the door gripping two open bottles of beer between the fingers of one hand while he fidgets with the collar of his jacket with the fingers of his other. "Need help with your gear?" he points down the hall.

I shake my head *no*. "Just my camera, my monopod, and one pocket strobe. It's all in the bag. Don't want anything that might draw too much attention."

"Ah." Rob smiles. "I'll wait for you at the top of the steps." He opens the front door. "There's usually a nice puddle of moonlight."

The door swings open. He watches me more than he watches where he's going as he backs out. "Don't take long."

The door clicks shut and Rob Quidell vanishes into the hallway, leaving only a slight hint of microbrewed beer behind.

I think he wants a moment alone before we're off into the wilds of the night to shoot in the dark. To center himself. It's time to be jolly and friendly.

I grab my smaller, cheaper DSLR case from my room, along with one Speedlight and my rope-and-monopod homemade tripod set-up. It's a lightweight and will get me good, real-looking photos.

With my real-life friend. I duck out the door, careful to close and lock it behind me, my jacket in my hand and my bag over my shoulder.

Rob sits on the top of the stairs with his back to the hallway. When the tumbler lock clicks, he looks over his shoulder. I can't see his face. He's backlit by the moon streaming in through the big window over the building's foyer.

I walk down the hall and set my bag next to the railing. I drop my jacket on top of my equipment and dust the top step before seating my backside next to Rob's.

Outside the apartment, I smell the lives of all the other inhabitants. Cooking grease and fried meats waft up from the second floor. Cat from down the hall. Cold air and exhaust fumes from outside. And pizza and beer from our apartment.

Sounds filter out, too. Faint hints of someone's television echo up the stairs. A voice rises against the background noise of the street outside, then vanishes again.

Next to me, Rob breathes. Moonlight reflects off his skin and shines in his eyes. He grins and scoots toward the rail to make room for me.

I take one of the beers. "Probably should leave these here." The bottle glints as I hold it up first to Rob, then to the moon.

"Aye." Rob winks and takes a pull before setting his next to his thigh. "I'm going to miss you."

I look away. The moon's not full, but it's close, and silver light spreads up the stairs and across the landing where we sit, filling the moment with a surreal sheen. Edges sharpen. Colors blend and turn blue. It's beautiful.

"You know," I say, "I had this fantasy that I'd write 'Isa's boyfriend' on your chest and take a picture so I could make another assistant—a jerk who ogles me—feel bad about himself." I don't know why I tell him this. Maybe so he knows *he's* not a jerk.

Rob grins and looks up, and after a shake of his head he takes a long pull on his beer.

The moonlight plays over his face and the bottle, and an ethereal glint flits through the space between us. It sparks and vanishes, a moment of subdued brightness that sums up perfectly my relationship with Rob. There's power there. A burst of brilliance that only appears when we're close to each other, the way we are right now. But then the world interferes, first by tainting his reflective surface. And now, by warping mine.

Rob winks. "Ah, yes. That old fantasy."

I chuckle and he sets down his bottle. And it seems, once again, that possible connection, that brilliant flare, vanishes.

Why do I let it go? Why don't I snap a photo and hold it up for him to see? Show him the caring in his eyes and the desire for connection radiating off his chest and his shoulders and his face? Because I'm good enough to capture those moments. I'm good enough at my job to gather evidence of his body language and play it back for him.

Which, really, is the problem. I'm good. And California is where I need to be to become excellent. California, Australia, Africa. Europe for months on end.

Rob will be here, becoming his own version of excellent. Not alone because he has his family. And he has my brother. And, I suspect, he'll have a girlfriend in no time after I'm gone, another woman capable of seeing all the brilliance I see sitting next to me. Someone who can see beyond his handsome face and his strong, gorgeous body. Someone who will love him as much as I do.

Maybe I sigh. Maybe I, too, have body language I don't realize I have. Because Rob reaches around my side for my bag. "You got a pen in there?"

His arm against my skin feels miraculous. My fantasies whirl through my head, fueled by his proximity and the light of the moon: Semi-public sex. Tying him to the railing and jerking him off until he comes all over my hands. Rob pressing me against the wall and growling like an animal as he takes me from behind.

But that's not Rob. That's my fantasy man I use to bottle up my sexual attraction to this person who is my friend.

"You can't be serious," I say. He can't actually be playing out one of my fantasies, even the silliest of the set.

But he's got my bag and he's rooting around in the front pocket. "Hah!" Out comes the felt-tipped marker I use to mark memory cards.

And off goes his shirt.

He twists in the moonlight of the landing, his fingers gripping the edges of his ratty t-shirt, and the fabric wisps as it scrapes over the skin of his face. He shakes his head a little as if the action will resettle his hair, and blinks. The shirt slides down his arms, over his well-shaped biceps, and down his beautiful and strong forearms. For a second, he glances at his hands bound up in the fabric. They sit on his lap, two masculine fists clenched around the cotton of his shirt, making his entire upper body tighten.

I have a flash of carnal need so strong I almost grab his hands and tie that shirt into a knot. An immature little voice in my head wants to punish him for all the times he acted like an ass. To hold him down and ride his cock and taste his lips and the warm wonderful skin of his neck and shoulders. To feel the heat of his stubble against my nipples as he takes one into his mouth then the other. To whisper that he'd better not come until I have at least three times.

But they're just more fantasies I need to release. That time's past.

Rob drops his t-shirt next to his beer. He looks down at his chest and his mouth screws up as he tries to figure out how to write in a way that would be readable in a photo. "Like this?" He pantomimes writing his name with his finger.

"You're insane."

His gaze feels like it's boring a hole through my skin. "If he's a douche who gets off on making you feel uncomfortable, then I say we fuck with his head."

I can't help but smile. It's a juvenile fantasy. Rob's my friend and he wants to support me doing something silly and... naughty. Because he's my best friend.

I reach for my bag. Quickly, I work my camera out of its straps, determined to distract myself by setting up for the low light. And taking a good photo.

The moonlight sparkles across the apartment building's long hall-way. I twist a little and motion for Rob to twist too, to get his chest into the light. He nods and moves, and watches me for cues.

"Good." I could set up my mini monopod and wrap the rope around my legs, but I'd miss this moment. I brace my back against the wall and one elbow against the railing instead, the other against my knee. I crank the shutter speed down and the aperture open. "You'll need to hold as still as possible."

Rob takes off the pen's cap and a small snap echoes through the hallway. He watches me, his eyes bright, and I snap the first photo. There's motion blur, but it adds a shimmer to the moment. I snap another photo.

Rob leans back and the line between the moon's light and the wall's shadow falls over his face. His features vanish. He raises a knee, bracing himself to hold still, and slowly starts writing.

My name appears first, three letters followed by an apostrophe and an 's' of possessiveness. He's mine, this man. Robert Quidell writes my name on his chest and it feels real even in this surreal moment. It feels as if he's giving me something he's never given anyone else. And he's doing it in a way that's both public and for us, very, very private.

In front of me, Rob moves in and out of the light, a body writing "Isa's boyfriend" across his flesh. This gesture goes beyond any of the social media haze around his past. I may never show these photos. It's about him giving of himself, not just of his skill with his body, and I feel showing the images would diminish his gift.

And it feels as if he's more naked, right now, than he was when we were in the cage down three floors, below our feet. More naked than when he pulled off his shirt to tease me after his workout. This feels as if he's peeling off his armor.

He looks up and I snap one more photo. Rob holds the pen between his fingers, just off his skin. "How's that?" he asks.

I turn off my camera and cap the lens. Carefully, I return it to the bag. I zip its pocket, listening to the sound fill the cool air of the hallway. And I take the pen, snapping on the cap, and return it, too, to its pocket.

Rob doesn't speak. He doesn't touch, either, though I see his hand move as if he wants to stroke my cheek.

His face is more raw than I've ever seen it. More emotion plays through his eyes than I thought possible, and I can't take it anymore. I can't take what I'm doing to this man.

I run my finger over my name, tracing the letters one at a time. As my fingertip twists around the bottom curve of the possessive 's', Rob closes his eyes. His chest tightens and I wonder just how ticklish the skin of this gorgeous man is. But when my finger glides over the 'b' at the beginning of 'boyfriend,' he opens his eyes.

His hand curls around mine, his fingers weaving between each of my own, first his pointer, then his index and ring, his skin warm and gentle and as brilliantly wonderful as the color of his eyes. When his pinky hooks around mine, he smiles.

And Rob Quidell nods his head *yes*.

CHAPTER 23

Robert

Isa glides her finger over my chest. I feel her touch, smell her warm scent. I hear only her breathing. I see the woman who I want to be more than a good friend.

"I'm leaving in two weeks," she whispers. "I won't be back. Not for a long time. This can't be."

"Yes, it can." I'll do whatever she needs. We can build what we need it to be. "I'll do the work—"

Isa's arms curl around my head. Her fingers weave into my hair. She pulls me to her, all of her, and her lips, her chest, her body presses against mine.

She's not gentle. One hand moves to my shoulders and her nails bite into my skin the way a woman's nails dig deep when she's about to come and she can't stop herself. Isa's body responds right now as if I've been fucking her for hours.

My cock is instantly, completely hard and the rush that comes from the change in blood flow makes me almost lose control. I can't think but I can touch her breasts and smell the faint musk of her arousal. "Isa," I growl.

I yank her onto my lap.

"You deserve... a real girlfriend." Her hand works into the waistband of my jeans. "Not someone who..." She sucks in her breath before my lips steal more of her air. "... leaves for months."

I pull back enough to see her eyes. She's serious. She doesn't think we can do this long distance.

Maybe she's right. Maybe she's not. But tonight, I'm proving to her how much she means to me.

I pull her hand out of my hair. Carefully, I stretch her fingers, flattening them along my own. Her palm presses against mine and I want to clasp my hand tight around hers but that's not going to get my point across.

I lay her palm over the words on my chest. And over my heart. "We have two weeks. It's going to be real, Isa." *As real as I can make it for you.*

Because every single moment I've spent with her has been real. More real than any other time with any other woman. I've been fucking ladies since I was fifteen and not once was it more than solving the puzzle of the moment. How do I make her feel comfortable enough with me that she'll fuck me? How do I get myself off while making a woman feel good? How do I live with myself in the morning?

Never how do I connect. How do I build a relationship.

Isa's lips glide along my neck. Her tongue touches my stubble. Her arms curl around my chest. She's closer than any woman has ever been, holding tighter than any other woman.

I can't let this end.

"Two weeks with you?" she asks.

She holds onto my front and the closeness, the connection, vibrates through my muscles. I almost whisper the truth. Tell her the strength of the emotions flowing through me. But I can't find the words. No sound I make could possibly express the need I feel right now.

So instead, I kiss her with my lips, my shoulders, my entire body. She needs to know.

"Two weeks." Two months. Two years. Spending two *centuries* with her would make me the happiest man in the world, but I don't say it. She'll run if I do, saying she can't hurt me by breaking up when she leaves.

But we have this moment.

I scoop my hands under her bottom and turn us so her back presses against the wall. The moon plays over her lovely features and across the lenses of her glasses. For a second, her eyes vanish. But I know I hold all her attention.

I press her against the wall, shifting her hips enough to press my now-painful erection against her crotch.

"I'm weak, Rob." Isa moans and arches her back. "I was weak when we met at the party. I'm weak now. My responsible brain is telling me to be responsible but I want to be with you."

I snake my hand under her shirt. She's wearing one of those thick-cupped bras, the formed ones which I hate. Can't feel nipples. I yank on the damned cup hard enough I think I hear it rip.

I bite through her t-shirt. "Fuck responsible," rumbles out of my throat. "You're staying with me tonight."

"All night?" Under her glasses, her beautiful eyes are open and wide.

When I stroke my thumb across her cheek, she kisses my fingers.

Every night, I think. "Tomorrow morning, I'm going to wake you with kisses and cuddles and a pot of *good* coffee."

A moan makes it through Isa's smile and her mouth opens just a bit. "I fantasize about you all the time," she breathes. "*All the time*. No one sparks my imagination the way you do, on so many levels. It's why I want to take pictures of you."

My entire body vibrates. "You get off on torturing me, don't you?" She better fuck me tonight. I'm not going to be able to handle wanking myself off. I need her body, her touches. I need Isa. "Being mean."

She chuckles. "One of my fantasies is tying you to the bed and teaching you a lesson."

In my head, words stop forming and my brain toggles over to making only images. The rush is fast and intense and exhilarating. I see her straddling my hips, her luscious breasts bouncing so close I feel a little breeze every time they go up and down. Her ass in the air as I pound her from behind. Her with my cock deep in her throat.

"I have other fantasies," she whispers. "Some involve your revenge the next day."

More images: Shuddering as I pinch on nipple clamps. Her begging and begging for me to fuck her again and again.

I tighten my core and stand up. Isa's back slides up the wall, her legs around my waist, but I don't let go. I don't let her fall. "Condoms in bedroom." Goddamn, I sound like an animal.

"Get my gear." She's growling, too.

I'll have to let her go.

Isa grins. Her lips land on the hollow above my collarbone and she suckles on my skin. Gently at first, then with a little teeth. I shiver.

"I like that I can read you so well." Her lips move up to my neck. "I know what you want before you do. You want me naked like this, against the wall, pounding me so hard everyone in the building thinks we're in an earthquake."

I'm beyond exclamations. I need to fuck her now. I cover her mouth with mine before she responds and I sweep my tongue over her teeth and inhale, to form a vacuum in her throat.

"Oh...." Isa moves with me when I try to pull away.

Which is exactly what I wanted. But I pop the seal. "You feel that? I'm going to do that with my cock."

Another, breathier "Oh..." flows from my beautiful girlfriend.

"I told you two orgasms while fucked, one licked." I rub against her pussy. "I expect the same from you, woman."

Isa drops her feet to the floor. She yanks away fast, and swipes for her equipment bag and coat. Her hand snags my jacket and t-shirt too, but she abandons the beers. Before I know it, she's down the hall and in front of our door.

"Damn it, my hands are full." She looks up at me, a smirk on her lips. "Key's in my front pocket."

I flatten her against the door and press my erection into her back. I could come on her now, out here in the hallway in the silver moonlight. Yank down those jeans and rub against the cleft of her ass and come all over her. Maybe I will.

I jam my fingers into the front pockets of her jeans, diving in deep, pressing on her hip bones and her pelvis. Her ass thrusts against my cock. Her legs spread. I grind my fingertips into her flesh as close to her pussy as I can.

"*Fuck*..." she breathes.

I swear she's going to come now and it makes me want her all the more. I yank the key out of her pocket and slam it into the lock, but I can't wait. Quickly, I glance side to side, listening for doors or voices or anything else that might mean a neighbor. Only Isa's moans fill the hallway.

I unzip her jeans. If I had a condom, I'd fuck her now. But I can finger her until she screams.

My hand works between her jeans and the soft skin of her belly, roaming down, looking for the fabric of her panties. God, they're tiny. Just enough to cover the trimmed hairs on her mound.

I press harder against her back and fight the need to bite the nape of her neck.

But then I remember what she said about fantasies.

She's slick. I slide my index finger into her folds, but don't rub. I just press on her clit. My mouth descends toward her hair. I use my teeth to flick away her ponytail before I latch onto sweet skin just below her hairline. And I nip at the same time I flick my fingertip across her clit.

Isa's entire body quakes as an orgasm rips through her. A moan rolls out, loud and sexy as hell. I yank my hand out of her panties and push open the apartment door.

Isa falls through.

And right into her brother.

CHAPTER 24

Isolde

I have never been so embarrassed in my entire life. My fly is open and I have my half-naked, hard-as-granite boyfriend with his arms around my waist.

Why the fuck is Mack in the living room?

He's ruining the moment. And giving me the same exact I-do-*not*-approve stare Dad gave me every time I brought home a date. As if his continued love was predicated on whether or not my boyfriends lived up to his standards.

Or maybe Mack is disappointed in Rob, and not me.

My brother's face alternates so fast between totally shocked and totally *not* shocked I think he's going to pull a facial muscle. "Oh for God's sake, what the hell are you two doing?" he yells.

"None of your business." Menace colors Rob's voice. His arms tighten around my waist and he pulls me against his front. His shoulders curve forward and one of his hands moves to cover my open jeans as I set my equipment on the floor just inside the door.

My breath hitches. When I look up at his face, I see why he's responding the way he is: No one yells at his girlfriend. Not some random person. Not my brother. In Rob's mind, my safety—both physical and mental—comes first, even if it means he might piss off his roommate enough to get kicked out.

I don't think he realizes what he's doing. Or how barely he's controlling the protectiveness in his stance.

I turn in his arms and hug his chest. He blinks, surprised, and returns the hug.

"We won't bother you anymore." Rob's attention flits away from Mack and returns completely to me. A kiss lands on the bridge of my nose, and another on my cheek.

I take his hands, folding my fingers into his, and squeeze.

"How is this a good idea?" Behind me, Mack sounds like he's about to throw a pillow at us.

Rob tenses again and his gaze flicks to my brother. I see a snarl start on the corner of his lips.

"Rob," I say. He's wound up like a spinning top and he's going to burst. But it can't be onto Mack. I want it on me.

The snarl turns to a smirk when he sees my face. And the next thing I know, he's pulling me down the hallway to his room.

"Don't be stupid! Either of you!"

Mack yells, but I don't care. I slam Rob's door the moment he pulls me through.

He doesn't flick on the light. The moon's light floods through the open curtains and it's perfect. He's perfect. Tonight will be perfect, no matter how much my brother yells.

Rob understands. He knows I won't ask more of him than I think he can give me. The future might pull us to different coasts but we have right now. We don't have to hold back.

His room is cramped, filled wall to wall with a large bed, his dresser, and his desk. The closet door's mirror reflects his gorgeous, naked back. A desk chair sits in the middle of what little walking space he has. And a small, three-drawered nightstand stacked with books and a lamp sits next to the head of the bed.

The condoms must be in there. The condoms I don't want to use, but I'm not on any form of birth control, so we don't have any other options.

It's never been an issue. I travel too much to form intimate relationships. But tonight, I feel a little annoyed by my lack of planning.

I want all of Rob Quidell.

He yanks up my t-shirt and his face descends into my cleavage.

"Thank you," I groan.

His hands yank down my jeans but he can't get them off with his face in my chest.

I've never had a man respond to me like this. Not even my first boyfriend that night at the charter house when we both lost our virginity. Not my only long-term boyfriend in college who told me he loved me, even though I don't think he knew how to love anything other than his BMW. Not the couple of random guys I've had sex with because we were both so horny we needed release.

No one wanted to be this close.

Rob pulls his face from between my breasts and I feel as if I'm truly exposed. He's my protection from the world, not my clothes or my equipment, and when he moves away, I don't like it.

Having his strong arms around me holding so tightly I can barely breathe feels right. I feel as if I've found a place of peace. Rob Quidell wants to be the steady rock in my life.

Rob, the player, who's never been anyone's rock. This man who has always pushed away everyone wants to be my center for as long as he can.

For the next two weeks.

"Thank me for what?" he asks.

For loving me, I think. I almost say it, but I don't want to terrify him. I'm selfish. I don't want him to realize the connection we're forming and to pull back from it. But I also don't want him to associate anything bad with allowing out this part of himself. He needs to learn to love as much as I need to be loved by him.

He touches my cheek, his fingers gliding over my skin. His ocean eyes shimmer in the moonlight, wonderful and full of life. My beautiful Rob looks happy.

"You are beautiful," he whispers.

The intensity in his voice flows into his next kiss. We aren't naked. He doesn't have his hand on my ass or cupping my breast. He holds me as close as to his chest as he can, his wonderful lips gliding over every micro-inch of mine. He tastes warm and a little like the beer, but genuine and healthy and fresh.

I step back. I need to see his face. His body. I need to watch him move and to feel the strength of his wonderful arms. I need Rob to be the living man he is.

His fingers caress my arms, gently gliding over my biceps to my elbows. He sweeps his palm along the outside of my forearm and an intense, bone-vibrating shiver runs up my arm and into my chest. A moan escapes.

Rob smiles. "I'm good at sex, Isa." He dances his fingers over my wrists, pressing and tickling the cleft that forms at the base of my palm when I wiggle my thumb. "I'm going to make this the best two weeks of your life."

Even if we stop now, even if I say no we can't do this because it can't last, even if we are just friends, I think these next two weeks will be brilliant. Special. And I don't think I'm going to want to leave.

"Hey." Rob kisses me again. "What's wrong?"

What do I say? Do I tell him the truth? *I shouldn't love you but I'm head over heels.*

So I give him one more opportunity to escape. One more moment before we tangle together. "Are you sure you want to do this?"

Rob's forehead contracts. He closes his eyes for a long second, then opens them again. "I want to be with you. If it's two weeks, it's two weeks." The look of consternation turns to one of concern. "Do *you* want to do this?"

I press myself against his chest, my face against his neck. The temple of my glasses rubs but we adjust. "Two weeks," I whisper.

I'm with him now and I'm not letting go.

Rob pulls back. His hands cup my shoulders, then my cheeks. Carefully, he takes off my glasses. When he steps away to set them on the nightstand, I feel cold. I need his touch and his warm skin.

All of the room's edges fuzzy out. Life without my glasses is soft and sort of shimmery. It's out of focus but not so bad I can't function. But it fogs distant places.

And, maybe, distant times. Two weeks from now, we will deal with breaking up. But right now, right here, Rob is hard and close enough to see clearly. And my focus returns to where it needs to be.

CHAPTER 25

Isolde

Electricity fires between my fingers and to the skin of Rob's chest. He closes his eyes and tips his head upward. I see the edges of his teeth and they glow just a little in the moonlight. When a low groan filters out over his tongue, his entire torso elongates. His wonderful chest. The waves of his exceptional abdomen. The words he wrote on his skin.

"Isa's boyfriend" ripples and I feel a surge of possessiveness course through my belly. It's stupid and childish but it feels so damned good. The gods offered me two weeks with Rob. The man I love brings out a level of pure, primal lust I didn't know I had.

Or maybe I did. My imagination's vivid enough.

I rub my palm over his constrained cock. My prize is about to burst out of his jeans and it makes me want to vacuum him until he comes in my throat.

His belt clinks and rubs under my fingers as I move him backward, toward the bed. I make quick work of the buckle and his fly, and push his jeans down his hips. They're off before I suck in another breath.

"You too." Rob's voice sounds dark, smoky. His eyes mirror his voice, as if he's looking at me from a new place.

I think he's a little afraid. His fingers vibrate as they undo the clasp of my bra. His palms too, when he cups my breasts. Nothing predatory moves from his skin to mine, but there's energy. Strong, wonderful, new energy.

His thumbs alternate flicking one of my nipples, then the other. The oscillation adds another layer to my lust and I can't take it anymore. I can't worry or whimper.

So I give in to my not-so-responsible self. And I let out the fantasies.

I wiggle off my jeans. They rub down my legs, constricting and lashing them together, and another rush of thrill strikes like lightning right into my pussy. Which do I want more? To be the animal first? To teach Rob his lesson? Or lie back and let him release his lust onto me?

I need both. I will have both. And more.

"Every one of those pretty-boy models you work with wants to fuck you." Rob's smoky voice takes on a dreamy edge. "No straight man would pass up *you*."

Why his words affect me so, I don't know. I float along their surface, buoyed by the lust I hear woven into the love in his voice. His certainty catches me off guard. Rob sounds as if he's hooked into the male hive mind and he knows, without a doubt, that he speaks the truth for every man on Earth.

And he's the one who won the prize.

I chuckle and run my palm over the soft cotton covering his diamond-hard cock. The vein running along the underside of his erection pulses against my fingers. The ridge of his cock's head quakes as I tickle it.

Rob groans and looks up at the ceiling again, his mouth slack and his shoulders tensing. "Jesus above," he breathes.

He wears super-soft boxer-briefs. The ones with the fabric covered elastic and the smooth, flat stitching. I hook the pinkies and ring fingers of both hands into his waistband and pull the fabric up and out, and stroke my thumbs and index fingers across the ridge of his crown.

A "*Fuck*," rides his breath as he grabs my shoulder and neck.

His kiss bends me backward and pushes against all my effort. My mouth opens on its own, my tongue dances with his all by itself. He tastes exactly right; exactly like Rob—savory and a little like sea salt touched by deep earth minerals forced up by a volcano. Rob, my man with more strata than he shows the world.

His lips work down my chin to my neck. His hands squeeze and massage my breasts. The head of his cock rubs against my belly and I almost come right now, standing inches from his mattress in my little black panties.

Can we make this last all night? Or is the need too strong? When it erupts, will we both let loose everything? I don't think I'll be able to control myself.

I push him toward the mattress. He slides his feet backward but keeps his grip on my breasts. His thumbs work my nipples again, sliding left to right, up to down. I know my mouth opens. I know I'm shuddering.

He flops onto his back, bringing me with him, but I break his hold on my nipples. And yank his boxer-briefs off his hips.

Heat rises off his long, thick cock and over his trimmed hair as I kneel between his legs. A thin line trails up to his navel and I dance my fingers through its soft hairs. Rob chuckles and the ridged muscles of his abs tighten under my touch. I massage along the groove between his abs and his hips and he wiggles again.

"You're ticklish," I say. Watching him squirm makes me want him more.

"Am not." Yet he squirms again and pushes up on his elbows.

"I want to taste you." I want him all the way in my throat and hitting against my gag reflex. I want to ride that edge. God, he's thick and I want to run my tongue over his crown.

Rob's face takes on all the dark smokiness from his voice. His eyelids droop. And I know that once I take him between my lips, he won't be able to hold himself up any longer.

The first lick pulls a loud groan from Rob. With the second, he drops onto his back again. Gently, I massage his inner thigh, working toward his balls, doing my best not to tickle too much. I want this to be the best blowjob of his life, not the time he spasmed because I wasn't paying attention.

A hint of his sea salt spreads over my tongue when I close my lips over the tip of his cock. I relax my throat and slowly slide him in, my lips cupping over his crown, then his shaft. When he hits the back of my throat, I suck hard to keep him in, even as I move up again. I take him deep again and again, one hand helping my mouth and the other caressing his balls.

His hips tighten. He likes my mouth so much I can tell he wants to pump.

I *want* him to thrust. I want to feel him on the verge of losing control. So I pop my mouth off his cock and strip his boxer-briefs completely off his legs. He sits up, his beautiful cock right there, right in front of me, and I pull him off the bed.

Rob kneels next to me. He grabs for my breasts, for my hair, and catches me in a deep, soul-burning kiss. "My turn," he groans. His fingers work into my panties. "I'm going to lick you until you scream."

The desire in his voice sends a real, bone-rattling quiver through my body. The man gives me nipple-hardening, orgasm-making chills. But I'm not done with him yet.

I crawl up onto the bed, ass away from him, my lips right where I want them. Leaning over the edge, I massage his hips, running my thumbs over the muscles of his lower abs. "I'm not done torturing you."

Rob chuckles. "You're *mean*."

He tries not to thrust when I pull his hips toward my mouth. I feel his glutes harden and his abs tighten. But he's off balance and he buckles forward, his chest coming over my head.

I take him deep again. His lips rest in the middle of my upper back and when he groans, it vibrates through my ribcage.

It feels good. So damned good. I suck hard on his cock, twirling my tongue against his shaft, and feel his pleasure roll through my shoulder blades.

The next thrust goes deeper than I expect but I hold the gag. Rob works his hands up the side of my body, his fingers digging into my flesh, until he reaches my ass.

And the next thing I know, I get another pump into my throat and a good hard smack on my right butt cheek.

I almost come. It almost happens. Rob must have realized because he shifts enough to curl an arm under my chest.

He clamps my nipple between his finger and thumb at the same time another slap hits my ass. And another thrust into my mouth.

The orgasm reverberates from the sting on my backside to the sting in my nipple. I moan around his cock but he pulls out of my mouth and flips me over.

He looks pleased. "That's two."

What is he going to do? "Fuck me now," I plead. "Please. I don't need—"

Rob presses the entire length of his body against mine, and his cock against my hip bone so hard it hurts. His kiss silences my pleas. I forget everything but him, sense nothing but his lips, and curl myself into his embrace.

My focus shifts from his taste to his touch. The vibration I noticed earlier dances again across his skin to mine. His lips find mine and his kiss is more intense, more alive, than any I've experienced in my life.

"Rob," I whisper. He's wonderful. Right now, he's everything.

"I want this to be the best sex of your life." He sounds as if he doesn't believe he can finish what he started. Rob Quidell seems to think he's not up to the task.

"It is. It already has been." I stroke his cheek and kiss the tip of his nose.

His kisses, how he embraces me, the touch of his fingers, are better than any other time. Better than any fantasy. "I'm with you."

Rob strokes my hip. When his fingers find my mound, I buck against his hand. "I want to make you come and come again and I want to be in you when it happens. I want to see your face and hear you sigh."

I think beautiful Rob who just spanked me to an orgasm wants sweet, missionary sex. He wants to see my eyes and feel my breath and see me respond to every thrust and every kiss.

I stroke his cheek, wondering if he's ever experienced the connection he craves. If sex has always been acrobatic and more about one-upping each other with skills than about feeling one another.

But that's not what he wants with me. Not our first time.

"Yes." I want to share this with him. To be, in some ways, his first.

He digs in the nightstand. I pull off my panties and scoot up the bed next to him, and curl my arms around his waist. We're both naked, both bathed in light from the moon outside. He tears open a condom, and the wrapper crinkles when he drops it on the floor. He makes fast work of rolling it on before snapping open the cap of the lube.

I kiss his shoulder. "Just a little." I'm wet enough.

He explores, his fingers rubbing over my clit and my opening, and I shudder. A new kiss finds my mouth as Rob moves between my legs.

Slowly, gently, he presses into me. His first inch sends an intense wave of pleasure through my belly. The second makes me whisper his name. With the fourth, I'm ready to scream. When his sixth and seventh move into me, I grasp the muscles of his backside. I need all of him. Every inch, every thrust.

He watches my face, his eyes wide open. Oceans swirl above me, glinting with emotions I never thought I'd see on a man's face while making love. But they're there and they're real.

I kiss his neck and grasp his back. He rocks against my clit, his hips as intense as his expression. He moves gently, slowly, making it last.

Making it real.

"Rob," I whisper. I want to cry. I want to speak the emotions welling higher in my belly and chest each time he slides into me. I want him to know.

He leans on one elbow to keep his leverage and strokes my face with his other hand. "I..." No other words move out of his throat. No other sounds but his breathing and his moans. He thrusts, a few shallow, a few deep, and kisses me again.

Greens and blues dance in his eyes. His dark hair blends into the shadows. Silvers spark and moonlight highlights. His hard body presses into mine, against mine, rocking, thrusting, and I read his desires. Rob wants this moment. He wants to move beyond arousal and simple touching.

His lips lock onto my neck, his shoulders hunching over, and he moves higher along my body to hit my clit with more force. The loud groan rolling from my throat surprises me, but not Rob. He knows how to do this right.

Hot-cold rakes every nerve in my body. My skin feels too big at the same time it feels too small—I feel each of his finger wisps and the gentle brushes of his breath. But I also feel the weight of his solid body. How much he stretches me. Every swirl of his cock caused by the rolling of his hips.

Rob ignites the upper limits of my body. He's found the edge beyond which my nerves will simply disintegrate. We glide along it, kissing and fucking. And, I think, loving.

My fingers dig into his shoulders. A new moan erupts. I spasm under Rob's thrusts and the world blanks out.

"*Oh*..." Rob pumps one last time.

My orgasm matches his, pulse for pulse, stuttered moan to stuttered moan. New kisses land on my neck, my cheek, my oversensitive lips. His fingers weave into mine. Each kiss is gentle, sweet. I kiss the tip of his nose and he grins, his eyes happy and, I think, amazed. But also a little sad.

All I want is to make sure I see only his happiness. I don't want to let him go.

"I need to take care of the condom," he says.

I nod. Rob lifts off me but I sit up too and lean against his shoulder. His arms curl around me for a long, strong, entwining hug. Rob holds me as tightly as I hold him, and his lips dance over my ear.

"I'm sorry for every stupid thing I did. For the stupid things I said to you," he whispers. "I'm so sorry."

I press my lips against his jaw and his cheek, and I give him my own apology. "If I had chosen you over my lust, it never would have happened." And we would have been together much, much sooner.

I know we would have been together. But loving longer would make leaving him much, much more difficult.

Rob kisses my temple and my forehead. He pulls away only long enough to roll off the condom, but he's paying more attention to me than his work. He ties the condom and drops it in the wastebasket and he's immediately back in my arms, curled around me, exactly how we were when we both orgasmed.

A new kiss lands on the bridge of my nose. "We'll figure it out," he whispers.

I nod and press myself against his chest. We will. I just hope I have the strength to do what's right.

CHAPTER 26

Robert

Isa fell asleep in my arms. Beautiful, fun, adventurous Isa cuddled against my side and fell asleep with her head on my shoulder.

For the first time in my life, a woman wanted to *sleep* with me.

I didn't say anything more than "We'll figure it out." I knew what would fall from my lips if the words continued to roll out: *Don't leave. I need you here. We can do this.*

I love you.

Part of me still wondered if she would be gone in the morning. If she'd sneak out the moment I fell asleep and that we'd be doing the cordial nods and embarrassed smirks over coffee. But she's here, sleeping next to me, her lovely hair fanned out over my pillow, snoring softly and smelling of sweat and sex and love.

Isolde Wellington, my roommate's "mean" twin sister. Isa, the woman I love more than I thought I was capable of loving. She's here. She stayed. Slept with me because she's my friend and my lover and I'm happier than I should be.

Maybe seeing my brothers with their new loves rubbed off on me.

Maybe I just needed examples of relationships worth fighting for that haven't ended in ripping metal and...

I blink and rub my face. I won't think about the accident.

But Isa travels a lot.

I kick that irrational thought in the gut. I'll hold it down and beat the snot out of it if I have to. The ten years of therapy can't be for nothing, no matter how hard I worked at making sure it didn't take.

But it did. My girlfriend is with me this morning.

My stomach growls and my cock does its normal morning stand at attention even though it got plenty of satisfaction last night. My girl-friend's adventurous. Which, I suppose, shouldn't surprise me one bit. She flies around the world to take photos of moments ranging from skinny models standing on beaches to poachers murdering elephants.

And for some reason, my globetrotting lover chose boring, shallow me.

For two weeks, she chooses to be with me.

I'm not giving her up. If I go six months without her in the same room with me, then I go six months. But when she flies home, it's going to be to me and not to some tiny, pathetic, lonesome place in California.

No, we're not breaking up when she goes. I'm not giving up without trying. I'll work myself to the bone for her.

I think she feels the same. I hope she feels the same. But I need to be careful. Can't come on too strong or she will run. Then we *will* have the awkward smirks and sideways glances over breakfast. And I'll never see her again.

Sun filters in through my window and I swear Isa glows. She snorts. Her nose wiggles. A hand bats at a few stray hairs wrapped around her face and she pretty much slaps herself across her cheek.

I can't help but chuckle. She's amazing and wonderful and real.

Her eyes open. "Oh!" And she sits up so fast I'm afraid she's going to smack against the headboard. "Rob!"

Worry whacks me with the same force I thought she might inflict on herself. What if she regrets last night? What if she would have snuck out, if she'd woken up first? "You okay?" I ask.

Isa rubs her eyes. "I was dreaming."

She reaches for me. I pull her into my arms and her luscious breasts flatten against my chest. My skin tingles where she touches.

I can't help but kiss her hair and her forehead. "Not bad, I hope."

"It seemed important." Isa cuddles in close. "I'm glad I woke up with you."

I think perhaps I suck in my breath. It's not manly. But I can't let her go.

Her kiss feels better than anything in my life. Better than a birthday party. Better than the time Tom dared me to climb over the roof and down the other side of the house and I did it in less than ten minutes. Better than my no-debt-accumulated scholarships.

I squirm when she traces her finger over the words on my chest. "I'm getting it tattooed on." I wink. "I'm thinking blacklight ink."

Isa chuckles. "My boyfriend-for-two-weeks is insane."

Not two weeks. It won't be two weeks. But I don't say the words. "You like me insane and you know it." I kiss her with enough energy my morning wood notices.

"Hmm..." Isa runs her hand over my hip. "Two weeks of waking up to this is going to be heaven." A new kiss lands on my shoulder. She glides a finger up my firm cock, base to tip, and smirks.

I try not to groan but her touch is brilliant.

"You are a thing of beauty, Robert Quidell." Her hand wraps around my erection and she strokes up once, then slowly down again.

My worries flop into the pond of subconscious buzz in the back of my head. I'll deal with them later. Right now, I have my woman.

I glance at the clock. I also need to be on campus in an hour and a half.

Groaning, I pull away. "I need to go to class." I'd rather spend the day fucking my girlfriend into pure bliss.

Isa makes a wide-eyed, exaggerated pout. "But it'd be a shame to waste a good, hard cock." She strokes me up and down again.

Playful and adventurous. I hit the jackpot with this one. "It's a renewable resource." God knows it won't go away and I'll be spending my day uncomfortable and distracted.

"I'll drive you to campus if I have to." Isa rolls over and reaches for a condom.

The perfect twin mounds of her gorgeous ass are right there, waiting for my attention.

I grab hold and press my thumbs into her flesh, spreading her cheeks to get a good look at her pussy in the bright morning sun.

Goddamn, I think I'm going to skip class this morning. I'll email my TA later. Say I'm sick. Or maybe I'll just tell him the truth—spending the morning boning my sex kitten girlfriend trumps stats lectures any day.

Isa wiggles her ass higher at the same time she widens her legs. "You're not going to get kicked out of grad school because of me, are you?" She wiggles her ass again. "If we're quick, you'll get to class on time."

I get a quickie before my boring day of classes and office hours? I think I like waking up with someone I love.

The condom flicks over her shoulder and lands on the curve of her ass. "Do me, baby," Isa drawls.

She glances over her shoulder, her expression cocky and naughty and full of a different emotion I don't quite understand. Acceptance, maybe. Desire, for sure. The desire to share this moment of bad behavior with me. We're intimate in our juvenile disregard for authority's hourly schedule.

"You're a bad influence." I smack her left ass cheek before kneading the muscle.

Goddamn, she's gorgeous.

"Oh!" But her expression just gets naughtier and she wiggles her ass again.

I'm directly behind her, using my knees to spread her legs farther apart. The condom sitting just at the top of her ass's cleft slides a little toward me. I grip her backside and wiggle it, to move the wrapper back to its original position.

"I need to take a shower." I smack her other cheek.

She responds by wiggling again and pressing her ass toward my belly.

I run my palm over her slick pussy. Her trimmed bush is slightly darker but the same basic blonde as her hair. Her inner lips blush and quiver when I rub my fingers over their warm, slick surface.

Yes, I'm missing stats class. "Can't miss my office hours this afternoon. Have a student coming in."

Isa bites her lip as she glances over her shoulder. "So you're not as bad a boy as you claim to be?"

And she calls me the brat. I smack her ass again, then knead her flesh, squeezing hard.

"I never liked spanking before." Her head drops down. "But when you do it, it's amazing."

Chuckling, I pull up on her ass cheeks. Her back bows and she drops her front down onto the bed, her chest flat and her arm out along the pillows.

I could tie her up. But I'd have to leave the glorious pussy in front of me. I ask anyway. "Blindfold?"

Isa looks surprised when she pushes up again and looks over shoulder. But her face quickly changes back to the naughty expression I saw earlier. "You like it?"

Sometimes. "I want to see you writhe because you can't stop coming."

"Oh..." Isa plants her face in the pillow and stretches out her arms. "Please."

"Don't move." I move to the head of the bed and dig around in my nightstand. The silk scarves wait in the back of the drawer, one for her eyes and one each for her arms.

The purple one, I brush along the back of her neck. She shivers and wiggles her ass and I want to fuck her right now. No toys, no playing, just a hard, fast fuck.

Maybe tomorrow morning.

I make quick work of tying the scarf around her head. Isa lifts her front off the bed. Just a little, but it's enough I see her open mouth. Her tongue darts out and I know immediately what my fiend of a girlfriend wants.

Slowly, so she knows what I'm doing, I lean over the side of her face and rub the underside of my cock against her cheek. Electricity flickers up my shaft and into my lower belly. Is she going to turn her head enough to take me in her mouth? Is she going to give me another mind-blowing blowjob, like she did last night? This morning, I'm not sure I could stop myself from coming on her face.

"Tie my hands," she whispers.

I immediately tie one end of a red scarf around the wrist of her hand opposite me. The effort rubs my cock against her face again. It's distracting. I can't think. But I manage to pull the long end of the scarf toward the headboard.

When I shift, she rolls slightly. Her lips wrap around the head of my cock and her tongue traces the tip.

I try not to groan. I try not to thrust. *Feel it*, I think, but shit, it's like I'm fifteen again and this is my first, formative moment of a woman sucking me.

When I move into her mouth, she pulls her head back, not taking me deep the way she did last night. She wants only the head of my cock.

Fuck, I think. *She's killing me.*

Her lips pop off and she wiggles her wrapped wrist. "Work first."

I immediately tie the scarf to the headboard, allowing some give, but not a lot, and do the same for the arm close to me. Isa lies on my bed on her chest, her ass in the air, the condom still perched on her lower back, her arms spread and her eyes blindfolded, ready for me to delight her senses.

Or just fuck her as I please.

I run my hands over her shoulders, teasing and tickling. She whimpers and pulls against her restraints, and her muscles tense under my touch. I move one hand around to the front of her neck and gently stroke her jaw. I run a finger over her lips.

"Hmm...." I hum into her ear. My other hand roams down her spine and over the curve of her back. I press the condom packet into her flesh. Then I move my hand around her hip.

Isa pants against my fingers. Slowly, I press a finger into her pussy, then another, and mirror the movements with my other hand, pressing one, then two fingers into her mouth.

"I will tell you when to come," I breathe into her ear. She can come and come again, but this is our first time playing this game. Better play by the conventional rules.

"What are you going to do?" She sounds wistful. Faraway. Which means she's enjoying the game.

"Fuck you." Quickly, I take hold of her head, positioning my hands to make sure she's not torqueing her neck or holding her head in a way that will hurt, and lift her shoulders off the bed. And just as quickly, I thrust deep into her mouth once, twice. Three times.

A sigh tickles my cock at the same time her tongue presses against the underside of my shaft. God, she knows what to do and it's divine. "Before you leave for California, I'm coming in your mouth," I growl.

Another sigh tickles along my shaft. I pull out of her mouth and rub my cock over the side of her face and up to the sensitive skin around her ear. Isa drops her face to the pillow again and I press my cock against her shoulder, her side. Each point of contact elicits a moan.

Her responses make me want to plunge into her. To just lose control and slam her hard.

I move between her legs. Slowly, I grind my palm against her glistening, upturned pussy. The condom slides to the side and I glare at it. That sheath of latex is going to keep me from feeling all the wonders of Isa's tight, hot pussy. For the first time in my life, the desire to be completely in contact with a woman almost overcomes my safety protocols.

I let out my frustration and nip her left ass cheek.

A breathy "Best boyfriend ever..." rolls out of Isa on the back of a moan.

No woman has ever trusted me this much. Even my "lifestyle" girlfriend was more into power games than trust and connection, no matter what she told me. But Isa likes what I do and wants everything I have to offer.

This can't be only two weeks. It can't. So I'm going to make her addiction to me as strong as her feelings.

I widen her legs again and flip onto my back. Digging my fingers into her ass, I pull it down until her pussy is right above my lips.

And I blow on her clit.

"Rob..." Her belly shakes and I swear she just came a little.

"No orgasms until I say." I accent my growl with a new slap to her ass.

"*Ah...*"

I lay a quick, gentle lick across her clit. Her pussy tastes like the rest of her skin—sweet with a hint of rose—but stronger. I lick again.

A new moan rises from my trussed up girlfriend. She wiggles, pulling against her restraints, and it makes me want her more. I suck on her clit and roll my tongue around her opening, lapping at her like a starved puppy.

She presses her pussy into my face, grinding and whimpering, but I keep licking. I keep sucking. And I slap her ass one more time.

Her orgasm spasms through her body and I feel her contractions against my lips. Pulses I want around my cock. I slap her ass again.

"I didn't say." I roll out from under her. The condom fell off while I ate her and now sits on the sheet next to her hip. I run its edge along her skin and rip it open next to her ear. "Time for your punishment."

I swear she quakes again. That another small orgasm rolls through her body.

Yes, I think. *I'll get what I want.* I want to feel her come while I'm buried in her, the way I came last night.

I roll the condom on. My balls burn. My cock feels ten times too big for my skin. And once again, I hate the damn latex.

I'm not careful. I thrust in, feeling the friction before her slickness takes over. Isa bucks against my hips and I pump deeper. She stretches more with each thrust but I bottom out and hit her cervix. She groans and shakes, and I think it might be the wrong kind of pain.

So I yank on her hips and reposition her ass to hit a different spot, at a different angle. The next shudder around my cock feels right—hot, intense, perfect. I slam into her again.

Fast, deep, I pump my hips against her ass. We slap together. The bed rocks and creaks, and I'm sure the neighbors below are getting an earful, but I don't care. Her sweet scent mixes with my lust and I'll fuck her this way all day if I can.

I can't hold my orgasm. I need release. She's gorgeous and tight and we fit together exactly right. Finding her spots is as easy as walking. And she's already found all of mine.

She arches back toward me, taking every thrust. "I'm going to come..." Another loud moan pushes from her throat.

"*Shit*," I groan, and pound into her again and again, faster and faster.

My orgasm hits me like a slam into a wall. It's sudden and surprising and reverberates from the point of impact through my entire body. My brain bounces against my skull. My knees buckle. And my entire weight drops onto Isa's back.

Isa twists her wrists and her hands pull out of the scarves. The blindfold comes off. She rolls under me and pulls me up to her shoulder, her entire body curling around mine the way she did last night.

I don't usually like being touched after an intense orgasm. I want the woman to let me be, at least for a moment or two, but not with Isa. I want her as close as I can get her. Tasting the set of her lips and her joy in her breath.

Like now. She grins and chuckles and presses the entire length of her body against mine and I'm in heaven. Real, wonderful heaven.

I move only far enough away that I can pull off the condom. She's breathing hard and so am I. We're both warm and bordering on sweaty. The sheet rubs over my skin as she pulls it up but cuddling together is what I need. Quickly, I return to her arms. And my bliss.

But the clock says if I shower now and run to the bus stop, I'll only miss the first part of my stats class. "I gotta go."

Isa sits up. She pulls the sheet over her chest and cocks her head to the side, watching me. "Go be otherwisely brilliant, gorgeous." She pats the mattress. "I think I will spend the morning lounging naked in your bed."

No pout. No frown. My girlfriend smiles and sends me out into the world to work my job and it's the best post-sex moment of my life.

I kiss her cheek knowing full well I'm not letting her go.

Not at the end of the two weeks. Not in two years, either. Or twenty. She's who I need. "Shower with me."

Isa wags her finger and flops onto the mattress. "Tomorrow."

Leaving her in my bed takes considerable will power. Showering without her, even more. I don't scrub the words on my chest. If they fade, I'll trace them. They're staying all fourteen of our days.

I brush my teeth, but don't shave. I'll get food on campus. Back in my room, Isa props herself up on an elbow and nods approvingly the entire time she watches me dress. Her gaze feels different from the dismissive lust I'm used to. She seems to enjoy watching me move even when we aren't having sex. It's nice.

"I gotta go," I say again.

Isa rolls off the bed and pulls my t-shirt from last night over her head. It falls over her exceptional breasts and down to her exceptional hips. Quickly she pulls on her panties.

"What time does Mack leave?" Isa cracks the door and looks into the hallway. "We alone?"

"He was out of here at dawn. Early class." I wrap my arm around her waist and pull her out to the living room with me. Once again, letting go takes more effort than it should. She fits against my side. Her warmth gives me calm.

But I have class. And office hours. "I'll be back around four." I toss my bag onto my back. "So will Mack."

Isa nods. When I swing open the outside door, she kisses my cheek. "Be careful."

I don't want to go. For the first time in my life I've found someone good for me and I want to spend every waking moment with her. But duty calls.

I nod. "Miss you already."

A blush rises along her cheeks. She looks down and away but squeezes my fingers. "You're wonderful."

"Let's talk tonight, okay? Figure things out." Then sit down with Mack. He can't be mad. I'm staying with Isa, no matter what happens.

She nods yes. "We need to sort out permanent addresses."

She wants to stay with me. I see it in her eyes and in the set of her cheeks and I almost blurt out how I feel. I almost say it. But I have class, so I kiss her instead. "Four."

Isa nods again. "Don't be late."

I back through the door. "I won't."

"Bye." She watches me step into the hall.

"Bye." I walk backwards toward the stairs.

"Go on." She shoos me away, but her face says *come back*.

I nod and turn away. The door clicks closed and I hear the lock tumble behind me. I should run for the bus, but I can't. Not yet.

I knock.

When she answers, confusion twists her face. I step in and hoist her up in my arms. My kiss steals her breath. I want to take away her worries and replace them with comfort and joy. "I'm going to think about you all day."

More blush creeps up her neck. "Go *on*. You're already late."

This time, I wait until I hear the lock click again before I dash away, toward the bus, my head full of possibilities and plans. My future wants to be with me. And we're going to make it happen.

CHAPTER 27

Robert

I don't remember my stats lecture. Don't remember sitting in my cubicle for office hours, either. But I do remember sexting with Isa all afternoon.

We sent back and forth more than naughty innuendos. Turns out, she managed to convince Mack to let her borrow his car tonight. Looks like I'm going on a real date with a gorgeous woman. She spent the day planning the whole thing.

I glance out the bus window and watch the dorms go by. It's nice today, warm and bright, and the air smells fresh. A night out will be fun, though so would another night full of fantasies.

I shift in my seat. Two excellent rounds of excellent sex within the last twenty-four excellent hours but my balls ache anyway. And I've been semi-hard since she texted me the first *I just took a shower* this morning.

Which she followed with *You like my black panties, don't you? I have a red pair I'm pulling over my thighs right now.*

Smart, talented, and a bad girl. I'm marrying that woman.

The bus lurches and I blink, suddenly aware of my own thoughts. I need to convince her we can handle a long-distance relationship first.

Hell, I need to make sure we can handle the next two weeks. It's not like I have a good track record. Neither does she, to be honest. Traveling has always taken priority to intimacy.

My sudden awareness of my thoughts shifts from future plans to the very real present. To expectations. Finishing school. And to likely sacrifices.

I shift again in my seat and tuck those thoughts away. It's not like I'm proposing. My beautiful girlfriend is taking me out for a night on the town and we're going to talk. Make plans.

The bus groans and rolls up to my stop. I jump off the step into the spring sunshine and the bus exhaust, my pack on my back and enough dance in my stride to make me smile.

Because this is going to work. For once in my life, I'm going to make sure I play for two people and not just myself.

I dodge a puddle. Birds sing and cars honk. A beer awaits, as do the cuddles of my glorious girlfriend. Though I do have a stats assignment due in a couple of days. At this point, I doubt Mack will help me with the programming. I don't think Isa can, though some of the image software she uses looks more like moon rocket controls than cropping tools. She'd probably figure out my stats program in under an hour.

Grinning to myself, I pull out my phone and tap my brother Tom. Time to get some relationship advice from an expert.

Though "expert" is more "lucky dumbass" in his case. Still, Sammie moved in a week after they met, so he's got insight on the whole "living together while you establish your relationship" problem.

You around? I tap out.

After a moment, *Why aren't you in class?* pops up.

Walking home. I glance around more to make sure I'm not going to run into someone as I stride along the sidewalk. *Got a woman question.*

To spank or not to spank? You need to ask Dan that, not me.

I shake my head. *TMI,* I tap out.

What's your problem, little brother?

I don't know how to phrase what I want to ask. When did you know Sammie was the one? When did you decide you wanted to marry her? Or maybe it's not so much deciding you want to make it permanent, but deciding to put in the effort to work toward making it permanent.

I think I'm in love, I tap out.

The pause before his answer is excruciating. What if my responsible brother chastises me? Tells me I'm too immature to even consider a real relationship and that I have way too much work to do on myself before I should open up *that* line of communication with Isa?

His answer isn't what I expect. *Don't hide something that important from her.*

I should speak up. Lay it all out. *What if I—*

I didn't see the guy squatting in the bushes next to the sidewalk. I didn't expect the punch.

Or the knife.

CHAPTER 28

Robert

I'm bleeding. I'm... *bleeding.*

I'm—

A person. Someone I don't recognize. "Hey, dude, hold on. We called 911. They're coming."

I can't see his face. The sun's too bright. "What?" He's pressing on my side.

A warm, metallic tang sits on my tongue. It fills my nose. I think I hurt but I don't know.

"Hold on. I hear the ambulance. You're going to be okay. Hold still."

Sirens. I'm *bleeding.*

Two new faces appear, one an older cop and another a woman in blue with a medic patch on her shoulder. She's wearing bright blue latex gloves.

"Son," the cop says. "What's your name?" He fishes around my pockets. I think he's looking for my wallet.

"Rob..." Breathing's harder than it should be. "Robert Quidell." I try to point at the apartment building. I was almost home. Why didn't I make it home? "I live there."

The cop looks over his shoulder. "What unit?"

"3E. My girlfriend..." Why can't I talk?

The cop yells something over his shoulder. The woman wearing the blue gloves puts a mask over my face.

I hear the screaming.

Isa's *screaming*.

CHAPTER 29

Isolde

The waiting room of the University hospital smells like puke and bleach and dirty diapers. The television blasts some stupid daytime show. Canned laughter blares from the speakers and hits my eardrums as a concussive wave of emotionally manipulative noise.

I want to punch something. Someone. Putting my fist through the wallboard might relieve some of my anxiety but it won't help Rob.

Mack paces. He's on the phone with Rob's brother Dan and I'm pretty sure they're making plans for Dan and Tom to fly in tonight.

Rob's been in surgery for two hours. The doctors won't give us information even though I rode in the ambulance, but they will talk to Rob's brothers, so Dan is telling us everything. Rob lost a lot of blood. The slash runs across his entire stomach but the puncture looks to have missed his organs. The doctors say no major damage. But they need to check. And sew him up.

I almost lost him, keeps spinning through my head. At the end of our two weeks, I would have at least known he's alive.

But he's going to be okay. He *has* to be okay.

I'm up, off the ugly orange burlap of the waiting room couch and pacing right alongside my brother. How did this happen? Rob was out in broad daylight on a busy street. The perp snatched his phone. Why did he need to slash too?

Mack touches my arm. "Dan will be here around midnight. One of us will need to pick him up."

I nod. I'm not really paying attention.

"He can sleep in Rob's room."

I nod again. A doctor in scrubs appears in the waiting room and I don't really care about the sleeping plans of another Quidell man.

The doctor who walks into the waiting room is a short, skinny guy. Muscular too, like a cyclist. He saunters over and stands in front of us with his feet apart and his fists in his waist like he's a superhero. Or a cowboy. Or a superhero cowboy.

Or a narcissistic workaholic cowboy surgeon. At least he's got enough of an ego to always be correct. Which means he more than likely stitched up my boyfriend correctly.

"You are Mr. Quidell's girlfriend and his roommate? The nurses tell me his brother faxed the consent to allow me to talk with you about his recovery." The doctor extends his hand. "Dr. Patel."

I shake his hand. He looks genuinely relieved to be talking to us. I don't think he likes dealing with family out of state.

Mack waves his phone. "I'm talking to Dan right now."

Dr. Patel nods. "Mr. Quidell is stable. He is in Recovery and we'll move him to the post-op ICU shortly." He turns away from Mack and addresses me directly. "If you wish to stay tonight, you will need to make arrangements."

Mack throws me a disapproving look, but doesn't argue.

"Thank you," I say.

Dr. Patel drops onto one of the waiting room chairs and motions for us to sit, as well. Mack sits on the couch across from the doctor and I plop down next to my brother, my ass on the edge of the cushion, and try very hard not to tap my foot. What if Rob's not okay? What if the doctor is only telling me this to keep me calm?

But that's not how surgeons work. Protecting people's feelings isn't important. Sewing up body parts is.

Dr. Patel drops his elbows to his thighs and leans forward, toward Mack and me. "He required several units of blood. No major damage. Thirty-seven sutures." He sniffs and waves at Mack's phone. "We've started antibiotics and anti-inflammatories. He's lucky he's as strong as he is. He responded quickly and with the correct rotation away from the assailant to protect his organs."

The unsaid words weigh heavy in the air between the doctor and Mack and I: *Any deeper and his guts would have been all over the pavement.*

Any deeper and your boyfriend would be dead.

I can't stop the hiccup. Nor can I stop the suck in of my breath. Or the tears.

Mack wraps his arm around my shoulder but talks to Dan on the phone. "I'll pick you up." A pause. "Isa's staying."

He gives me a little squeeze.

Dr. Patel nods once. "I estimate a week before he will be cleared for release. We will watch the wound and make sure it is healing well. Once he's home, he can't be up and around. No extra walking. No power lifting or skiing, either." He grins at his joke. "And I suggest six to eight weeks before he returns to classes."

Mack nods. "Thanks, Doctor."

We watch the skinny Dr. Patel swagger back into the halls of the hospital. Rob's going to need care for at least two months.

Not two weeks.

Six weeks beyond the point in time where I was going to accept the most important opportunity of my career.

We were going to talk. I was going to suggest, perhaps, we try long distance until the end of summer. Then regroup before school starts in the fall. Decide if we can honestly do this. Or if my sexy gorgeous boyfriend needs more touch than I am able to offer.

More contact, more caring, more support than globetrotting me can provide.

Rob's degree is as important as my photography career. I figure I'd commute. And when he's done with his coursework, maybe, just maybe, he might consider moving to California.

But I'd need to be making enough money to support both of us.

Which means I need this job. But he's going to be recovering for six to eight weeks.

Mack pats my leg. "Dan will be here tonight. I'll bring him around tomorrow morning."

I nod.

"Listen, he'll want to take Rob home to Minnesota until he fully recovers." Mack frowns and stares down the hallway Dr. Patel vanished into.

Where Rob would spend his recovery hadn't crossed my mind, but Mack's right. Rob needs to be with his family, not here in a student apartment.

Mack pats my shoulder. "I need to go to the department. We need to find someone to teach his section. And I need to get the paperwork started to set up incompletes for him for this semester."

My brother stands up and rubs the top of his head. After a moment, he frowns and adjusts his glasses. "Tell Rob I have the department under control."

I nod again.

"Are you going to be okay here by yourself?" Mack digs around in his pocket for his car keys.

"I won't go outside by myself if that's what you're worried about." The hospital is on the opposite side of campus from the apartment. It's a half hour walk. But Mack's question wasn't about leaving me here without transportation.

Mack shakes his head. "That's not what I meant."

No, it's not. "Are you worried I'm going to pull a Dad?" Because I think deep inside I'm worried I'm going to channel our father and retreat from the entire situation. Retreat from Rob.

Mack's expression says very clearly that I'm right. And, I think, that his worry was the underpinning of his anger when I fell through the door into the apartment last night.

"Why would you think that, brother?" I shouldn't snarl. Now is not the time for me to be fighting with Mack.

He frowns and looks at the floor. "I'll be back in the morning with at least Dan. Not sure if Tom is coming tonight or not."

So Mack's avoiding. I watch him for a long second, not at all surprised.

"Call me if there's issues." Mack twirls his keys around his finger. "Let me know when he wakes up, okay?"

I nod again. "We're both stronger than our parents, Mack." Neither of us needs to fall into the narcissistic bullshit that's kept our parents in serial relationships their entire lives.

"I used to think that when Lisa and I dated." Mack scratches at his stubble. "You know how that turned out."

Yes, I do. Sacrifices weren't going to be made even though they ended up at the same school. And, at least according to Lisa, they tried. Communicated. But professional life is professional life.

And here I thought I could make it work with Rob across two time zones.

"I'll text as soon as I pick up Dan."

Mack squeezes my shoulder again and walks away, down the hall toward the hospital entrance.

CHAPTER 30

Robert

I don't open my eyes but I hear beeps and buzzes and indistinct chatter. Feel air blowing up my nose. My tongue sits like a weight in my mouth more than functions to taste. When someone shuffles and a curtain rattle-shrieks open, I still won't look around.

"Mr. Quidell?" A maternal hand touches my forehead before moving to my shoulder and I know part of my brain thinks it belongs to Mom. But it doesn't. And I'm lying in a hospital bed watching my body from behind closed eyes as it processes smells and touches and thinking that it's a little boy again. Because that would mean Mom and Jeanie are still here. And I almost didn't die, too.

"Can you hear me? You're in Recovery. We'll be moving you soon." The nurse touches my face again. "Your girlfriend is here."

Isa? The muscles around my eyes don't want to cooperate. They don't want to raise my lids and they don't want to focus my eyes. But I make them, because Isa's here.

"Hey, handsome." Isa runs her finger over my cheek. "Doc says no skiing for at least eight weeks."

All sensation of Mom vanishes. I'm floating on antiseptic hospital noises and I think someone stabbed me but my girlfriend's here. I blink because my eyes refuse to adjust but my girlfriend's with me.

"I love you." I have no idea if I say it or just think it, but I'm pretty sure Isa hears me.

"Oh, Rob." Isa kisses my cheek.

Her expression might be surprised, or it might be angry. Or she might be happy. I can't tell.

Behind her, the woman who touched me like Mom and must be the nurse, smiles. She's a round woman wearing round green scrubs and a round blue puff of plastic hair constraint on her head. She leans close and winks. "All the nurses think you're a keeper, young man." Her hand waves at my chest.

"What?" My chest?

Isa snickers. "She's referring to your mark of boyfriend-hood."

"Oh." I remember writing something on my skin. "I love you." She needs to know how I feel. I almost died.

Isa bites her lip. "I love you, too."

She loves me. "Will you marry me?" I almost died. I can't live life regretting losing her.

The nurse chuckles as she fiddles with the tubing running in and out of my body. Isa, though, blinks rapidly.

"When I'm done with school I'll get a good job and you won't have to travel anymore." She won't be out there waiting to get in a car crash. Or knifed. "We'll buy you studio space. You can take photos wherever we land."

The rapid blinking turns into a full rounding of eyes and mouth. Is she shocked? She shouldn't be shocked. I almost died.

"Hey there, young man." The nurse is throwing me a stern maternal look. "You're not thinking clearly because of the meds in your system, so be careful, huh? Don't pull the pretty stitches Dr. Patel wove into your belly." She runs a thermometer over my forehead.

Isa's sitting back in her chair, still wide-eyed. Still as round as the nurse and her plastic puff of hair containment. "I think we need to talk about this when you're... coherent."

"I want to marry you." I don't feel my arm reach for Isa but the nurse stops me from twisting. I glance at my wrapped-up, IV-encrusted wrist. "I love you and I almost died."

The nurse pats my shoulder. "No, you did *not* almost die. You'll have a showroom-worthy scar but the EMTs got you here in plenty of time."

The nurse leans toward Isa. "We see this all the time. In two hours, either he won't remember what he's saying or he'll be so embarrassed he'll try to crawl under his bed, so don't be too freaked out."

Isa nods but doesn't stop making the round expression at me.

I don't care what the nurse says. I *know* I almost died. "I'll remember. I love you. Will you marry me?"

"Rob, please don't. We'll talk about it later, okay? You need to rest." Isa pats my arm.

She doesn't move closer. She doesn't blink. She looks as stiff as the splint on my IV arm.

The nurse glares at me and makes a small *Quit it* shake of her head.

"But..." I'm suddenly very tired. Tired like I ran a marathon. Or got knifed in the belly. I close my eyes.

When I look again, Isa and the nurse are talking outside my curtained-off recovery area. I can't hear them, but I see the nurse squeeze Isa's arm. Isa hiccups and wraps her arms around her chest.

She glances up at me but she won't look at my face.

And I don't understand why.

CHAPTER 31

Isolde

The ICU waiting room smells like turpentine. The chairs squeak and the lights flicker. But I need to be someplace by myself for a couple of minutes.

I can't leave. I promised Mack. And what would that say to Rob if I just up and vanished? What kind of girlfriend would I be?

The kind who's terrified by the demands of her white-picket-fence-wanting boyfriend.

The nurse said Rob babbled because of the anesthetics and the pain killers. That he'll be back to normal by morning and probably begging for my forgiveness. But I don't know. If he wasn't thinking it, he wouldn't have said it. And some of his words made my stomach lurch.

My gut gyrated and jumped as if I got knifed, not Rob.

Did he understand what he said? *Settle down, Isa. Become a good little wife.*

"Oh my God," I breathe.

I'm overreacting. I *know* I'm overreacting, but I can't help but see my mom's flat expression anytime she speaks about her career. About her camera or her brief year and a half photographing wildlife in northern Canada. About the polar bears and the moose.

Rob asked once why Mom's house didn't showcase my photos. It doesn't showcase her photos, either.

It showcases Dad's surgical career.

I pinch the bridge of my nose and try very hard not to rock back and forth. "Oh my God," I breathe again. How do I handle this?

A nurse swings around the corner into the little alcove where I'm hiding out. She's young, probably my age, with pretty blue eyes and a bouncy brown ponytail. "Ms. Wellington?"

I look up. "Yes?"

"I made up the cot in Mr. Quidell's room." She points over her shoulder.

I'm sleeping here tonight. Someone needs to be here. To keep an eye on Rob. He needs care, now. "Thanks," I say.

Machines beep and pumps whiz but he's sleeping soundly when I come in. The nurse said that if he wakes up they can increase his pain meds, but she figures he'll sleep until morning.

Quietly, I wash my face in the room's sterile bathroom and brush my teeth with the tiny, flimsy hospital-provided toothbrush.

The cot's lumps press into my back and neck but it'll do. I just need to remember what the nurse said: He'll be embarrassed in the morning. And we'll laugh it off.

But I don't know.

I don't know if I can.

⚜

ROB'S BROTHER DAN IS THE LARGEST MAN I HAVE EVER MET. HE'S A good four inches taller—and wider—than Rob. He's also just as square-jawed and handsome, but a lot less scruffy. His head of chocolate brown hair sits tidy and well-trimmed next to his scalp. He stands with me in the wide, too-bright hallway outside Rob's room and watches the world with the same blue-green ocean eyes.

Rob said Dan used to be a firefighter. I swear the first thing Dan did when he and Mack walked onto the ICU floor was to make sure he knew the locations of all the exits.

I can tell he's trying not to be imposing.

He glances into Rob's room. We're in sight of the nurse's station out here in the hall. Two of the nurses are trying very hard not to watch over the countertop. Dan obviously gets his share of the stares, as well.

"Ms. Wellington," he says. His giant hand engulfs mine when he reaches out to shake. He's got the same smooth, warm baritone as Rob, as well.

"Sorry we had to meet this way," I say.

Behind us, in the room, Rob stirs. Dan squeezes my hand and walks by, his attention diverted. I watch him pull a chair around and drop next to his brother.

Mack touches my elbow. "Tom will fly in when Dan goes back to Minnesota. They want to make arrangements to get his stuff. Dan wants to take him home as soon as the doctors okay a plane trip."

"What are you going to do with the apartment?" My brother's rent effectively just doubled.

Mack shrugs. "I might list for a new roommate. Or not. Depends on what Rob wants to do."

I can tell he's anxious about it.

In the room, Dan laughs and squeezes Rob's shoulder.

"I need to go back to California, Mack." I blurt it out all high-pitched and as anxious as Mack seems to be about the apartment.

My brother inhales slowly, and exhales even slower. His mouth twists and untwists as if he doesn't know what to say. "I think Rob's the one you need to talk to about that."

He's right. I do. I also told Rob that I love him.

Which I do. But, I think, I need space.

"Just be careful about causing him extra stress." Mack points over his shoulder. "I'm going down to the cafeteria. You want me to get you something?"

I give my brother my order and follow him into the room to ask Dan. And I watch as the men make food-eating plans.

Rob lies on his crumpled hospital bed, turned on his side, and watches me more than his brother. When Dan asks to go with Mack, Rob waves him away.

And reaches for my hand.

CHAPTER 32

Robert

My brother Dan pulls a chair toward my bed and sits his big ass down across from my head. "Nurses say you only get one day on the costs-more-per-hour-than-a-Porsche floor." He waves at my room. "Then it's off to a regular person's room."

If anyone knows about hospitals and costs and all that bullshit, it's Dan. He spent two months in the burn ward after his accident.

"Why didn't you tell me the pain meds were this good?" I'd sit up on the bed but the nurses won't let me and my belly doesn't want to bend.

"They alter parts of your brain you don't think they're altering." Dan laughs and clasps my shoulder. "The doc won't let you take the meds home when you leave, so don't get *too* used to them."

I want to make some snarky comment but my brain's not up to it, so I shrug. "I'll miss the pretty robes, though."

Dan laughs again, but this time he leans close, his face serious. "The pain meds stop being nice when you don't need them anymore. Remember that."

I sniff. "Geez, you look like you think I'll do something stupid."

Dan sits back. "Why would I think that?"

I close my eyes. They took the oxygen tube thing out from under my nose when they moved me onto this floor, but I'm still surrounded by buzzing, wheezing machines. At least my beeps are strong and rhythmic.

And so is my tendency toward bratty behavior. Dan's warning comes only because I have a track record. Not with drugs or things mostly illegal, but it's there. And he's been dealing with it all his life.

"I'm trying to grow up, Dan." I'd roll over but the nurses don't want me to do that, either.

Dan twists his lips and glances into the hallway. "I like Isa. She's nice. And concerned about you."

"I said something in Recovery. The nurse said I probably wouldn't remember." *Shit.* I do. "Motherfucker." I slam my hand into the mattress.

"What'd you do this time, Robert?" Oh, the number of times I've heard that tone of voice from my dear brother. Every time I pulled a penalty playing soccer while we were kids. That one time I made the neighbor girl cry. But she deserved it. She was spreading rumors about Tom. I made sure her mouth bit her in the ass.

And now I'm wondering if what I said in Recovery is about to bite me in the ass, big time. "I told her I love her."

Dan grins and shakes his head. "Well, that might or might not go over well."

"It probably would have been fine, if I hadn't asked her to marry me." I'm an idiot.

Dan laughs. "It's going to be fun watching you clean up this mess."

"It's not funny." It's not. She withdrew. Goddamn it, she clearly, completely withdrew from me when I said I wanted to marry her.

What the hell did I do?

Dan watches Isa and Mack outside the room more than he watches me. "I take it Ms. Wellington thought your proposal was med-fueled and inappropriate?"

"I don't know." I don't know shit anymore. "She's going back to California. She has a wonderful opportunity to advance her career. It's big. She can't miss it. We were going to talk about trying a long distance relationship."

Dan looks like he wants to sigh. His face draws down and his corners of his mouth make a father-frown. But he nods. "I'll talk to the doctors. Mack, too. We'll figure out the best way to deal with your recovery. I'd like you to come home. But if that doesn't work, we'll see what we can do. Maybe Dad will come up from Sedona. Who knows?" He sits back and sniffs, still watching Isa more than me. "But you can't go to California, Robert. Not until you're healthy and done with your schooling."

"Yes, Dad." At this point, I'm not sure Isa would want me in California, anyway.

Mack knocks on the door. "Hey, Dan, I'm getting food. Want to come along?"

Dan pats my shoulder. "Your only option is to talk to her about it." He pushes back his chair.

"When did you come to the conclusion that communication is the best course?" When I left after Bart's birthday party, Dan was in full not-talking-about-it mode with his girlfriend, Camille.

Dan pulls his wallet out of his pocket and checks his cash, I'm assuming to see what he can afford in the cafeteria.

"Therapist." He sniffs but seems satisfied with his fund supply. "Doing the needed work." He stuffs his wallet back into his pocket. "I'll be back in an hour or so."

My brother and my roommate wave, and disappear into the hallway.

Isa, though, stands in the door, watching me.

CHAPTER 33

Robert

She sits in the chair Dan pushed back from the bed. She doesn't move it closer. She stays too far away to touch.

The machines around my head beep and buzz. I don't hurt too much at the moment, but the dressings around my belly feel tight. The stitches and staples in my flesh constrain.

Pretty soon, the slash is going to start stinging. And, I suspect, that little energy boost that came with the fresh and happily donated blood pumping in my body will wear off. I'll be lying here wrapped like a mummy with only my own sad body to keep me company.

"Doc said it could have been a lot worse," I say.

A small grin appears on Isa's perfect lips.

"Nothing important got pierced." Lucky me only got slashed.

"If you need anything, or if Bart needs anything after I go back to California, or if you want to talk, text me. Or call. Okay?"

Is she breaking up with me? *Fuck*, I think. She already decided. I see it on her face. "What happened to our two weeks?"

Isa blinks and frowns and her shoulders slump. "I haven't left yet. You'll be out before I go. I just…"

She trails off and looks away, out the window.

"What, Isa?" What's going on here? I can't parse her responses. I'm suddenly too tired from talking to Dan. And too spaced on my meds.

"We're friends," she says. "I want us to stay friends. But I need to go to California. This job is a make or break for me. I can't stay here."

"I know. I don't want you to pass up an opportunity that's going to catapult you where you need to be, Isa. I'll do anything you need to help get you there."

Isa looks at her hands. "Anything, Rob?"

Anything? My brain freezes up. The fatigue suddenly rolls over me like a wave of hot, humid air and I can't think. I'm not processing. "Isa, I'm not thinking well, here. Can we talk about this later?"

After a long moment, she nods. "I'm sorry I brought it up now."

"It's the meds." I think I must have closed my eyes for a moment. When I open them again, she's leaning over me.

"Go to sleep," she says.

"Okay." But part of me cringes. Part of me thinks she's never coming back. "Miss you already," I whisper.

Isa's breath hitches. But she kisses my cheek anyway. "You *are* a keeper, Rob. For someone, even if that someone isn't me."

"What?" She said something I didn't catch.

But I don't think it was good.

I hear her shoes on the tile floor and I hope she's giving me another good-bye kiss. One that says *I'll be back later*. But that's not what I hear.

When I open my eyes again, I'm alone in my whining, beeping hospital room.

❦

OVER THE NEXT WEEK, ISA BRINGS ME ARTICLES I ATTEMPT, BUT fail, to read with my med-crossed eyes. We do puzzles and word searches together. I do my best to quiz her about her travels and spend most of my waking time staring at her pretty photos.

We don't talk about what she meant by *Anything, Rob?* It's... too much right now. But she's here. She didn't completely withdraw.

Dan leaves, citing work. Tom arrives and trades off sitting at my bedside with Isa and Mack. A few friends stop by to check on me, all as equally wide-eyed as they are freaked out. Classmates deliver assignments and balloon bouquets from the department. I'm set to take the rest of the semester at the pace I need. All my professors agree and are helping out.

Cops ask questions. Attorneys offer no answers. I mostly sleep and feel tired. The slash alternates stinging like a son of a bitch and aching as if Satan himself crawled into my gut. The nurses give me more pain meds to make it stop, but *everything* stops, and I wonder if I can even handle incompletes.

So I ask Isa to show me more photos, because at least then I'm thinking about beautiful things.

The doc says I'm healing remarkably fast. The shit they swab onto the slash smells like bug killer but it gets the job done. I'm suffering very little inflammation. No infections, either. So they're going to send me home in a day or two.

I'll need to use a wheelchair for a week or so. No walking up the steps until I'm cleared by the docs either, so I get to ride our building's rattling, mildew-smelling elevator. Tom rolls his eyes and calls me a whiner when I tell him I don't like being in a windowless box hanging from some random cable. But he nods because I know he doesn't like elevators any more than I do.

They send me home with a strong prescription and orders to continue with my newly formed sleep habits. Mack drives. Tom and Isa sit in the backseat, courteously chatting about Bart and Tom's art career. I listen, chiming in only every so often, as I try not to look too sick because the bumps and sways of the drive pull on my stomach like I'm on a fair ride.

Tom pushes my rented wheelchair through the building's back door and up the first floor hallway. It's dark down here, darker than our floor, and kid noises bounce through the super's apartment door.

"Mack says he told the super you were coming home today." Tom sniffs and keeps pushing me forward. Like Dan, Tom needs to stoop to push the wheelchair. They're both taller than me, and wider. I'm the runt.

Isa did the same blinking *oh my God you're so big* expression with Tom that she did with Dan. And like a lot of people, she seemed fascinated by how well he paints, considering the size of his hands.

I got a bit jealous. I couldn't help myself. Tom, though, took it in stride. Spent a lot of time chatting up Sammie to Isa. Said his fiancé wants to start an official artist's representation and promotion company, and that she'd love to talk to Isa.

Tom pushes the elevator button. He leans against the wall with his hands in the pockets of his jeans, my giant eighteen-months-older-than-me big brother. "So, Isa's not your girlfriend anymore?"

Shit, I think. "What she say?" Because she hasn't said shit to me.

"I don't think she wants to stress you."

"So you're doing it for her?" My brother's got an eye for body language. Much better than mine. Especially right now, with the drugs in my system.

And the fact I don't want to think about it.

We have three days left before she leaves. Three days I hoped we'd talk. *Shit*, I think again.

Tom stands straight. "We talk about Bart, not you." He shrugs. "She does a lot of avoiding. Which made me wonder, that's all."

The door pings and glides open. Tom wheels me into the dark confines of our building's vertically climbing coffin and we both frown. I fucking hate elevators.

"Dan told me about the issue you two had in Recovery." Tom taps his finger on the handle of my chair. The vibration snaps through the back and into my spine. "Just realize you may need to talk about it several times before the problem is settled."

I hear a semi-groan. I don't think this is completely about Isa.

"And then you'll need to revisit." Another semi-groan fills the elevator. "Maintenance."

I crank my neck around and looked up at my frowning my brother. "You sound more married than Dan."

Tom shakes his head as the elevator door slides open, but doesn't say any more. Isa's standing at by the door, waiting.

She grins too, and points at my face. "You got him to smile."

Tom wheels me out. "That's because we were talking about you."

I don't know if he winked at Isa, or smiled, but his tone sounds genuine. And I swear she blushes.

CHAPTER 34

Isolde

Dinner the first night Rob's home consists of an ordered pizza topped with every form or savory ground-up animal available from the pizzeria, as well as chunks of what I suspect are mushrooms and onions. It's tasty and filling, and I spend the rest of the evening on the couch next to Rob wishing I'd eaten two fewer slices than I did.

Before bed, Tom moves his suitcase into my room. And I move into Rob's.

I'm weak. I should sleep on the couch but our two weeks aren't up. And someone needs to keep an eye on him.

And...

I'm going back to California. Responsible Brain nags me to act like a grown-up but Rob doesn't need the extra stress.

Even for the few days we have left. I need Rob. I need to be near him because professional life is about to step between us and call an end to our special time. I can't be the good little wifey. But I can, at least for the rest of our two weeks, be a good girlfriend.

Rob doesn't want to go back to Minnesota. His doctor is here and he has access to the University physical therapy department. Tom doesn't seem all that happy about it, but he shrugs and makes Rob promise to come home for the summer.

The sunset spreads golden-red light through Rob's room. I help him sit on the edge of his bed. He closes his eyes as obvious pain plays over his handsome face. The red hue of the light streaming through the window doesn't help and for a second I swear he looks like he's about to curl into a ball.

Or maybe it'll be me clutching my knees weeping.

What am I doing? How is it that I think this is a good idea? But...

I miss him already. It's going to end and I won't be coming back to the man who loves me and I know I'm going to spend the next three months crying myself to sleep every night.

Rob pats the bed. "Sit down."

I drop next to him. He watches me carefully, his beautiful eyes showing as much concern for me as they do for the ache in his flesh.

Slowly, he weaves his fingers into mine. "I'm going to miss you," he whispers. "A lot."

"Oh, Rob." I tuck myself in between his side and his arm and wrap my arms around his chest. "We'll talk, okay? Lisa and Mack are still friends. We can be, too."

Rob's lips glide over my forehead but his body vibrates. From anger? From pain? I don't know.

"So that's it, Isa? We're breaking up?"

I nod against his shoulder. "I'm going back to California in a few days." How do I say this? "I need..."

I think he wants to yell at me. I think he wants to pound on the wall and throw his nightstand light across the room. Because I think he knows what I'm about to say.

"You said 'I want to marry you.'" I back away. "Marrying me isn't a good idea." He deserves someone more in tune with his needs. "I'm not good at settling down."

He closes his eyes. "Don't blame me for wanting to share my joy about not dying. Blame the meds."

I hiccup. He *is* angry.

But he should be. *I* would be. Maybe I am.

When I don't answer, he opens his eyes.

His expression changes instantly from the hard tremor of anger to a wide-eyed concern. "Isa, don't cry. How is it that I make the woman I love want to burst into tears? Don't—"

My words burst out in a single breath. "You wouldn't have said what you did if somewhere deep inside you weren't thinking that way."

Rob leans back. His face moves out of the reds and oranges and golds of the sunset and into shadow. "Why is loving you a bad thing, Isa?"

Loving isn't the issue. "Don't ask me to sacrifice my career for yours." I wipe away a tear.

When did I start crying? Why can't I hold it together around Rob? My body feels as if I got the slash, not him.

"When did *Marry me* become a death sentence? Why would I ask you to sacrifice any part of your career? You're beyond talented."

The emotions swirling through my brain and my body make me nauseous. They're calling up memories from my parents' split and I see my therapist's office in California. I see the warm orange-red of the walls and smell the soothing sandalwood aromatherapy she always doused the room in. I feel the sun's heat on the breeze from her open windows. I see her face. I hear her voice: *Are you seeing what's in front of you, Isa? Are you looking?*

I'm a photographer. I'm a scientist. And I very clearly see what's coming.

So I stuff those nauseating emotions back into the pocket universe from which they escaped.

"You said 'When I get a job, we'll get you studio space.'" I sit up tall, because I need to be strong. "I know what that means. You intend to become a professor, like Mack. You're going to do the post-grad one year appointment move-around from one university to the next for what, five, six years until you get an associate professor position? Where?"

"I won't know until I graduate where positions are available. That's how it works."

"This is why Mack and Lisa broke up. They'd have to separate when they graduated, so they ended it before they combined their lives to the point it would tear them apart when they split." But it did anyway. I don't think my brother's recovered yet.

I don't know if I will either, when I leave in a few days. Why did I agree to two weeks? Why can't I control my impulses?

For the first time since meeting him, I don't think I can read Rob. It doesn't help that he won't look at me.

"Let's say we do get married." I'm whispering now. And trying not to sob. "I can't spend my life in isolation. I can't just take snapshots of the pretty flowers and do high school graduation pictures for the locals."

"That's not what I meant."

But I think it is. Rob looks more defeated, more exhausted, then incredulous.

Then something else rolls up to my surface. A terrible, tiny voice. One I didn't realize had been whispering to me all this time. "How long are you going to be willing to live with me traveling all the time? What happens when the department secretary flirts with you? Are you going to have a threesome with some buxom cowgirl and the local librarian because you're lonely? When I get home, are you going to ask for an open relationship because you're living that way anyway?"

I wipe away another tear. "Because that's not going to happen."

Rob turns away. His shoulders. His chest. His eyes. Every molecule of Rob backs away from me. "I like your other fantasies better."

What did I just do? I jump off the bed. I can't be this close to him. I can't see him suffering this way.

"I can't argue with you anymore." Rob waves me away. "I need to sleep."

I look at the floor. The only movements either of us make is to breathe in, then out.

In, then out.

"I'm not as immature as you think I am, Isa."

Rob rolls away and all I see are the last of the sunset's reds playing over his back.

CHAPTER 35

Isolde

Mack flicks the signal and changes lanes. I rebooked my flight to an earlier day. Seemed to be the kindest thing to do.

Rob will find a nice new girlfriend in no time. One who doesn't mind tagging along to Middle America University and who is willing to accommodate his career.

I don't have that option.

"What you did was cold, Isa." This from the man who gave me shit for giving into my desires in the first place.

"I said good-bye." If I'd been stronger, if I hadn't let my fantasies get the best of me, if I'd talked to Rob about my career before I slept with him, none of this would have happened.

But we also would not have had our brilliant few days together.

"I suppose you did."

"He knew I'd be leaving anyway."

Mack scratches at his cheek stubble.

"It's better this way, Mack." It is. "What if we'd gone the two weeks and made plans and accommodations and in a year he drops the whole

'Let's live in this university town!' bomb? I'm not doing that. I'm not going to become Mom."

Mack pulls into the parking ramp. I'm leaving for good so he wants to walk in with me. "So you've decided to become Dad instead?"

"No." I glare at him. "I'm ending it before there's any chance of cheating. Or children."

"Or responsibility." Mack pulls the key from the ignition.

I throw open my door but grab it before it slams into the sedan in the next space over. "I'll text you when I land."

"Will you at least explain to Rob why you're doing this?" He slams his door, too.

I lean against the car. Exhaust fumes fill the ramp and I'd like to go inside. Not that the inside of the airport smells any better. "Does it matter anymore?"

"To me? No. But I can tell you right now that it damn well matters to Rob." Mack opens the trunk and pulls out my bag. "At first I thought you getting involved with him was the worst idea you've ever had. He can be... immature. But damn it, Isa, I think when the meds wear off and he realizes you aren't coming back it's going to fillet his heart. Not just break it, but shred it into bleeding strips."

I pull out my suitcase. A loud *shink* echoes off the concrete pillar in front of the car when I yank up the handle. I think it's echoing off my heart, too.

Because I think I just *shinked* Rob and me. And maybe Mack, too. "What do you want, Mack? For me to tell you we can overcome our nurture with our nature?" Because I've seen what our nurture leads to. "Smart and talented doesn't always overcome the shit life throws at us."

"No, Isolde, I want you to use your smarts to figure out how to overcome those shitty little moments of nurture planted in the backs of our brains." Mack slams the car's trunk and the entire frame shakes.

A big pick-up truck rolls by, looking for a space. The airport's constantly-droning, canned overhead announcements bounce off the ramp's concrete. And I'm about to walk away from the man I love.

Because he loves me too much.

"You and I had it shitty, Isolde. Be we did not have it Quidell shitty.

So maybe you should cut him some slack." My brother walks toward the skyway to the airport proper, my equipment pack on his back. "Maybe talk to him instead of accusing him of behaviors you don't know if he will commit."

But maybe I'm saving him from *my* future behaviors. *I can't stay here, Rob. I can't be tied down.*

Again, the nauseous emotions swirl up in my gut. And again, I stuff them away into their little pocket. I don't need them right now.

"I still have to leave!" I yell. "I have work!"

Mack glances over his shoulder. He doesn't respond, but I very clearly see on his face what he's thinking: *Just like Dad.*

Somewhere, out there, an airplane takes off carrying people to someplace or another. People leaving. People returning home. People with a calm place of roots and anchors. People a lot different from me.

Mack's right. But the sad thing about all this is that I know I'm right, too. And our rights don't overlap into the true correct path out of this situation.

So I'm taking the path I know will lead to the type of fulfillment I want the most. I'm going to photograph the world.

Alone.

CHAPTER 36

Robert

She's not coming back.

Mack looked away when I asked him why and he mumbled something about family history. Then, out of nowhere, he hugged me and said he's sorry.

I wish she'd talk to me about why she's so scared.

Tom stayed for a couple of days, then flew home. My dad will be here tomorrow. But Isa's gone forever.

I think I cried myself to sleep last night. When Mack asked about it I said I need more painkillers.

I try to focus on my classes. Mack's helping me catch up in stats and a couple other students in the department come by every day with notes and assignments. One of my professors even worked with the department to set up a video conference link during class so I can participate.

Dan was right; the meds do make basic thinking difficult. But I need to try. I need to keep myself busy.

They caught the guy a month after he slashed my belly. He confessed to get a reduced sentence on another aggravated robbery charge. I haven't heard if he's going to be back on the street menacing people. I figured there's nothing I can do about it either way. My job from this point forward is to pay attention to the world around me. And, I think, to buckle down. Work harder. Make sure I make the most of what I've got.

My doctor pulled the staples out of my scar a couple days ago. They numbed it but feeling the metal yanked out of my skin was weird and nasty. Felt like someone had put down a very small vacuum cleaner nozzle to suck up my skin along the scar, then did it again. And again.

Doc said I can fly next week, if I want to. So I think I will go home for the summer. When I tell Dad, he nods and pats my shoulder and mumbles something about doing what's best for the family.

I don't have the energy to fix our father issues right now, so I don't try. I just wave when Mack takes him to the airport, too.

So I immerse myself in articles. And writing my next paper. And producing the slides to share with my afternoon class. I'm almost caught up, meds or no meds in my system. I figure a couple more hours tonight won't hurt.

Mack's finished his comps and is now officially All But Dissertation. It's teaching and data gathering for him from this point forward.

Keys rattle in the door lock and I look up from my studies and my spot on the couch. Mack walks in and immediately wags his finger in my general direction. "Why are you awake?"

"Hmm?" Carefully, I stretch out my legs. My physical therapist—a sweet middle-aged guy with a bald spot—has me rubbing some sort of scar-care stuff on the slash. It smells like horseshit, but it's helping with the pulling and tightening. Still, I need to be careful.

"Shouldn't you be sleeping like the invalid you are?" Mack tosses his keys on the coffee table and seats his ass next to mine.

Mack's been amazing. It's not like we were good friends before all the shit went down. I was just his kid roommate who started a fling with his sister. But he stepped up and took care of all the department paperwork and questions for me. Without his help, I probably would have had to drop out for the semester.

I'm fortunate, that's for sure.

"Studying. Almost caught up. I'm thinking I'll be able to go into campus and to take my finals on time." My therapist and my doctors want me to start "low impact exercise" again, which means walking. No rock climbing or soccer yet, but it's a start. As long as the scar doesn't hurt too much, I'm good.

Mack nods. "Finalized summer plans?"

I think he's worried I won't be around to pay rent over the summer, but hasn't wanted to ask because of the whole "stressing Rob" business. Which, I suspect, has more to do with his sister than my lovely scar at this point.

"I think I'll go home for a while. Can't TA until Fall Semester anyway." I shrug.

"Are you moving out?" Mack stares forward and doesn't look at me.

"Are you kicking me out?" Because this is the first he's insinuated that I may not be welcome. I close my textbook and set it on the table. It thumps louder than I intend it to, but Mack doesn't seem to notice.

"No. Would you be upset if Isa visits on Friday?"

Dumbfounded, I stare at Mack. Isa visiting is totally out of the blue. I know he's been talking with her but he's been kind and not doing it in the apartment where I can hear him.

"This week?" I ask. She must be coming to celebrate his ABD status. "She's willing to be in the same building with me?"

Mack's nose crinkles. "No. I lied and told her you were visiting your family for the weekend."

I snort. Which quickly turns to a chuckle. Which turns into a full-on laughter roar. "Oh my God that hurts." I wrap my hand over the scar.

Mack shakes his head, laughing too. "She totally deserves me fucking with her." His laugh turns into a loud, honking snort out of his nose. "It's payback for that time she told my first girlfriend I was secretly fucking the lonely housewife down the street."

"She did that?" Now I'm laughing uncontrollably. "And she says I'm the brat."

Mack pokes me in the arm. "Oh, you two are way too alike for your own good. That's why I yelled at you. If you haven't figured it out yet, you were sleeping with the female version of yourself." He snorts. "Except for the sex with every woman on the planet bullshit. Or the not pulling your nose out of your books. Or the lovely cheekbones and the pouty lips."

Mack makes a kissy face. "Or the fact that you're talentless and my sister has the gift." He rolls his eyes.

"That's not fair. I draw a mean happy face, so I'm not a complete hack." I can't stop laughing. I don't know if it's because it feels good to laugh, or because if I stop, I'll start crying.

Crying and yelling and ripping apart the couch cushions.

"She was afraid, Rob. We grew up with a mother who sacrificed her dreams to tend to our father's career. Then it fell apart and we dealt with a lot of drinking and random men." He shrugs.

"I'm not like that. I would never do that." Why didn't she talk to me about it?

Mack inhales sharply and cuts off his chuckles. "That's not what she heard in the hospital. At the time, I don't think you two talking would have done any good, anyway."

He pats my knee. "I'm picking her up tomorrow." Then frowns. "Mom says she cries herself to sleep every night."

"She does?" My words come out a whisper, reverent and real. I feel it in my chest. Around my heart. And until this moment, when the possibility that I'd see her again became tangible, I didn't realize how much I miss her.

Isa, another vanished woman I don't think about because I can't.

But she's coming back.

Mack nods. His words come out reverent and real, as well. "If I were you, I don't know if I could forgive her." His eyes look vacant and distant.

He's serious.

Isa isn't the only Wellington with trust issues.

"It's not about forgiving," I say. Forgiving is the easy part. "It's about growing out of the hurt." And learning not to let the hurt fester to the point where it coats the entire world with its slime. Or so I supposedly learned from my therapist, all those years ago.

"It's a lot harder to do than it is to say." I pat the couch cushion. "Maybe that's why I'm so easy, you know. With the forgiveness."

Mack snorts. "You're just *easy*."

Maybe I am. Maybe my family has an easy way about us. Tom's certainly easygoing. And Bart's quite the charmer....

A plan bubbles up. I grin and shake my head.

"What?" Mack looks rightfully suspicious.

"So, you okay with a little revenge?" Maybe the meds aren't cutting into all my brain spaces after all.

My roommate laughs. "Always, my friend. Always."

CHAPTER 37

Isolde

I'm pretty sure my brother's fucking with me. The whole "Oh, Rob's gone so let's celebrate me passing my comps," and "Oh, Rob flew to Minnesota so you can sleep in his bed," is total bullshit. The way he's trying not to smirk as he pulls into the lot behind the apartment building clinches it.

My brother thought he could pass off his ABD status as a reason to party so I'm about to come face to face with the man I jilted.

"I hate you, Mack." I slap the roof of the car. "This is *not* a good idea."

"It's a fine idea." Mack scowls. "You know what was a bad idea? You fucking my roommate in the first place. But we already discussed that, haven't we?" He pulls my bags out of the car. "So why don't you go upstairs and make nice with the guy you're going to end up seeing again sooner or later anyway. Because he's my friend and he lives here too and I am *not* flying out to Mom's place every time you need a freakin' hug."

Mack slams the car door and walks toward the building.

I look around, making sure no one's in the lot with us, and follow him to the back door. "Take me to a hotel!" This isn't fair. To me, to—

The door swings open.

"What's not fair, Isolde?"

Rob grips the door as if it's going to run away from him and launch itself into space. He wears baggy sweats and a huge t-shirt I suspect is his brother Dan's. He looks thinner, like he's lost some of his muscle tone. The smudges under his eyes cast a shadow of exhaustion, as does his scruffy, unshaven face.

He needs a haircut, too. But he's up and he's alive and he's made it through his ordeal intact.

Or mostly intact.

"A lot of life's not fair, Robert," I say.

He snorts and grins. Shaking his head, he moves to the side to let us pass.

I'm surprised, to be honest, that he didn't just lay into me the moment he opened the door. *I* would have laid into me the moment I saw me. I know I broke his heart.

But better I broke it before we'd combined our lives. Cleaner, this way. Less pain in the long run.

At least I'll keep telling myself that.

I move by and start up the stairs, but stop and look over my shoulder. "You okay walking up three flights?"

"Yes." Rob shakes his head again and slowly, steadily, starts up the steps.

I smack my brother's arm. "You let him climb steps like this?"

Mack's expression says he would have given me the finger if his hands weren't full. "Doctor cleared him for exercise."

"Sex, too." Rob doesn't glance over his shoulder at us, though I know he's smirking. I see it in his shoulders.

Mack snickers.

I think the boys are picking on me.

At the top of the stairs, Rob steps by the spot where he wrote "Isa's boyfriend" on his chest and continues his slow and steady pace toward the apartment door.

When he swings it open, I hear a little boy.

"Bart's here?" I ask. What are they doing, running an intervention on me?

I balk, refusing to step in. "What the hell is going on?"

Mack rolls his eyes and pushes me through the door.

Rob's laptop is open and sitting on the coffee table next to a pile of books.

On his computer screen, I see a room brimming with little artist toys: An easel. Multiple boxes of action figures and crayons and paints. And another open laptop, this one connected to the camera Rob gave Bart for his birthday.

I must be looking at the living room of Dan's house.

A little head bounces into the bottom of the frame. "Uncle Robby! Are you back?" The little head bounces in again. "Is Ms. Isa with you? I want to show her my pictures!"

"Dan set the webcam on top of the television." Rob walks into the living room. "Bart's figured out how to toggle, haven't you?" he calls.

"I have!" The screen switches to the web cam on the computer hooked to Bart's camera. "See?"

Five-year-old crystal blue eyes smile at me through the web cam and little Bart waves. "Hi, Ms. Isa! I took pictures." The camera and its cable wiggle.

A stream of photos blips by. Most are his classes at the Community Center. Several are a dark-eyed woman with black hair I think is Dan's girlfriend, Camille. A few are a five-year-old's angle up at Bart's very tall father.

They all show remarkable intuitive framing. He's learning how to use his camera's depth of field, too.

I drop my bag on the floor and kneel in front of the computer. "How are you, Bart?"

The display switches back to my little friend. "I graduated from the Community Center!" He jumps up and down but stops and looks over his shoulder. Quietly, he leans toward the computer. "Ms. Frazier moved in *for real* on Saturday," he whispers. "She's going to be my mommy."

I touch my mouth. He looks so happy I want to cry.

Or maybe I want to cry because I'm not moving in. For real.

"Uncle Robby is coming home this summer and we're going to the lake!" Bart bounces around again. "Uncle Tommy and Auntie Sammie are bringing Mr. Pickles!"

I glance up at Rob. "Mr. Pickles?" Does Tom have a horse I don't know about?

He nods toward the computer. "Cat."

"Ah."

"Will you come, Ms. Isa?" Bart bats his baby blues at me. "Please?"

There it is. I'm being expertly manipulated by the world's cutest five-year-old.

"Depends." I don't know why I say it. I should just say *No* and be done with it, but Bart's showing real talent.

And he's a great kid.

"Please?" He holds out his kid's camera. "Will you teach me how to take *good* pictures?"

Oh my God, I think. "Did your Uncle Robby put you up to asking me to come to the lake?"

Bart bats his eyelashes again and makes the unmistakable Quidell pout. "He said I'm supposed to say no if you ask."

Behind me, loud chortles burst from both Rob and Mack. I look over my shoulder. Rob smirks and shrugs.

Mack mouths *Don't be a douche. Tell Bart yes.*

From the laptop speaker, I hear a woman call from the kitchen behind Bart. "Is your uncle back?"

Bart points over his shoulder and smiles a huge smile. "My mommy."

Every little bit of anger and frustration that had been stewing in my gut melts away. How can I say no to Bart? No one with a soul could say no to that boy. "I have a shoot in California but then I can visit."

Or stay at home, alone in my crappy little loft. I frown.

"So you'll come to the lake?" Bart jumps up and down again. "Daddy! Ms. Isa's coming to the lake!"

I throw a *What the fuck did you just get me into?* look at Rob.

"Go get your daddy, Bart. So we can finalize plans." He looks right at me, one eyebrow cocked and his bad boy smirk all over his face.

You're terrible, I mouth.

Yes, I am, Rob mouths back.

"Okay!" Bart runs off.

"Only as a friend," I say. "I'm going to spend time with Bart."

Rob nods. "I know." Slowly, he drops onto the couch and waves good-bye to Mack, who walks off toward the kitchen.

I think Rob wants to groan as he settles into the couch. He's been through hell and how did I help? I ran off and left my brother to tend to the misery. "I'm sorry about what I did."

A sadness the exact opposite of Bart's joy descends over his face. "Good."

I feel my eyes narrow and my mouth thin to a flat line. "I know you're not okay with what happened."

"With what you *did*."

I deserve this. I do. "I'm sorry. I am. Do you want to talk about it?" He's not okay. I can tell. It's going to take him some time. It's going to take *me* some time. But maybe being friends will help.

"Yes." Rob shrugs and leans against the back of the couch. My grandparents' throw is still there, still soft and intricate, and I swear it's mocking me.

Why did you hurt him? it's asking. *Why didn't you try?*

"I'm here for a couple—"

"We do it on *my* timeline, not yours." He waves his hand in my general direction.

"What?" What does that mean? But Dan appears on the laptop before I have an opportunity to ask.

"Hey, Isa. How are you?" Dan asks. His smile looks as sad as Rob's. "I hear you're coming to the lake to teach the little master the fine art of photography."

"She is!" Bart bounces into the frame again.

Rob leans forward and the three of us make plans. I'm totally locked into this trip. There's no getting out of it, now. I'm off to a Minnesota lake to teach a brilliant five-year-old how to hold his camera.

Dan signs off and I wave good-bye to Bart.

It's going to be the best week of my life, I think.

I shake, wondering where that thought came from. Or why I would think it, especially with Rob's obvious anger.

Slowly, he closes his laptop. "I still miss you." He speaks hushed, as if Bart, or the world, might overhear. "I miss the time that was stolen from us, even if it would have been brief." Rob looks away. "I told myself seeing you would be good for me. That it'd be a nice dose of exposure therapy. I'd get used to Mack's mean sister again."

"We would have broken up anyway." I might as well be honest.

Rob chuckles and shakes his head. "Yes. As you decided already. For both of us."

I look away. My body feels as if it's crunching in on itself. Because he's right.

"I need to study." Rob looks like his scar hurts. "In my room. By myself. Though some days focusing through the meds makes it difficult."

"I'm sorry." I want to squeeze his hand but I don't dare touch. "I'm sorry you've gone through all this."

Rob absently scratches at his belly, right over his scar. "Maybe by the time you visit the lake, we can talk."

This time, I don't stop myself. I take his hand. "I'll see you again at the lake."

Rob stares at our hands. His fingers twitch as if he wants to wrap his digits through mine, and I think the dark circles under his eyes turn a deeper shade of purple. "If I text, will you talk to me?"

Responsible Brain screams *Clean break!* But Not-So-Responsible brain yells *You miss him as much as he misses you!*

And I'm weak. Head-to-toe, heart-driven weak.

"Yes," I say. "Every day, if you want to talk."

Every single day.

Rob nods. "Good night, Isa."

CHAPTER 38

Isolde

Every day, I wake up to a new text from Rob. Some are random quotes. Others, forwarded pictures from his little nephew. I think he's engaging in more of his "exposure therapy."

I throw on my clothes and I drive to the studio and some days, I shoot photos. Some days, I production assist. Some days, I edit. But every day I check my phone at lunch time, hoping to see what new wonder Rob's sent my way.

The second week after Mack's ABD celebration, Rob began texting questions about the many places I've visited. Asking things about the people and the cultures and if any of them interested me enough that I'd want to go back for an extended time to do in-depth work.

We video chatted. Turns out he's doing preliminary planning for his dissertation. His advisor wants to see a concrete idea of Rob's future by the time he returns in the fall.

He left for Minnesota the third week. I got a lot of lake photos. He's right; it is beautiful. I pack accordingly.

The fourth week, I borrow Mom's crossover hatchback with the storage space and the good gas mileage. The studio owner takes his vacation this month, so I'm taking mine, too. I'm driving through the Rockies, all under the guise of teaching the little master, and photographing the wilds on the way back to California.

It takes me four days to drive from Los Angeles to the wonder of green freshness that is Minneapolis and St. Paul. Dodging road construction and evening traffic, I settle in for the final four hour drive north to the Quidells' lake house.

I roll down my car's window as I slowly make my way along the dirt drive toward the house. The air here smells just as fresh, but heavier, than it did in the mountains. Insects and frogs buzz. Water laps a shore not too far off. Animals rustle in the trees. Something dog-shaped scurries out of the way of my headlights. Gravel crunches under the tires.

I feel as if I'm being drawn in by a giant magnet. Teaching Bart will be fun, but I know the real pull. The Quidell family has me in their orbit. *Rob* has me in his orbit. Maybe I need to admit it. Maybe I should settle in and enjoy the ride.

Enjoy this time of exposure therapy. Because ultimately, Mack's right. I'm going to see Rob again and again. He's my brother's room-mate and friend. He's part of my life.

The car sways as I inch it down the drive, and I sway right along with it. I think I need to admit how much I want to be here. How much I've been looking forward to spending time with a functional family, even if it's the family of my ex-boyfriend.

The drive curves and opens into a wide, cleared area in front of a big, two story cabin that looks, architecturally, as if it was built quite a few decades ago, and added onto in the fifties or sixties. Natural cedar siding sucks in my car's headlights and make the cabin's shape slightly blurry, but I see a wide porch that I suspect circles the entire building.

Off to the side, down an open walkway toward the beach, the Quidells all sit around a big, roaring fire pit. Bart's off his dad's lap and running toward my car before I finish parking next to the other vehicles in the clearing.

"Ms. Isa's here!" Bart, dressed in what looks like superhero jammies, a hoodie, and hiking boots, bounds up the walkway, his arms wide, with Dan and Rob right behind him.

When I open my car door, I'm greeted with the nicest, strongest five-year-old hug I've ever experienced. He smells like bonfire and burned candy. I drop down to my knee and hug him back, though he's pretty tall for a kindergartner. "Hello, Bart."

"Daddy said I could stay up until you got here." Bart yawns. "You drove all the way from California?" He looks over my shoulder. "Did you bring your camera? I brought mine!"

My back complains about standing straight, but at least I don't have to drive anymore. "All my gear is in the back of the car."

Rob stops at the end of the car, watching me. Dan, though, steps up. He's wearing a long-sleeved t-shirt and cargo shorts, and big hiking boots, much like Rob. Grinning, Dan offers a quick hug. When he steps back, he places a hand on Bart's shoulder. "Bart, what did I say earlier?"

"Oh!" Bart stands tall. "Thank you for visiting our lake house, Ms. Isa. Thank you for being my teacher, too!" He offers his hand to shake, even though he just squeezed the life out of me with a hug.

I shake his hand. "You are welcome, Bart."

"Do you want a roasted marshmallow?" Bart points at the fire. "Mommy's making s'mores but I'm supposed to go to bed now." He frowns.

Rob pats Bart's shoulder, but he's still looking at me. "Let's get Ms. Isa's suitcases inside first, okay?"

"Okay!" Bart jumps up and down next to my car.

Tom, also dressed in a t-shirt and cargo shorts, saunters up and pats Rob on the shoulder. "Take Isa down to the fire and introduce her around." He nods toward the car. "Dan and I will take her things in."

Rob nods. "What do you say, Bart?" But he's still watching me more than anyone else. "Should we go get those s'mores?"

"Okay!" Bart takes my hand as if he's the only person allowed to touch me.

Grinning at Rob, I let Bart pull me by.

Dan opens the back of my car. "Your room is upstairs, first door on the left. You want everything in?"

"Please," I call. Bart's got me half way around the cabin by the time Tom and Dan start unloading.

Rob walks behind us with his hands in his pockets. "The drive tire you out?"

He's back to his normal level of scruffy, with his five-day beard and his messy, almost luminescent hair. He looks refreshed, too, less exhausted. The lake's done well by him.

Bart pulls me down the path. "A little," I say. "How are you doing?"

Rob points. "Watch your step."

"Oh!" I dance down a short set of stairs toward the long, wide dock. The big Quidell cabin comes with a small boathouse, a wide, flagstoned patio area bordering the pebbled beach, and a long dock. The fire pit sits at the edge of the patio, next to the sand.

Two women get up from camping chairs and wave. The taller of the two, the one with the auburn ponytail, must be Sammie. I recognize her from Tom's opening. The other dark-haired woman I recognize from Bart's photos.

She extends one hand toward me and another to Bart. "Camille," she says as we shake. "Bart, careful so Isa doesn't trip."

Next to me, Rob chuckles.

The other woman also offers a hand. "Sammie," she says.

"Hello," I answer. They're both quite beautiful, and very different from each other. I think I'll be getting some interesting photos.

Camille looks at Sammie, who looks at her. "We were just going in," she says. "Time for Bart to go to bed."

Camille makes a show of yawning. "We came up late last night and the little man here got us up early this morning, didn't you?" She ruffs Bart's hair.

"I heard Mr. Pickles meowing." Bart frowns.

Sammie smiles. "Rob said you're not allergic, correct?" She points at the house.

"Kitties are fine." I ruffle Bart's hair, too. "You get a good night's sleep, okay? I brought lots of stuff to do. We'll start tomorrow."

"Can I have another s'more?" Bart pouts.

Camille and Sammie look at each other, then both look directly at Rob.

"Tell you what," he leans toward Bart. "We'll do another fire tomorrow and make a lot of s'mores for everyone, okay? I think Ms. Isa is tired."

Bart yawns again, but doesn't argue. "Okay, Uncle Robby."

I think he really is tired.

Camille smiles and takes Bart's hand. "Good night." She takes Bart and Sammie with her toward the cabin's back screen door.

I watch them go. "I brought a stack of travel magazines and atlases, and a scrapbook, so Bart can help plan the return drive."

Rob's standing close enough I feel his warmth. The breeze flowing off the lake adds a misty chill to the air, and the water gently laps at the pebbles. The fire crackles and sparks twirl upward from its licking flames. In the circle, Dan and Tom chat about the cabin and, I think, about adding on studio space. But it's Rob who holds my attention.

"Bart will like that." He doesn't move.

I could wrap my arms around him if I wanted to. Right now. Out here, with his brothers in front of the cabin working diligently to bring the trappings of my life into theirs, and their soon-to-be wives tending to Bart in the kitchen, on the other side of the door.

"Do you want to go inside, with your family?" Instead of staying out here, with mean me.

Rob watches Camille through the window as she wipes Bart's face. "In a minute."

Inside, Tom walks into the kitchen. He curls an arm around Sammie and kisses her cheek. When she smiles, he waves to us through the window.

They vanish into the hallway.

"Your stuff must be in." Rob looks out over the lake. The fire crackles and he moves away, toward the camp chairs. "Want a marshmallow? Some water?" He holds up a bottle.

"Thank you for inviting me." My voice all but vanishes into the pops and snaps of the fire.

Rob looks out over the lake. "We're friends."

I sniff. He's looking away, thank God, and I don't think he notices. Because if he did, I'd fall apart right here.

I'm not over him. I wasn't when I left after the attack, and I wasn't when I visited for Mack's celebration. And I definitely wasn't on the four day drive through the mountains.

My brain made new fantasies. Begging ones, with Rob on his knees with his arms around my waist. Fuck-buddy ones where we ignore everyone and spend the next few days in the woods fucking under the bright sun. The fight ones, where we wrestle and get sweaty and I always win. Always ride him until a mind numbing orgasm shudders through his gorgeous body.

Or the one where we spend two days talking and kissing and making love.

Why was I so cruel? Why did I think two weeks was enough? Or that maybe, just maybe, long distance might work?

The screen door opens. Dan sticks out his head. "Gear's in your room. We locked your car." He points over his shoulder. "We'll see you at breakfast."

"There's only one shower in the house." Rob watches his brother shut the door. "There's another in the boathouse."

The firelight plays over his cheeks and when he sighs, I think it sets his pale eyes blazing. For a moment, Rob burns as bright as the bonfire.

The pull I felt driving up to the house wasn't from the lake. Or the Quidells in general. It came solely from Rob. From the magnetic connection I've felt for him since the moment we first met in the dead center of winter, in the cold, under his bee hat.

The symbol of family he doesn't need now, because he's embedded in it. Here, he's safe. He has Dan and Tom and Bart. No one's going to knife him here. Not physically.

Not emotionally, either.

Rob picks up a bucket and dumps it on the fire. "Let's get some sleep." When the fire vanishes, he offers his hand.

"Okay," I say, knowing full well that he's sleeping alone tonight.

But not alone. He has his family around him.

Me, he's keeping in a separate room, where I belong.

CHAPTER 39

Robert

Isa spends the next few days teaching Bart how to take photos. They sit on the dock with her magazines and her scrapbook and my nephew plans out my ex-girlfriend's overly circular route back to California.

Dan and Camille hold hands a lot. Tom and Sammie touch, but they seem edgy. And exhausted. They're both working two full-time jobs, with their corporate work and Tom's blossoming art career.

I take a lot of naps. And a lot of walks with Bart and Isa. We don't talk about why we broke up.

I'm being mean. I know it. Dan and Tom know it. Isa obviously wants to talk but I'm letting her stew.

A lot of things get hard, though, when she puts on her blue bikini and goes swimming with Sammie and Camille.

Tom and I sit on the dock in our camp chairs with our beers, watching the show. Out on the float off the end of the dock, the women laugh. Tom gets his *I'm going to paint this* look on his face. Sometimes I envy him his visual memory.

He takes a sip of his beer. "Bart's been asking Dan why you're moping. He doesn't understand, since Ms. Isa is here. He thinks you should be as happy as him."

Out on the float, Isa laughs at something Sammie says.

God, they're beautiful, our three muses, with their auburn, black, and blonde ponytails and their skin glowing in the sun. Yeah, I understand why Tom wants to paint this scene.

I shrug and take a sip of my beer.

"It's childish not talking to her the way you are." Tom chuckles. "Though I'd do exactly the same thing."

Now I chuckle. "It was Mack's idea."

"Seriously?" Tom laughs. "To keep her uncomfortably uncertain for an entire week? Damn, he's more of a player than you."

I don't know how much more I can take, though. How many more longing glances I can handle. How many more walks in the woods holding Bart's hand and not hers.

Sammie waves from the float.

Tom sets down his beer and stands up. "Ladies be returning." My brother obviously has adult activities on his mind. He and Sammie might be having a difficulty here and there—not that he's said—but it can't be too bad.

I chuckle again.

The women walk up the beach. Tom's right there, handing out towels, like a cabana boy. Camille wraps hers around her middle and pats Isa knowingly on the shoulder. Moments later, Sammie and Tom follow her up the steps to the porch.

Isa towels off her hair as she watches them go. "I like your family," she says.

I motion to the dock and we walk up to the railing. Gnats buzz in the shade thrown by the boathouse, but it's cooler, and not so bright. Somewhere off in the reeds, a fish *plops* in the water. A turtle scuttles around on the beach. The lake smells fresher today than usual, with its warm, not-quite heavy scent of plants and animals. Birds chirp and the high notes of Sammie's laugh peal from inside the cabin.

"I like them too," I say.

Isa wraps her towel around her chest. "Mack and I grew up in a very different environment."

I lean against the rail. The boathouse blocks some of our view of the cabin and out here, only the golden glow of the lake throws shadows. They creep over Isa, across her face, into her hair, and hide the sadness in her eyes.

I can't take it anymore. The uncertainty. I need to get the emotions out of my system. "How could you *not* see that the guy who wrote 'Isa's boyfriend' on his chest was head over heels in love with you?" I want to slap the railing but I grip it instead. "In permanent marker!"

Her mouth opens and closes. "Rob—"

She reaches to take my hand but I step away. The anger's surfacing. I've kept it down. Kept it tucked away, mostly for Bart. It's good for no one. But I don't think it's willing to stay buried any longer.

"How the hell could me saying 'I love you' and 'I want to marry you' have been such a shock?"

"But that's just it! It *was* a shock, Rob!" She throws her hands in the air. "When I realized—really, truly understood—I got scared."

The lake's calm, like I need to be, so I look out over the water hoping to internalize at least some of the stillness. "And you tell me I'm the one unaware of my emotions."

"That's not fair."

"Not fair, Isa? You know what's *not fair*? You unilaterally deciding that we're through. You, all by yourself. Why'd you do it? Because I'm a bad boy?"

I understand intellectually the reasons. Mack explained their childhood. But emotionally, it doesn't make sense. I'm not her father.

I see her chest tighten. She's holding in a sob. "I don't see you that way!" she yells. "I've never seen you that way!"

The volume of my voice drops. I'm almost whispering. "I don't do that anymore." My words float over the lake. Somehow, I need to declare my confession. This goes deeper than my social media persona. Or my undergraduate years. I'm not immature anymore.

"Rob..." Gently, Isa touches my wrist.

She doesn't stroke or glide her fingers, she settles her hand onto my skin. I think she's hoping to offer a small moment of comfort because I'm angry. Even though her face says she wants to yell *You're mean!*

"I'm sorry." Isa can't hold her sob any longer. "I'm so, so sorry. I shouldn't have..." A hiccup interrupts her words. "I acted like..." Another hiccup cuts off her voice entirely.

"Isa..." I pull her to my chest. Part of me is yelling that she deserves me being mean. Another part wants only to drop to the dock and cradle her on my lap.

She sobs against my shoulder and it feels as if she's holding onto me for dear life.

"No one's ever loved me like this," she whispers. "No one's fought for me. Or supported me the way you do. Unconditionally."

She blinks and stiffens in my arms. "Not even Mack's been so... open about supporting my goals. My parents, never. Mom lets me live with her, but doesn't show my photos. Mack lets me live with him too, but I saw him walk away from the love of his life because he wasn't able to compromise."

I don't say anything. What can I say? She needs to get this out.

"Yet I pushed you away and you still wanted me to teach your nephew, even though me being here obviously causes you pain."

I bury my face in her hair. She smells like the lake, but hints of her sweet, organic shampoo cling to her scalp. My beautiful Isa. "Your photos are still the backgrounds on all my devices. New phone. Laptop. Everything."

"Really?" She pulls away enough to see my face.

"You look like you just licked an electric fence." I suspect my expression isn't much different.

The anger still bubbles inside my chest. It's like a fountain in the middle of a pond brimming with every emotion my body can produce. I want to swing at the wall of the boathouse at the same time I want to curl up into a ball. I want to hunt the asshole who slashed me at the same time I want to cry like a baby.

I want to love Isa just as much as I want her to understand how much she hurt me.

Gently, she lays her fingers over my scar. My t-shirt rubs over the ridge, flicking slightly as she touches. "This is going to sound really stupid," she says.

I almost snort. My well of contradictory emotions sloshes inside my gut and the scar tingles. Isa pressing against my chest feels both comforting and uncomfortable. She touches, but is she really touching? She wants forgiveness, but can I give it?

I've bottled it up. I've stuffed it down. Exposure therapy should have made this easier but really, I asked her here because one way or another, I need closure. My emotional fount needs to pick which color filter it's going to use on its lights.

Bitter, angry, scab-colored red or the warm, sweet gold tones of Isa's hair?

"How stupid?" I ask.

She looks like she wants to bite her lip. "I've been watching you and your brothers."

I let go and cross my arms. My desire to punch the wall of the boathouse makes my muscles twitch.

"Watching and marveling at how good you all are with Bart. How no matter what he does, he's always loved."

My brows pull together. Of course we're good with him. "He's a good kid."

"Yeah, but you'd all love him even if he wasn't. You did a lot of naughty things as a kid, didn't you? Acted out? Your brothers still love you." The towel loosens and she readjusts it so it doesn't slide off her sweet hips.

Horniness rears its head in my overflowing fountain. It swims around like a snapping turtle, lapping through all my bratty meanness, and my bubbling anger, and right through the need to rock back and forth crying.

How is she doing this to me? Why the hell did I let a woman get this far under my skin?

Why the hell won't she just say what she means? "Why wouldn't they love me? We're family."

Isa sniffs and looks out over the lake. "Mack and I acted out, too. Dad won't talk to us. Says we need to 'learn from our mistakes.'"

Jesus, I think. "That's stupid."

She glances at my face before wrapping her arms around her chest. "See, I told you it would sound stupid."

My inner brat screams *Stupid!* and I want to walk away. Or pick her up. I don't know which. "Are you blaming your shitty father for your shitty behavior, Isa? Because that's shitty."

She wipes her eye with the back of her hand.

I realize I'm pushing her toward real tears. But this time, I think it needs to happen.

"I'm explaining why I acted the way I did." Her face and her body harden. "Because I thought what we had was a fantasy. I didn't believe it could happen in real life. No one's that good to me."

"You're right. That's stupid." I uncross my arms and slap my palm on the railing. Is she always going to be like this?

She clamps her mouth shut, then opens it with a pop. "I don't have the right to ask you for a second chance," she says. "You're past your limit. I went over the edge and there's no turning back and I should just be grateful you're willing to be friends."

Isa blinks and steps closer. "I'm so sorry. Will you...?"

I stand up straight. She's going to say it. "Will I what?"

Isa nods as if she understands. "Even if there's no turning back, will you forgive me? I'm being selfish asking. I shouldn't. I'm sorry. But I—"

I can't talk. The words don't form, so I let my kisses carry my need and my anger. My frustration.

And my love.

CHAPTER 40

Isolde

A fish surfaces just off the dock before flicking its tail and vanishing again. The air buzzes with the sound of crickets and cicadas and gnats. Someone in the house slams a door.

Rob's breath heats the skin of my neck. He yanks me toward him, his fingers digging into the flesh of my upper arms. His slight scent of ocean mixes with the humidity in the air and I swear I hear waves crashing on the shore. Waves of his anger. His frustration. Every ounce of his love.

He's crashing into me.

"I will *never* hurt you again," I breathe.

He nips at my skin just under my ear and I shiver. "Say it again," he growls.

"No more hurting you. I won't do it again." My towel drops to the slats of the dock. The only things between me and his erection are his cargo shorts and my bikini bottom.

I rub against his front.

"Are you going to talk to me?" His grip tightens for a moment, but he seems to realize how strong he is and he backs off. "If we're together, then we make decisions together."

I curl a leg around his. God, I want to climb on him now, out in the open. Or drop to my knees and suck him off right here. "Together."

One hand releases from my arm. He glances up and at the cabin before turning me slightly to block any view of what he's doing to my front.

Rob works his fingers under the cup of my top. "If you get any more of those *he's just like Dad* notions you forget them immediately, you understand?"

"Yes," I breathe as I nibble on his chin.

"Because I'm not."

"You're not." He's Rob, my boyfriend. And the man I love. Oh, God, *love*. Head over heels. "I'm sorry."

"That's right, you're sorry. You're very sorry, aren't you? You've never been sorrier in your whole life, have you?" He flicks my nipple.

My breath stutters. I can't speak.

"Tell me how sorry you are." The authority in his voice makes my legs quake.

I can barely hold myself up. "I'm very sorry." Why did I push him away?

"Do you still believe I'm going to consign you to some shithole backwater and make you spend the rest of your life taking pictures of raccoons?" His anger growls out through his constricted throat. His skin reddens across his neck, too.

"No, I don't."

"You better not. Because that's not going to happen."

"It won't." Even if I didn't believe him, the commanding tone of his voice makes me. "I need to do a better job of separating fantasy from reality."

"Yes, you do." Rob twists me again so my back is completely to the cabin. His other hand works into the front of my bikini bottom.

But he only strokes across my pubic bone.

I want to scream. "I will. I swear I will."

"Do you have any idea how in love with you I am?" Both his hands pull out from inside my suit and his arms curl around me. I'm suddenly, completely enveloped by Rob's embrace. By his strong forearms and biceps. His wonderful chest. He's all here. All with me.

"Rob..." I kiss his ear, his neck. "I'm sorry. I'm so, so sorry. I love you." The next kiss finds his lips. "I absolutely love you."

"Don't push me away again. Please." His hold is so tight, I can barely breathe.

"I won't. I swear."

Another thump echoes down from the house, followed by a laugh. Rob backs away enough to take my hands. "Boathouse?"

I blink and look over my shoulder. Can't have Bart bursting out of the screen door.

I snatch my towel off the ground and pull Rob toward the little house's entrance. The door slams against the wall and Rob chuckles as he pushes me inside.

He still sounds angry. And his grip is still firm and demanding. The boathouse is a rickety place big enough to nestle in their fiberglass motorboat, along with a shower opposite the door, two canoes hanging from the ceiling, and several shelves full of tools. A lawn mower sits unused in the corner.

The water sloshes against the boat's hull. The lake side door of the boathouse is closed and locked, but there's still a good three foot gap between the structure and the waterline. Sun sprinkles in, reflecting from outside.

My bikini top is off before Rob presses my back against the cabin-side door. My bottoms follow. I'm naked between the dirty window and a couple more camp chairs hanging on the wall just inside the door.

Rob strokes my mound and his index finger works between my folds. "How much do you want me to fuck you?" His other hand twists and kneads my breasts.

"I think about you every time I'm in the shower," I groan. "By myself. Taking care of my urges."

His kiss floods my senses. I'm under its surface, bobbing in its wonder and praying for air. He's the world I see. The world I hear. He's all I taste.

"I don't want an open relationship, Isa. I want you. I don't want you fucking other guys when we're apart, you understand? I love you."

"I won't. I'll call you. Ask you to talk me through it."

Rob responds with a crooked grin, but his face quickly turns serious. "I will never cheat. Even if we're apart for years, I will never cheat."

He's offering a level of commitment I didn't think I would ever get... or deserve. "I can't put you through that," I whisper. "I won't—"

His kiss silences my worries. "Trust *me*, Isa. Not the version of me you've built up in your head."

"Oh." He's right. That fantasy can't rear its head anymore. It can't.

"I'm real."

And he loves me.

I work at the buckle of his belt. "Take off your shirt."

His t-shirt flips up and over his head.

I stop with my fingers on the button of his shorts. The scar curves across his belly and around his side. Rob got slashed coming home to me. I run my finger over its raised edges. He almost died.

"I know what you're thinking." He looks down at my face. "I didn't die. I'm fine now. I'm going to finish school and we'll figure out how best to make this work. If it means me finding a non-academic job in California, then that's what I do."

More commitment. More love. "Are you sure?"

The anger's gone. Rob strokes my cheek and gently kisses the tip of my nose. "I've never been more sure of anything in my life."

"Oh, Rob, I love you." More than anything. "We'll figure it out."

"We will." He unzips his shorts.

Slowly, carefully, he picks up my naked backside and sets me on the edge of a bench next to the lawnmower. I push down his shorts, then his soft boxer-briefs. He's rock hard in my hand, and when I stroke him, he shivers.

"I want to feel you," he whispers. "But I'll go in for condoms if you need me to."

We shouldn't do this. We should be careful. "I need to feel you as much as you need to feel me."

"Are you sure?" He presses his cock against my belly. "Because I'll go inside. We can both go in."

"I'm sure." I don't know why, but I am. Sure the way I knew after the party that I couldn't be just a conquest for this wonderful man. But also sure the way, I think, his mother was the night she eloped with his father.

Carefully, Rob presses into me. He feels so good, so real. I've never been with anyone without a condom. Never trusted someone this much.

My Rob with his wonderful, ocean-colored eyes. His scruffy stubble and his brilliant, quick mind. His incredible body.

He feels amazing as he slowly pushes into me. Slowly gives me an inch. Then another. And another. I'm the luckiest woman on Earth.

"I love you," I moan. More than anything.

He shivers again and his face falls to my shoulder. His strong arms tighten around me once more, cinching in a hold that could keep me stable for years. Rob thrusts deliberately, with a wonderful, slow rhythm. "Isa..." A new kiss takes all my breath. "Marry me." Another thrust. "Even if it's ten years from now. Marry me."

I hold his shoulders as he pumps into me, and press my face into his neck. "Yes..." I whisper. "Oh, God..." With each thrust my voice grows. "Yes, Rob." And my pleasure. "Rob! This is... *ah!*" An orgasm rolls through my abdomen and out to all my fingers and toes. Whimpering, I fall backward, against the line trimmer sitting at the back of the bench.

He kisses me again, but his face is serious. Intense. He feels so damn good when he shifts his hips and slams me hard. "Jesus, Isa..."

Rob pulls out but keeps pumping against my mound, rubbing against my naked skin. He groans and his lips latch onto my shoulder. He bites. Lightly, but it's going to leave a mark.

Oh my God he's *marking* me.

Rob's back tightens. And hot cum spurts onto the underside of my breasts.

It's unbelievably sexy. I don't know why, but seeing Rob so excited by my body makes me immediately horny again.

Incredibly nipple-hardening, panting because I need him again now, *horny*. But a lot of guys don't like being touched right after coming.

But I need him and—

He must sense my horniness because he flips me around. His mouth latches onto the back of my neck and I almost howl. Almost let it all out.

"God *damn* you are hot," Rob rumbles into my ear. "I am the only man who touches you, do you understand?" The anger's back. I feel it pulse from his hard, newly re-tensing body. "You fantasize about them. Think about them. But those pretty boy models don't touch. Only me."

Rob presses his still-hard, still-perfect cock against my ass.

No one compares to Rob. No one occupies so much of my thinking, or my feeling. "Why would I fantasize about anyone but you?" He's all I need. My gorgeous Rob.

Possessive hands roam over my back. Possessive hands smack my ass. "I'm still angry, Isa." He sounds almost apologetic.

Almost.

"It keeps welling up, even though I think it's gone. Part of me wants to fuck you until you scream, just to prove my point." He rubs against my ass but doesn't thrust against my skin. "I want you every way I can get you."

He fingers my anus.

Holy shit, I think. "You are so much better than *any* fantasy."

A low *heh* rolls from Rob's lips into my ear. "We have our entire lives."

He's not going to—

Rob flips me around again. "Into the boat," he orders. "On your back. Now." He pushes me toward the small, rocking craft.

I crawl in, looking for a place to lie down. It's cramped. Two benches cross the middle, both with storage underneath. I won't fit between. There's really nothing I can do.

Rob's shorts and boxer-briefs drop onto my bikini bottoms and he jumps in, not paying attention to the boat's position. It rocks to the side, almost dipping all the way into the lake, and a big wave spreads out across the water.

Rob braces the boat with his feet and it suddenly, completely stops rocking. His incredible cock is right at eye level, glorious and springing against his lower abs. He came on me once already, and he's already good to go again.

I am most definitely the luckiest woman in the world.

I move forward to take him in my mouth but he grabs my ponytail. "Up on the back of the boat." He nods toward the curved fiberglass sweeping over the squared end of the boat. A low, rounded wall houses the interior parts of the motor and makes the back end of the little boat a smooth arch.

I immediately lie on the arch next to the motor housing. My back curves away from Rob, my breasts up and out, my pussy presented and waiting for him to do with as he pleases.

A new growl rolls from his throat and he grabs my waist, hoisting me higher until my head almost hangs over the boat's end. And my pussy is easily accessible to his roving fingers.

And tongue.

I drop my head back. I'm looking out at the open, upside-down lake, at the sparkles and the surfacing fish and the sun's sheen. Rob cups a breast, massaging with a tight grip. With his other hand, he spreads my legs.

Two fingers glide along the edges of my slick parts, one on either side. He runs them up, then down, then up again. On the final up stroke, he flicks my clit.

I shudder, but I won't come again. This needs to last.

"This time, you do as I say." He stares at my pussy, his face and body humming with his desire and need.

Before I can respond, he slaps my clit.

"Oh!" No one's ever slapped me there. It's... intense. I don't think I'd like it if another man did it, but with Rob, it's amazing.

I grin.

"No orgasms until I give you permission." He slaps me again. His other hand trails over my abdomen, touching gently, the exact opposite of the slaps.

"*Fuck...*" My head drops back over the edge of the boat. The dissonance is going to set me on fire.

Rob works his tongue across my bellybutton and I moan, wanting his lips working my clit instead. He knows exactly what to do and how long to do it. The right pressure, the correct tease. God, he's incredible.

His tongue flits across my opening before drawing ever tightening circles around my clit. Just before I think he's going to kiss or suck or lap, he pulls back.

I see the lake, the water where the sky should be, and I feel nothing from where Rob should be, between my wiggling thighs and licking me to splendor. I pull up my head and look, trying to frown at my gorgeous boyfriend.

His hands latch onto my hips. Slowly, he works them up over my waist, to the underside of my breasts.

The look on his face is one of fierce, animalistic joy. "You have the most spectacular breasts." His thumbs work over my nipples. "When I'm at school and you're off shooting in South America, I want topless selfies."

I blink, my mouth rounding. "You are so *demanding*."

"Still mad." He slaps my pussy again. "Do you want me to lick you to an orgasm?"

Oh my God. "Yes!" I hiss like I'm deflating. When he runs the pad of his thumb around the outside of my opening, my hips buck.

"I want to watch you shower." A finger probes. "I want you to call me. I want to know how horny you are. How much you miss my kisses and my cock."

Rob blows on my clit. I shiver. Even if we're half a world apart, he wants to see me every day. I don't think Rob will ever give in to separation.

It works both ways. I don't want to be apart from him anymore than he wants to be apart from me. "Only if I get to watch you jerk off," I growl.

One of Rob's eyebrows arches. A grin appears. "I serve only my goddess."

His mouth descends onto my pussy.

It's heaven. He flicks his tongue. He probes and massages my thighs and my ass. One second, suction makes me squirm; the next, kisses make me moan. The ecstasy spreads like a tingling, warm presence over my entire body, across my breasts, into my shoulders. Up my neck and into the roof of my mouth. Down to my toes and my fingertips. Robs licks and my world flips upside down, like my view of the lake.

"I'm going to..." I can't stop the orgasm. I can't.

"Come," Rob commands.

The orgasm thunders into my belly, riding on the tingly, hot brilliance already woven into my body. Rob rides it too, first changing his pressure, then his speed, to draw it out as long as possible.

I snort, maybe squeal, and slap the hull.

The next thing I know, I'm being pulled down the slick fiberglass into the boat. I can't fight, I can't do anything but continue to gasp and quake. My knees buckle. I fly forward, legs spread wide open, onto my kneeling man.

Rob's cock thrusts deep into my pussy. "Yes..." he groans. "You're still coming..." Another deep thrust and a new spasm rocks my core.

An arm threads under my ass and Rob presses me against the part of the boat I just slid down. He pounds me hard and steady, thrusting with all the strength of his thighs and buttocks.

His gaze locks to mine. "This is what I want." Another deep, powerful thrust. "You looking at me this way." A warm kiss dances over my lips. I taste myself, but mostly I taste Rob's slight saltiness. "In love with me."

The warm tingling of my orgasm changes into an electrical tingling around my heart. It dances through my chest, up my neck, and onto my face. My cheeks round. My eyes widen. And I kiss Rob with everything I feel as he thrusts again and again.

Rob will care for my heart as carefully, and as well, as he cares for my body. He won't withhold because he's upset. He's proving how unconditional his love is right now, with each plunge into me. With each touch to my cheeks and kiss to my lips.

And all he asks is the same in return.

"Will you..." My words barely form. "... marry me?" Part of me can't believe I just asked him. Another part dances with joy.

A new orgasm rips through me, one held steady by Rob's embrace and strong body. A soft *Ah...* floats to my ear. He bucks against me one last time, his cock jerking sharply inside me.

The boat rocks as the final kinetic energy of our lovemaking dissipates. He holds me against his front, still buried deep inside me, still warm and wonderful.

His next kiss gives me his answer. Joy fills his eyes and his smile. "My goddess," he whispers. "I'm yours. Now and always."

He's what I want. He's what I need. Now and always.

For the rest of my life.

CHAPTER 41

Robert

I peer at the video feed on my phone. Bart's messing with something out of the camera's view. "What you doing there, buddy?"

His head pops back into the frame, along with one of the atlases Isa gave him before we drove away from the lake house together three weeks ago. Road-tripping through the Rockies with the love of my life sounded like just what I needed to finish my recovery.

Mountain air does wonders. As do the touches of a loving woman. I'm now as right as rain, even if Reno is too hot and a bit dry for my tastes. Colorado, though, is beautiful. We spent three days in Grand Mesa National Forest alone.

Bart waves his atlas. "Where are you, Uncle Robby?" He pages through the maps. "Are you still in Colorado?" He folds back the book to show me the big yellow circle he made around Denver.

"We're in Reno, Nevada. Do you know which way we drove to get to Nevada?" My nephew's been closely following our travels. He drew a picture of Mr. Pickles for us before we left and Isa's been photographing it on every boulder and bush we come across. In Denver, she did an entire series of random people—a cop, some kid on a bike, one of our waitresses—holding it up, just for Bart.

He jumped up and down and clapped for three minutes straight when he saw.

Bart's head disappears below the frame again. "I'll find Reno!"

The webcam pans back to my brother. Dan chuckles and adjusts his laptop. "I've never seen him this interested in anything outside his paints and crayons."

"It's because Isa sends him new pictures every three hours." Or at least every time we stop and she's got good wifi.

Dan chuckles again. He leans toward the webcam like he's going to tell me a secret. "Tom and Sammie postponed the wedding, by the way."

I shake my head. I'm surprised but I'm not that surprised. "Why?"

Dan shrugs. "First it was her family. Then it was all 'let's have a double wedding!' Now, I don't know." He shrugs again.

Bart pops up. "Found it!" He holds up the map. "Will Ms. Isa send me new pictures?"

"Of course, little man." He really is excited. His atlas looks well thumbed. "Later, okay?"

Bart frowns but nods. "Where are you going next?" He holds up the atlas again.

"Tell you what. Why don't you look at the map and find me the closest big city, okay?" That'll keep him busy for about thirty seconds.

"Okay!" Bart vanishes again.

Another chuckle rolls out of my brother. "So, what are you two up to in Reno?" He peers at his screen. "Are you in some cheap-ass theme hotel?" After a moment and an exaggerated eye roll, he sits back. "You are."

I grin and pan my phone around the room, to show off our evening's accommodations. All of Isa's equipment is stacked in the corner under a huge, hanging, bright red lava lamp. Shiny silver wall-paper decorated with little red hearts glints on the walls. The entire place smells like stale champagne, but we couldn't turn up the opportunity to spend a couple of days making love on the massive, heart-shaped rotating bed in the middle of the room.

"Are you in the honeymoon suite?" Dan sounds incredulous.

I can't stop laughing. "Yep." The most obnoxious honeymoon suite this side of old school Vegas.

"Why the hell are you in the—" Dan stops talking when I hold up my hand and my wedding-banded ring finger.

"You didn't." Dan peers at the screen for a long moment. "You did." He shakes his head and turns around. "Camille! You have to see this!" Then back to me. "You're an idiot."

"Sure. I'm the idiot. When *you* going to make it legal, brother?"

Camille stops about five feet behind Dan and lets out a scream loud enough it overtakes my phone's speaker and turns into a buzz worthy of a hive of bees. "Oh my God!" She jumps up and down behind my brother.

Before Dan can say anything, Bart pops back into the frame. "What?" He looks around, all five-years-old and confused.

"Uncle Robby and Ms. Isa got married!" Camille gives her soon-to-be stepson a hug.

"You're making me look bad, little brother." Dan frowns. I can't tell if he's happy for me, or in total shock.

I shrug. I am, to be honest, the last one of us anyone expected to get married. But I'm no longer falling down to expectations. Mine or anyone else's.

Neither is Isa.

Camille drops onto Dan's lap and adjusts the screen and the cam again. "Where's the bride?"

"Getting ice." She hasn't been feeling well the last few days, but I don't tell them that. They'd get worried.

"Oh." Camille gives Dan a hug. "So I take it you're staying in L.A. until school starts?"

"I'll be bicoastal as of September." It's only a year and a half before I'm ABD. "I'm thinking I might write my dissertation about how social media affects the boundaries between the various subcultures in Colorado." Both Isa and I like the state, and there's a lot to study. "Isa's thinking of doing a photo essay at the same time."

Maybe doing a gallery show, too.

Camille smiles. "I knew you two would figure it out." She hugs Dan again.

"San Fran... Fransisto!" Bart holds up the atlas. "Highway 80 goes into California." He points. "Is that right?"

"That's right, buddy." Dan lifts him onto his lap when Camille stands up. To me: "But you'll be home for Christmas, right?"

Camille waves and walks back toward the kitchen. "You better!" she calls.

I nod. "Probably. I don't think Isa's family is big on holiday celebrations."

"Well, hell." Dan sniffs like a dad who smells weed in his son's bedroom. "Bring Mack, then."

My brother-in-law might like spending time with my loud family. Or he might be overwhelmed. Either way, it'll be a new experience for him.

Dan traces a road on Bart's map. "See here? That's the Monterey Bay Aquarium. We'll look it up when we're done talking to Uncle Robby, okay?"

Bart's eyes get big. "Do they have sharks?"

I chuckle.

Dan rubs his son's head. "We'll have to look."

"Okay." Bart folds up his book. "Can I have a cookie?"

Dan pats Bart's shoulder and nods toward the kitchen. "Go ask your mom."

A big smile lights up my nephew's face. "Bye, Uncle Robby!" he yells, and runs off toward Camille and his snack.

"Listen, I gotta go," I say. Isa's been in the bathroom a long time and I want to check on her. Besides, my battery is running low.

Dan shakes his head. "You got married first."

I wave. Dan waves. We sign off and I glance around our honeymoon suite as I plug in my phone. The chair next to the window is upholstered with the ugliest crushed red velvet I suspect was available in the early eighties, when the hotel opened for business.

The place is truly the tackiest room I've ever been in. Which, I think, just makes it more special. It makes Isa happy. Which makes me happy.

We have a few more weeks, then I need to fly back to school. I'm going to be walking through LAX, lonely and frowning and missing her terribly. I miss her now, and she's just in the other room.

"Honey?" The bathroom door's open and I hear her moving around inside. "You okay? Still feeling queasy?"

I push open the door.

My beautiful wife looks up, her face a perfect circle topped by her lovely blonde ponytail. She's in her pajama tank top still, and her tight little sleep shorts. Just looking at her feminine curves makes the deepest parts of my brain and body very happy.

But behind her glasses, her eyes are as round as her cheeks. As is her mouth.

In her hand, held in front of her chest like it's a hot poker, is a long white plastic stick that looks like a thermometer. But it's not.

It's not at all a thermometer.

Oh boy, flits through my mind. *Oh boy* followed by a very quick, intense tactile and emotional re-experiencing of our make-up sex in the boathouse. Our "marry me fuck," as Isa called it, when we were lying in our sleeping bag under the Colorado stars and she was looking for a good pounding.

She holds out the white plastic stick. A word shows in the little window next to her fingers. One word. One precious word that smacks the world upside the head: Pregnant.

I stare at the little window. And the word. "We're going to have a baby?" *Looks like we get a souvenir from our sexy fun time*, I think. But I don't say it. It's flippant and smartass and it popped up from the immature part of my brain. The one that no longer gets any say.

"Yes." She's still shocked. And her face is still round.

I'm shocked. My face is probably just as round as hers. "Is that why you've been feeling sick?" My wife has morning sickness.

"I think so." Isa blinks. "Rob? What are going to do?"

I pull her into my arms. She shivers and I feel as if she's holding on to my chest because I'm the only thing keeping her from drowning.

"We're going to have a baby." I hold onto her the same way. "This changes the logistics of the next few years." I kiss her forehead. "We're pregnant." I may need to work out taking a semester off and...

The reality of the moment hits me like I just stumbled into a wall. I fell in love, eloped, and now I'm going to be a daddy nine months later. Just like my father.

"Bart's going to have a cousin." I'm grinning like the idiot Dan likes to tell me I am.

"You're not mad?" Isa shivers again. "I didn't know yesterday when we went to the chapel. I didn't." I feel her crunch in on herself as she returns to clinging to my front.

She's genuinely upset.

"What?" Why would I be mad? My part in allowing this happy accident was as big as hers. "Of course you didn't know. You just took the test." I kiss her again.

"Oh, Rob." Isa hiccups against my chest.

I nuzzle her jaw, doing my best to make her feel better. "Guess you don't have to worry about going on the pill when we get home, huh?" I kiss her neck, playing up the naughty. "Hmm, pregnant woman sex."

Isa chuckles and hugs me close with her cheek over my heart. "I thought you might be mad."

"Why would I be mad?" I lean down and make her look at me.

"I don't ever want you to think you're trapped." She hiccups again.

I'm not trapped. I think, strangely, I've been set free. Or at least released into a whole, new, wild part of my life. It's out there, just waiting to be mapped and explored. "I'm the happiest man in the world."

Isa wipes away a tear. "I love you, Robert Quidell."

I hold her close in the surreal and tacky bathroom of an equally surreal and tacky theme hotel room in Reno, Nevada. A place I never thought I'd be, at least anytime soon.

Yet here I am with the most talented and wonderful person I know, ready to step into a whole new part of both our lives. "I love you too, Isa Wellington-Quidell."

Now and forever.

The Story continues
in book four, **Thomas's Need**

Careers and wedding plans swirl around Tom and Sammie until a parent falls ill and a job vanishes....

THOMAS'S NEED PREVIEW

CHAPTER ONE

Thomas

"**P**ut this on, Uncle Tommy." Bart holds out a child-sized, bark-brown vest complete with child-sized arm holes and a child-sized bug "abdomen" hanging off its back. "You can't go in unless you're an ant like me."

My nephew tugs on his own vest before looking up at me with his big, blue, five-year-old eyes.

Kids are exhausting. We've been in the Children's Museum for just over an hour and I already want to run for the hills, or for a beer. Either would work. But I promised my brother's boy an afternoon of "fun in the city" so here we are, a happy-if-precise kindergartener and his big oaf of an uncle, at the mouth of an indoor "anthill" play tunnel.

This particular exhibit has been a staple of the Children's Museum since I was a child. Hell, I think it was here when Bart's grandfather was a child. It was probably here before Minneapolis became a city. The first human to step onto this spot fifteen thousand years ago slammed a spear into the ground and declared, "Let's build the kids an anthill right here!"

Some things never change, including the murals rolling over the costume area where Bart now stands, and the air around us. An odd mixture of aged dust, cleaning chemicals, and that specific, sweet-yet-sour scent of child hangs in the air as thick as the shadows deep in the tunnels.

I run a finger over the pockmarked paint. Refreshing the blues in the mural would go a long way to adding a little brightness.

Funny how I never noticed the blandness of the colors when I was the kid playing. I just wanted to run fast and lose my younger brother inside the tunnels. It never worked; Rob always lost *me*. I suspect Bart would do the same.

I point at the vest. "I don't think that'll fit, buddy."

Bart frowns. He's already taller than all the other five-year-olds and I suspect he's destined for the full Quidell height and broad build, like his father and his uncles. Small we are not, which is fine, except when you're supposed to crawl through an insect mound.

"Oh." Bart's hand—and the vest—drop to his side. He looks at the floor for a moment, then out into the open area in front of the exhibit, his face open and hopeful. "Auntie Sammie can come in with me!"

My fiancé looks up from her task of stuffing Bart's action figures into his backpack. "What?" She smooths the front of her t-shirt as she stands up.

Sammie is slightly older than me—four years to be exact. She graduated from the University the same year I started. We'd crossed paths as students, but only in a disconnected, lost-opportunity kind of way. Thankfully, we met again last year when I started in the Art Department where we both work.

We've been making up for lost time ever since.

Her t-shirt hugs her curves, as do her jeans. Sammie's perfect female shape and luminescent auburn hair set her apart from the tired parents herding little ones through the exhibits. In my eyes, she's a vision.

But she doesn't seem as overwhelmed by the noise as I am. Sammie, unlike me, understands how to replenish her reservoir of energy.

"Bart would like you to be an ant with him." I point at my nephew. He smiles.

Sammie's face takes on an *Oh my God you are so adorable* look. The one every human with a soul makes when in the presence of kids or kittens. That wide-eyed pout, the one that only flits across features because everyone knows adults don't make that face.

But it's hard not to, when a kindergartener wants you to play.

And I think I fall even more in love with Sammie than I was after our quality cuddle time this morning, if that's even possible.

A little girl with golden skin and equally golden eyes runs around Sammie's side. Her big, curly ponytail bounces as she darts by me and right up to Bart.

"Hello," says the little girl. She's his height, which means she's probably slightly older than him, and she obviously knows her way around.

Bart doesn't say anything. He just stares all dumbfounded at the pretty girl.

Sammie's gaze shifts from Bart to me. She shakes her head as she walks over.

The little girl takes the ant-vest from my nephew's hand. "I'll be an ant with you."

Bart smiles a new, big, happy smile. "Okay."

The little girl slips the vest over her shoulders. "This way gets to the slide faster." She points behind me, then looks up at my face. "Are you his daddy?"

"That's my uncle," Bart says. He steps between his new friend and me as if I'm competition. "He's an artist."

I can't help but chuckle.

Bart throws me a look, but when the girl takes his hand, he's utterly, completely lost.

"Let's go!" she says, and my nephew disappears into the anthill with his new friend.

Sammie sets the backpack at our feet and leans her head against my shoulder. "Ah, young love."

I take her hand as I watch an older woman guide my young nephew through the tunnels. At least Bart didn't miss *his* chances.

I kiss Sammie's cheek. "I guess he's better at seeing his opportunities than his uncle."

Sammie looks up at my face. Her brows twist up for a second, and her warm, hazel eyes take on a shadow. But she shakes her head again and pats my elbow. "What's that saying? You make your own opportunities?"

"Yeah," I say, and kiss her cheek again. She's my muse, my Sammie. What would I do without her?

※

"HER NAME IS SERENA!" BART KICKS THE BACK OF SAMMIE'S SEAT.

There's not a lot of room in the back of my truck's cab. Sammie waves her hand over the headrest. "Watch the toes, please," she says.

Bart ignores her. He's too wrapped up in his cougar moment. "Like the tennis player." Bart swings his arm. "How do you play tennis, Uncle Tommy?" He swings his arm again. "Serena says she plays tennis and volleyball. She knows how to ski down hills!"

He makes a loud *whooshing* noise. Sammie throws me a bemused look.

Bart leans forward. "Can I learn to ski? I want to ski." His next noise sounds more like a monster truck than the swishing of snow.

I turn into my brother's neighborhood. It's nice—suburban and full of mature trees and well-maintained, middle-class split-levels. Dan says the schools are good and the streets safe. The area reminds me a lot of our neighborhood growing up, which, I suspect, is why he chose to buy a house here.

That's my brother, the painfully perfect family man.

"I think we've created a monster." Sammie nods over her shoulder.

Bart continues his monologue about the wide range of sporting activities available to today's youth.

The truck's engine grumbles one last time as I park in Dan's driveway. Dan's girlfriend, Camille, steps out onto the front step. She's freshly showered. Her damp black hair hangs over her shoulders and her muscles look loose as if she just finished a good workout.

"I think you and Camille need to pose for me." A full suite of classic painterly poses run through my head. "I could do a full series. Call it 'The Muses.'"

Sammie smiles as she opens the door and steps out. She helps Bart undo his seatbelt and he's running for Camille before I pull the key from the ignition.

Sammie taps the side panel of the truck as she watches him go. "I think he had fun."

I walk around the front of the truck and wrap my arms around her waist. "How could he not?" I gently kiss her upper lip. "He's a Quidell. We have a weakness for cougars."

Sammie slaps my shoulder. "Me-*ow*," she says, and saunters up the driveway, toward my brother's house.

I chuckle as I follow.

"Concert's at nine," she says over her shoulder.

We had an afternoon with the nephew. Now it's time to party like adults. I will never understand where Sammie gets the energy for it all.

Other than she sleeps better than I do. But I made a promise, so I smile. "We'd better get home so we can get ready."

Sammie's eyes brighten. Her hips swing as she follows Bart. She holds her back erect and her shoulders high, but her head tips just a little to the side as she takes in how Camille hugs Bart.

And again, I think I'm more in love now than I was this morning, even if I am tired.

My Sammie. My muse. I follow her into my brother's house for a quick good-bye with Bart.

I watch my nephew run off for a cookie and a juice box.

Sammie grasps my hand. "Ready?" she asks.

I guess it's time for a whole other anthill. I kiss her again. Any night with Sammie is special, concert or no concert. "Let's go."

The Story continues in book four, **Thomas's Need**...

THE WORLDS OF
KRIS AUSTEN RADCLIFFE

Hot Contemporary Romance:

The Quidell Brothers
Thomas's Muse
Daniel's Fire
Robert's Soul
Thomas's Need
Andrew's Kiss *(coming soon)*

*Genre-bending Science Fiction about
love, family, and dragons:*

WORLD ON FIRE
Series one
Fate Fire Shifter Dragon
Games of Fate
Flux of Skin
Fifth of Blood

Bonds Broken & Silent
All But Human
Men and Beasts
The Burning World

Series Two
Witch of the Midnight Blade
Call of the Dragonslayer (*coming soon*)

Smart Urban Fantasy:

Northern Creatures
Monster Born
Vampire Cursed
Elf Raised
Wolf Hunted (*coming soon*)

ABOUT THE AUTHOR

As a child, Kris took down a pack of hungry wolves with only a hard-cover copy of *The Dragonriders of Pern* and a sharpened toothbrush. That fateful day set her on a path traversing many storytelling worlds —dabbles in film and comic books, time as a talent agent and a text-book photo coordinator, and a foray into nonfiction. After co-authoring *Mind Shapes: Understanding the Differences in Thinking and Communication*, Kris returned to academia. But she craved narrative and a richly-textured world of Fates, Shifters, and Dragons—and unexpected, true love.

Kris lives in Minnesota with her husband, two daughters, Handsome Cat, and an entire menagerie of suburban wildlife bent on destroying her house. That battered-but-true copy of *Dragonriders*? She found it yesterday. It's time to pay a visit to the woodpeckers.

Fore more information
www.krisaustenradcliffe.com
krisradcliffe@sixtalonsign.com